COLD WIND

COLD WIND

A MYSTERY

PAIGE SHELTON

Minotaur Books
New York

First published in the United States by Minotaur Books,
an imprint of St. Martin's Publishing Group

COLD WIND. Copyright © 2020 by Paige Shelton. All rights reserved.
Printed in the United States of America. For information, address
St. Martin's Publishing Group, 120 Broadway, New York, NY 10271.

www.minotaurbooks.com

The Library of Congress Cataloging-in-Publication Data is available upon request.

ISBN 978-1-250-29531-6 (hardcover)
ISBN 978-1-250-29532-3 (ebook)

Our books may be purchased in bulk for promotional, educational,
or business use. Please contact your local bookseller or the
Macmillan Corporate and Premium Sales Department at
1-800-221-7945, extension 5442, or by email at
MacmillanSpecialMarkets@macmillan.com.

First Edition: 2020

10 9 8 7 6 5 4 3 2 1

For Charlie,
keeping me sane all these years
but particularly in 2020

COLD WIND

One

I lifted the curtain flap. Twilight was one of my new favorite things; an extended time here in my new neighborhood in Alaska before and after real sunrise and sunset. As we came upon the end of October, twilight in Benedict lasted about forty minutes at each end of the shorter days. We only had about nine hours of daylight now, and for whatever reason, I'd come to count on looking at, or maybe just noticing, the twilight bookends. It was comforting to look out there; it filled me with a sense of peacefulness I craved, particularly in the mornings.

I'd been working on peaceful.

We'd had a little snow—just enough to make the view pretty, but not daunting. We'd also had plenty of rain and a few surprisingly warmer-than-normal temperatures. The combination had caused a mudslide somewhere on the edge of town, but, though it seemed to be a main topic of local conversation, it hadn't hampered anything I needed to do. I'd heard Viola, my landlord, wishing for more snow and colder temperatures just to keep the mud from sliding farther. She'd be pleased by last night's freeze.

I took a deep breath, focusing on a shadow inside the trees. I didn't see anything unusual, nothing and no one looking back at me. I took another breath. It was as if I were perched on the edge of calm and comfortable, but couldn't quite dive in. Peaceful was hard work, and I hadn't been totally successful at acquiring it. But I wasn't going to stop trying.

I closed the curtain and gathered my laptop and the two burner phones I still had from my escape from St. Louis five months earlier. I used my satellite hot spot here in my room, but it wasn't as reliable as the internet and phone signals at the *Petition*'s shed, which I pilfered from the nearby library's signals. The librarian, Orin, had invited me to use whatever I wanted.

The *Petition*, the local newspaper I ran—I was the only employee— also gave me a place to work my other job, the one that, of my new neighbors, only Gril, the local police chief, knew about.

It was my job as a novelist that had garnered me the attention of a stalker, one who'd taken me from my front porch and kept me in his van for three long days. I still couldn't remember many details. And since he hadn't been found, I still didn't know who he was. Or where he was. So I'd stayed in Alaska, hiding, and trying to enjoy this primitive new world.

I put my things into my backpack and swung it over my arm. I wore good hiking boots, good socks, a great coat, and gloves that sometimes actually made my hands too hot. I was good at winter gear now.

I slipped a hat over my newly blond hair—the color change a re- sult of the trauma of being kidnapped—and the scar that announced I'd had brain surgery to clear a subdural hematoma. The haircut I'd given myself in the hospital bathroom with blunt-nosed scissors had grown out a little, but the scar might always be noticeable.

I didn't care in the least about how I looked, except that I didn't want to look anything like novelist Elizabeth Fairchild.

Mission accomplished, little lady. I smiled as I remembered the words being spoken in a different context, by the pilot of the plane that had brought me from Juneau to Benedict. Hank Harvington, with the help of his brother, Francis, ran the local airport and flew the planes, and both were my friends now. Friendships were formed quickly in this part of the world. You had to learn who to trust. Mother Nature could be brutal. I suspected we were closing in on the time when I'd really see what she was made of, but for now, I was enjoying the light snowfall and the milder temperatures. And that smoky twilight.

I slung my pack over my shoulder, left my room, double-checked the door lock, and made my way out to the lobby. I was surprised to come upon my landlord, Viola, and another woman.

"Beth, this is Ellen," Viola said. "She'll be staying with us, probably through the winter."

I tried to be cool, not let Viola see that the introduction had unsettled me. There hadn't been a new resident at the Benedict House since June, when the three who'd been there had been sent away—only one of them to supervised freedom. The other two had been in some trouble, though I hadn't received an update as to exactly how much. But it looked like we were going to have more company.

The Benedict House, my home away from home, was a halfway house, a place for parolees to spend some time under Viola's watchful eye and loaded revolver before they went to live on their own. I'd gotten a room there somewhat by accident, in my hurried planning. When you have only a few minutes to find a place to hide, details can get overlooked.

At first, I'd been thrown by the news that I'd be living with possible criminals, particularly after escaping from one, but I'd accepted it, and then enjoyed the reprieve when those first three had left. It was a place for female residents only, after all. And supposedly nonviolent ones at that, though lately I'd heard some stories to the contrary.

I had enjoyed sharing the space with just Viola. In fact, there'd been some talk that the Benedict House wasn't going to welcome any more "clients" because of some of Viola's missteps back in June. But all must have been forgiven.

"Hello," I said, an obvious forced friendliness to my voice. I extended my hand, though I'm not sure Ellen noticed either my tone or my hand.

The woman was strung out. It wasn't a difficult look to recognize. Skinny, with gray skin, a blemished face, stringy hair, glazed eyes. Twitching everywhere.

She didn't extend her hand but crossed her twiglike arms in front of her chest instead, tucking her hands into her armpits. Her glassy eyes couldn't quite focus on me as she nodded and bit her chapped bottom lip.

I looked at Viola.

Viola frowned and shook her head once. "Ellen's going to have a few rough days and nights. Sorry if she gets noisy. She won't be able to cook for a while, but we'll get her on it as soon as possible. Until then, you're still on your own for meals."

"Sure," I said. I'd been given kitchen access, but most of the time I ate at Food, our simply and aptly named local diner/café. One of Viola's rules for the involuntary residents was cooking duty. Just like for some royalty over the centuries, she'd have them taste-test the food before anyone else ate. If they didn't keel over, the rest of us could partake. For the record, I hadn't witnessed anyone keeling over.

Ellen sent a confused blink to Viola. She was in for a lot of surprises.

I wondered if Viola was equipped to handle Ellen's upcoming struggles with withdrawal. I was sure Viola had seen it all before, but it was going to get ugly. My landlord cut an imposing figure: a tall, stocky woman who wore her high-crowned fedora better than even Indiana Jones wore his. As far as I could tell, she never got sick even though she also never donned a coat thicker than what I'd call a jacket.

"All right." Viola grabbed Ellen's arm and guided her around me and toward the stairway that would take them up to the rooms where the clients stayed. "Let's go. Have a good day, Beth."

"You too," I said as they turned onto the stairs.

Originally built as a Russian Orthodox church, the Benedict House had spent some time as a real inn, one with moose tiles in the bathrooms and thick comforters on the beds. Twenty years earlier, though, it had been deemed structurally unsound. If a big earthquake hit, chances were pretty good the walls would come down.

But apparently it hadn't been unsound enough to raze, just precarious enough that the owners could no longer safely welcome paying guests. The State of Alaska purchased the building, and it suddenly didn't have to meet the same standards an inn would. How about a halfway house, someone thought. Twenty years and lots of earthquakes later, it was still standing.

Viola had only told me that story recently. I thought about the walls every now and then but didn't spend much time being concerned, even if I had experienced one quake that got my attention. I'd been in my room, and the chair I'd been sitting in had rumbled and creaked. I heard a loud noise like a freight train. After a few moments, everything calmed, and the walls remained upright. Afterward, I wondered if I'd truly felt what I thought I'd felt. Viola later confirmed that it had, in fact, been an earthquake. Since she hadn't been worried, I'd decided not to be, either.

Even after most of the summer tourists left Benedict and rooms opened at other lodgings, I hadn't found any other place to live that appealed to me, so I'd stayed. I liked having Viola close by: an imposing woman with a gun who I thought was smart enough to know when it was needed. I hadn't seen her draw it yet, but I knew she would if she had to. I hadn't told her about my kidnapping, but I'd been thinking about doing so lately.

I sent one more glance down the hallway, but Viola and Ellen were well out of sight. I wasn't there to work for Viola, but she and I had become friends. A part of me wanted to ask her if there was something I could do to help. But, no, of course there wasn't. That wasn't my job.

Besides, I had my own issues. And my own jobs.

Even with the overnight freezes and the layer of white snow, there was still a lot of mud everywhere. Viola had put a mat by the front door where we kept our mud boots.

I slipped my long brown rubber boots over my hiking boots, keeping my jeans tucked inside, and grabbed my truck keys from my coat pocket. As I stepped outside, twilight was giving way to sunrise. It was cold but the sky was currently clear.

I glanced toward the other buildings that were part of the small downtown corner. Their signs read "Food," "Mercantile," "Post Office." Randy, the proprietor of the mercantile, stepped out of his building and moved to the edge of the boardwalk. He put his hands in his pockets and seemed to be distracted, but he noticed me soon enough.

"Beth. Hey, how goes it?" he called; we weren't far away from each other.

"All's well, Randy. You?"

"I'm okay," he said after a long pause.

The boardwalk was covered by an awning that extended out from the front of the retail buildings but not in front of the Benedict House. I lifted my feet through puddled mud and walked toward him, glad when I came upon a drier patch, but not sure what to do with all the mud I'd gathered. I tapped the sides of my feet on the edge of the boardwalk, cleaning them off well enough to venture farther.

I did and didn't know Randy Phillips well. We hadn't shared a meal or even a drink, but I'd shopped in his store and he'd let me have an account. Our conversations had been brief and without substance, but I'd decided that I liked him and could trust him as much as anyone.

Randy was probably almost sixty, but seemed like he was still in his forties. The mercantile kept him moving, kept his joints lubricated, he claimed. He wasn't married and kept his salt-and-pepper hair just long enough to always look messy.

"What's up?" I asked as I joined him.

"Nothing."

I laughed. "Okay. I don't believe you."

He sent me a quick smile and then looked in the direction of the ocean. I turned that way, too, though from where we were standing, we couldn't see the water. The shore was a couple of miles away and the view was blocked by tall spruce trees, their tops currently threaded with fog. Carmel, one of the horses that roamed around town, came into view. He moved toward us, high-stepping along one of the only two paved roads. It seemed as if he'd seen us and thought we might be waiting for him. I wished I had a carrot or an apple.

I looked back at Randy. "Really, you okay?"

"Oh, I'm fine," he said.

"Randy?"

Another long moment later, he nodded to himself before he looked back at me. "Do you know where I live, Beth?"

"No." I might have assumed he lived in the back of the mercantile, but I hadn't given it any thought.

"Out past your *Petition* shed and beyond the library."

My *Petition* shed was where I wrote and printed a new edition of the paper every week. Its content included events like community center class times, local meetings regarding everything from the Glacier Bay Lodge gift shop hours to where a new concrete parking strip for some place or another might be poured come springtime, and if the diner had enough halibut to offer special prices to locals for a few weeks.

"Okay," I said. "That's pretty far out there."

"I live way out in the woods. I like it that way. I talk to so many people throughout the day that it's good to get away from the rat race, you know?"

I suppressed a laugh. I didn't know exactly how many customers Randy saw in his store, but there weren't very many people around, even when tourists filled the inns and the fishing boats during the summer. I hadn't seen any sign of a rat race since I'd left St. Louis. But Randy wasn't joking.

"I understand," I said.

Randy looked out toward the *Petition* office now, but there was nothing to see there but more trees. He said, "I heard some noises last night."

"What kind?"

"I don't know. I don't think I've ever heard anything like them before." He looked at me. "I've lived here six years or so, Beth, and I've never heard sounds like what I heard last night."

"Can you describe them?"

"Screams."

"Human? Animal?"

"Neither. Something in between."

"Did you go out and look?"

"I opened my door and flashed a light, but I didn't see anything."

"It's really on your mind. Maybe you should call Gril, let him know."

"I called Donner when I got in. No phone out there. Donner headed out to my place earlier this morning. I'm waiting for him to get back." He sent me another worried frown. "What if someone was in trouble but I didn't go help them?"

Donner, a park ranger and part of Gril's team, was the one to call if a wildlife emergency presented itself, among other things. If you could reach him, that was. There were only a few pockets of cell phone and internet coverage in the area. There were some landlines, but even they hadn't been put in everywhere.

I shook my head. "No, Randy, you know you can't think that way. You followed your gut; that's all you can do. You might have gotten hurt. You can't put yourself in a potentially dangerous situation, particularly out there where no one would find you in a timely manner."

My words came directly from one of the community center classes I'd taken. I'd promised Donner I would take any survival and self-defense classes that might be offered. If I was going to live in this wild place, I needed to have some smarts about it.

Carmel had stopped at the statue of Ben the Bear, a black bear. The statue wore a friendly smile, made for the tourists, as the horse sniffed the muddy ground around it.

"I know I have to be smart, but I sure wish Donner would get back," Randy said.

"He will."

"Sure." Randy took a deep breath and reached into his pocket. "Too damn muddy out there for me, but here are some carrots for the horse if you want to take them out to him."

"Sure. Thanks." I took the carrots as Randy turned around to head back inside.

But then he stopped and faced me again. I waited as he seemed to think about what he wanted to say.

"Beth?"

"Yeah?"

"Did that body ever get identified?"

There had only been one unidentified body discovered in the area since I'd moved to town, so it didn't take me long to figure out what he was talking about. Shortly after I arrived in Benedict, a body had been found near the ocean. It was a man, dressed in jeans and a white dress shirt. I still remembered wondering why the dress shirt wasn't dirtier as the cold ocean water lapped at the rocky shore and over his body. Later, I thought it had been a strange thing to notice.

Gril had called me to the site to ask me if I could see anything unusual. An earlier murder, one that had occurred right when I first came to town, had been solved partially because of something I'd observed.

I had a sense of spatial distances that wasn't common; it was how I'd come to help my grandfather, the police chief of a small Missouri town, when I was working for him as a teenager.

I shrugged. "Not that I know of. Why?"

Randy's mouth made a hard, straight line as he looked out into the woods and then back at me. "Just wondered." Then he pushed through the door of the mercantile and went inside.

I glanced toward the road I thought Donner would be traveling, but I didn't see his truck or anyone else coming in this direction. I contemplated following Randy inside to talk to him some more, even if I wasn't sure what there was to say.

Finally, I looked at the horse and whistled. Carmel looked up, and I held out the carrots. He walked right to me.

"Hey, you." I petted his nose.

He gobbled the carrots gently but greedily. He and the two other horses, Coffee and Cream, were domesticated enough that they roamed around on their own. They had a home and were, in fact, well taken care of. But they'd gotten out one day, and the literal and figurative barn door hadn't been closed since.

I worried about them mingling with all the other wildlife in the area, but had been frequently told they were fine.

When I first moved to Benedict and asked what wildlife I could potentially run into, I'd been told "all of it." I hadn't had any scary run-ins, but I'd seen my share of bears, moose, wolves, and porcupines—lots of porcupines. I knew how to keep a respectful distance, and though I didn't consider myself wildlife smart yet, I'd become less stupid. At least I hoped so.

Once the carrots were gone, the horse had no interest in me. He turned and carried on with his morning explorations, bidding me adieu with a noisy snort. I wondered if I'd ever again be able to live in the kind of place that didn't have horses roaming around freely.

I looked around as I pulled my cap down over my ears. It was early, just after eight. Maybe it was the conversation with Randy, maybe it was just the cold, but now, as I looked into the woods again, goose bumps rose on my arms.

"Just get to work," I muttered, shaking away the chill.

As I made my way back to the other side of the Benedict House, I glanced up to its second-story windows. One was illuminated, probably the window to Ellen's room. Was Viola there, too, or was Ellen alone and scared?

My truck was old, a purchase I'd made from Ruke, a local Tlingit man. His sister had driven it until she left to marry a man from another tribe. I was surprised every time the engine turned over, but it had never once sputtered. Even this morning, it started right up, and its almost-new tires got me onto the unpaved road that would take me to the *Petition*. The road had become covered in enough foliage that I wasn't mired in mud, but it wasn't an easy drive. Like Viola, I also looked forward to everything freezing over. Of course, other issues would come with that.

I was almost to the *Petition*'s building, an old tin-roofed hunting shed, when I saw vehicle lights coming my direction. I hoped it was Donner, and I hoped he hadn't found anything terrible.

I pulled over a little, put the truck in park, and rolled down the window, having to push in the crank with my right hand as I rolled with my left to keep the handle from falling off. I loved my truck.

The oncoming vehicle was, in fact, Donner's, but it didn't look like he was going to stop. I put my arm out the window and waved.

He sent me a look I couldn't quite decipher, other than that he wasn't happy. He slowed to a halt and rolled down his window. He was dressed in his brown park ranger garb, and a Russian-style fur hat covered his head. His beard took up so much of the rest of his face, I often thought it was a good thing he had such bright green eyes, or no one would be able to distinguish the back of his head from the front.

"What's up, Beth?" he asked, brusquely. "You okay?"

"I'm fine . . . I talked to Randy. Did you find anything out there?"

Donner squinted. "What did he tell you?"

"He heard a strange noise."

He nodded. "Yes."

"Donner?" I said when he didn't continue.

"Listen, don't go out there, and don't drive past the *Petition* building today. The weather has caused some unexpected shifts in the roads. Okay?"

"Sure. I never go farther than the library," I said.

There was something I could only describe as "tight" to his voice. It was more than shifts in the land, mudslides, concerning him. I was curious, but certainly not brave enough to go exploring on my own.

"Don't even go that far today. Just to the *Petition*. Got it?" he said.

"Donner?"

"Do what I say, Beth. Okay?"

"Sure."

He rolled up his window. His wheels spun for only a second as he put the truck in gear and drove away. I almost turned around and followed him back to the cabin that housed the local police to ask more questions, but no one cared about my position as "the press." It wasn't that they didn't respect me; this part of the world was theirs, Gril's and everyone else's who made this wild place a safe place to live. Freedom of the press just wasn't their priority. I'd stay out of the way for now.

I'd hear the details, probably in gossip form, soon enough. I'd head back to town for lunch later and learn what was going on. More than anything, I hoped Randy was okay.

I put my truck back into drive and continued to the *Petition*.

Two

Hey, baby girl—How's it hanging? Low and to the left, I always say. I have a little news, but it's not about the piece of scum that took you. It's about your dad. Hold on to your butt. I'm pretty sure he's alive.

I slammed down the screen of my laptop, an involuntary reaction to the first part of my mother's email.

She was "pretty sure" my father was alive? The man who had disappeared when I was a child, the man my mother had become obsessed with finding until a new man had come into our lives—the *piece of scum* who had taken me and kept me in his van for three days.

Though I always thought it a remote possibility that my father wasn't dead, my mother's note made me think she'd finally come upon some proof, and if that was the case, this was big news. I might not have acknowledged the fact that deep down I was sure my father was dead, but that was, in fact, what I'd come to believe.

The man who had taken me was still on the run, in hiding. For a time, I thought—was convinced—his name was Levi Brooks, but that had only been a name on an envelope I'd seen inside his van. I'd remembered that envelope on the same day the man's body had been found on the shoreline near where the Glacier Bay tourist ships docked, the body that Randy had just asked me about, the dead man in the white dress shirt.

I had to tell myself that though this was potentially big news from my mother, it was nothing to be concerned about. My go-to reaction to almost anything "new" had become panic; I thought it must be a post-traumatic-stress reaction, but I wasn't sure. Yet another deep breath was in order, and a silent reminder to myself that I was safe, that this wasn't bad news. I was far away from danger. I was fine. I lifted the screen again and it lit to life, the email still there.

So, if he's alive, that's the good news. Or maybe it's the bad news, hard to know for sure at this point. Fucker. It's good he might not have been murdered, killed, torn apart limb by limb, whatever. Maybe you can tell I'm having a hard time figuring out how to feel about all of this. What are we supposed to make of the fact that he might have left us on purpose? Hang on, though—I don't know all the details. Not yet, at least. I'm going to get them. I'm going to get him. I don't know what I'll do with him, but if he is alive, he will have to answer for leaving us.

Just wanted you to know the latest. I'll keep on keeping on and let you know if I find anything t'all about the scumbags in our lives. So you don't worry, I'm going to talk to Detective Majors about this too. I won't run off half-cocked. I'd rather be well armed with information and then cock-up all the way.

LURVE you so much.

Mom.

"Oh, Mom," I said when I finished reading the email. "Oh, Mill."

Millicent Rivers, my mother, would always be a force of nature. I loved her, but she could be exhausting.

I decided to try to look on a bright side, however dim it might be. The man who'd taken me—I'd been calling him my "unsub," for "unidentified subject"—was still out there, and I knew my mother would kill him if she found him. But if she was distracted by my father's possible whereabouts, then her priority was no longer killing the guy who had terrorized me. I wanted him dead, but I didn't want my mother to pay for the crime.

A surprise—though it shouldn't have been—twinge of pain suddenly ran along the side of my head, right next to the scar from my brain surgery. I stopped everything, stopped thinking, and sat back in my chair. I closed my eyes, placed my palms on my thighs, and did even more deep breathing as I tried to meditate, think about things that wouldn't take me back to either those three days I'd been held captive or when my father had disappeared—my two most traumatic experiences—and the resulting feelings that had just been stirred up.

Learning to rein in and control uncontrollable feelings made for hard work. I was determined to rise above everything that had tried to bring me down, but to do that, I had to learn to control not only my reactive panic but the blinding pain, the strange "spells" that sometimes came on during moments of stress.

Dr. Genero, my brain surgeon, told me the pain would subside over time. It had, a little. But when I talked to her about it, I lied and said it was getting *much* better. I don't know why I lied; maybe I didn't want to disappoint her more than I already had when I'd left the hospital without being properly discharged. She and I had talked some over the phone, but she hoped I could find someone local to help me. She said it would still take time for the pain to go away completely, but she thought a therapist of some sort might help with it as well as the unreasonable panic, too.

I still hadn't found a doctor or a therapist I could trust. I didn't want to talk to anyone in Benedict about the abduction—about who I truly was—except Gril. I didn't trust anything online, either, but I was still looking.

I was working on it.

The pain in my head rode an upward wave, but not for long. I was able to relax so that the threat of a sharp knifelike stab didn't come, and I was left with a low, dull ache. I could work with a dull ache.

I hoped to get to the point where memories were just normal thoughts, not things that sent me to places I didn't want to go back to.

Not long ago, I had a memory of my father rehearsing his sales pitch to me. He'd sold cleaning supplies—he'd "made women's lives easier and better." But there had been a moment in that memory when my father had seemed bothered by something he might have done, some wrong he hadn't righted. Maybe there *was* something more to those moments, but I couldn't be sure. I opened my eyes, dull ache and all, and decided that now wasn't the time to try to remember anything else. I should just get to work.

I had a newspaper to put together, and a thriller to write, which you'd think would have gotten easier after living one of my very own terrifying plotlines. No such luck. Writing books was still a one-word-at-a-time job that would never be easy. At least it hadn't become more difficult.

My office, the shed where the now deceased Bobby Reardon had created the Benedict *Petition*, was small. Bobby had written on well-used typewriters and used a newfangled copy machine as his printing press. Along with the two old desks in the place, he'd adorned the walls with old movie posters and kept a bottle of whiskey in a bottom desk drawer. I'd become accustomed to my visitors and their expectations of a drink and some friendly conversation. I still couldn't bring myself to leave the door unlocked, but most everyone knew to knock.

I'd kept Bobby's typewriters and added one of my own, an ancient Olympia I'd found years earlier in a Missouri Ozarks antiques shop.

I always wrote my first drafts on the typewriter. I'd been working on my latest thriller for two months now. The first draft was almost done. I'd gone with medical technology this time, a mix between Robin Cook's early book *Coma* and the 2001 movie *A.I. Artificial Intelligence*. It had been going well, and my editor had been pleased with updates I'd sent.

I'd considered writing about, re-creating, what I remembered going through with my unsub, but I wasn't ready to do that to myself; also, sometimes truth just really was way too off the rails to be accepted as fiction. If I could find a way to make the story therapeutic, then maybe. But not now.

My head was clear enough to get to work, but just as I threaded a clean sheet of paper into my typewriter, a knock sounded on the door. The locked door wasn't just because I was paranoid; it also gave me a chance to hide my work before I let anyone in, since Gril was the only person who knew I was also the novelist Elizabeth Fairchild.

I hadn't typed anything for either the newspaper or the novel yet, but I sat frozen for a moment, hoping whoever was on the other side of the door would announce themselves. They knocked again.

"Who's there?" I said.

A series of knocks, this time rapid-fire.

"Shit." I pushed away from the desk and walked the three steps to the door.

"Who is it?" I asked, one hand on the doorknob.

There was no answer, so I asked again. Still no answer.

Another set of quick knocks startled me back a step or two. The calm I'd gathered was gone. Why wouldn't they tell me who they were?

"I need to know who it is before I open the door," I said as I approached again.

I had no weapon. I looked around the shed. The most lethal things were a lamp and the typewriters. I could heave a lamp better. I took a step to grab it.

Then I heard something: a garbled noise that verged on an airy scream. Randy had said something about hearing something *like* a scream, something that was a mix between animal and human. Was I hearing the same thing?

If I could have put myself outside that moment and observed it, I would have yelled at myself not to open the door, but I couldn't help it, couldn't stop my shaking fingers from turning the lock and then the doorknob.

Three

Hello," I managed to squawk. I cleared my throat. My entire body was now shaking, my heart beating fast in my ears. But the grown-up part of me told me to get it together.

Two girls stood on the small stoop. They were young, probably not even ten years old. They were both dressed in boots, pants, and coats, it seemed, but it was hard to tell; they were covered in mud.

I could see their eyes. One girl's were brown, the other's blue.

The blue-eyed girl nodded and blinked at me.

The idea that something here was so very wrong began to solidify in my mind. My focus moved from my own nightmares to the fact that this just wasn't normal, even for Benedict, Alaska. As if a switch had been flipped, I stopped shaking. I looked out behind the girls and saw no one else, no attacking wildlife, but an urgency filled in all the places within me that had been overtaken by fear only a few moments earlier.

"Come in, come in," I said.

They didn't look at each other to see if the other would go. They didn't hesitate. The brown-eyed girl stepped forward first and the other one followed. I scanned outside again to see if there was anyone else around; there wasn't. I closed the door, threw the bolt, and brought two chairs to a spot where they could sit beside each other.

They stank. Badly. I tried to ignore the smell. I could feel the cold coming off them. How long had they been out in the elements?

"Let me get you some water," I said as I made my way to the water cooler. As I filled two paper cone cups, I continued speaking. "Are either of you hurt?"

They didn't answer, so I looked back at them. They were staring at me with wide eyes and more silence.

I handed each girl a cup. They drank greedily. I had the sense that I needed to tell them to slow down, but I didn't have time to get the words out.

They finished and then held their empty cups out toward me.

"More?" I asked.

The brown-eyed girl nodded, but the blue-eyed one only continued to stare.

I took the cups and filled them both halfway. "Can you tell me what happened to you two? Where are you from? Can I call your parents?"

Neither of them spoke. I made my way back again and handed them the water. They drank a little slower this time. I tried to assess the situation. The only good news I could suss out was that they didn't seem to be hurt.

Bottom line, though, this still wasn't good.

However, I knew lots of people lived out in these woods. I knew baths weren't a priority for everyone. I knew it was muddy outside. Okay, this might not be as strange an occurrence as it currently seemed.

But it *was* cold, and these girls *were* young.

"Can you give me a name or a number of someone to call?" I tried again, gently. "Anyone?"

They looked at me, but didn't extend the cups again.

"I'm going to need to call the police," I said, trying to keep my tone gentle. I didn't want to scare them, but if the threat of calling the police would get them to tell me who I really needed to call, I would use it.

Their eyes were glassy but aware, tracking me, and seeming to pay appropriate attention. They didn't argue or protest.

"Do you understand English?" I said.

They both nodded once.

"Okay," I said. They could hear.

Cell phone coverage was stronger by my desk than anywhere else in the shed. I moved back behind my chair and dialed Gril's number, using the burner phone with the number he would recognize.

"Beth, what's up?" he said as he answered.

"A couple of young girls just knocked on the door of the *Petition*. They don't . . . something's not right."

"Names?"

"They aren't talking."

"Are they hurt?"

"I can't be sure, but I don't think their lives are in imminent danger. They're muddy." Maybe someone had been chasing them. I looked toward the door, glad I'd locked it.

"Beth?"

"I'm sorry. I'm here. What should I do?" I said.

Gril thought a moment. "Stay put. I was headed out that way anyway. I'll grab Dr. Powder and we'll be right there."

"I've got the door locked," I said randomly.

"Okay. Are you worried for your or the girls' safety?"

"I'm just not sure," I said.

I heard Gril make noises like he was standing up. "Be right there. I'll get Powder. Stay where you are."

"We will."

Four

True to his word, Gril was there quickly. I hadn't realized that I recognized the sound of his truck engine, but when I heard it this time, I knew it was him and wasn't afraid to open the door. I was relieved.

The shed never felt too small with a guest or two. But when Gril and Dr. Powder joined the girls and me, the space became cramped. Gril talked to the girls first, asking them the same questions I had. Neither of them said a word. They didn't cry or seem frightened. They were strangely calm, alert but silent. Gril grabbed some paper and pens from my desk and handed them to the girls, asking if they could write down anything.

The brown-eyed girl wrote "Annie." The blue-eyed girl wrote "Mary."

"Your names?" Gril said.

They nodded.

"That's great. Can you tell me more? Your last name, parents' names, address?"

The girls looked at each other and then back at Gril before they both shook their heads and put the pens down. Were they deciding not to write anything else, or were they not able to? Gril didn't push them. Soon he stepped back and let Dr. Powder perform an examination as he made a call to the state police.

As I listened to this end of the call, I determined that two girls, no matter what their names were, *hadn't* recently been reported missing. Gril told the person on the other end as much as he could—he didn't really know ages or hair colors, just that one girl had blue eyes and the other brown. He promised he'd get pictures sent as soon as the girls' features weren't hidden under so much mud.

"Doc, do you recognize them at all?" Gril asked after he ended the call.

"I don't, Chief. Not even a little," Dr. Powder said. "I can't even tell you if they're from around here."

Probably sixty years old with strong, broad shoulders, Dr. Gregory Powder had been the picture of calm every time I'd seen him. I wondered if anything ruffled his feathers. He'd once inspected the scar on the side of my head and proclaimed, "Nicely done."

Though he was our resident doctor, I'd told him the same lie I'd told everyone but Gril: that I'd fallen off a horse—back in Colorado. He hadn't questioned me further, but I knew he wondered what my real story was. Benedict was one of those kinds of places, though, and it could be presumed that many folks had a real story they weren't telling.

He checked the girls' vitals, saying aloud that they seemed to be okay other than slightly dehydrated, and probably hungry, but it would be good to give them clear liquids first, just in case their stomachs were sensitive. He warned about potential nut allergies but said they should get something in their systems. Neither of them was frostbitten, but they'd been outside for longer than they should have. He looked inside their mouths and nodded at Gril. I saw the girls' tongues and I wondered if the doctor was letting Gril know they still had them. He suggested that Gril call Viola to ask if she would help get them cleaned up. He would examine them again afterward just in case all the grime was hiding something that needed medical attention, he said, but he didn't think he'd find anything new.

Gril said he wanted to step outside to make the call. He asked me to come with him.

I followed and noticed that he made sure to close the door tightly behind us. We had to walk to the back side of the building, where the phone coverage was strongest.

"Why does the doctor want you to call Viola?" I asked.

Gril shrugged. "She's the closest thing we have to a female official. Those girls are going to need some cleaning. They might be more comfortable with a woman."

"Of course." I didn't mention that Viola might have her hands full with Ellen. She'd let him know if she couldn't help.

I hadn't really looked at his eyes until that moment. He was upset, but the girls were, for the most part, okay, so I didn't think that was what was weighing on him.

"What do you think is going on?" I asked.

"Beth, something else has happened," he said.

My heart both fluttered and sunk. "Something about my case?"

Gril blinked and then put a hand on my arm. He was an old, grizzled man with unruly gray hair and a beard that never looked quite right. His bent and dirty glasses magnified his eyes to owlish proportions. I'd become fond of him over the last few months. He'd been my confidant, a friend and an authority figure I could trust. He'd even given me names of therapists in Juneau I could talk to about the trauma I'd lived, if I wanted to. He was also in touch with the St. Louis detective on my case, Detective Majors.

"No, no, Beth," he said quietly. "I'm sorry if I scared you."

I shook my head. Not everything was about me and my bag of ugliness. "No, Gril, my bad. Apologies. What happened?"

Gril took his hand from my arm and rubbed his chin. He swallowed and then looked farther into the woods, down the road Donner had been traveling when I'd seen him earlier.

"Donner found something out there," he said.

"What?"

"I'm going to tell you, but I need to ask you a couple more questions about those girls first, okay?"

I nodded.

"They haven't said a word?"

"Not one."

"Do you know from which direction they came?"

"No idea. I didn't ask. I didn't see them coming. I just answered the door. They knocked."

"Did they seem in distress?"

I thought a moment. "No, not scared. They seemed in shock, maybe. They still kind of seem that way; alert, but not all the way aware."

"But calm?"

"I guess." I paused. "Thirsty. They were thirsty."

"Okay."

When Gril didn't ask another question, I did: "What did Donner find?"

He hesitated a moment. "A body."

"Oh, shit." I hadn't expected that answer.

"Yes. Female. Middle-age. He didn't recognize her, but she wasn't . . . Well, he has no idea who she is."

"That's what Randy heard last night?"

He blinked at me, seemingly surprised. "No, the woman had been deceased awhile. When did you talk to Randy?"

"This morning. He told me what he heard. I heard a strange noise when I didn't answer the door right away. It sounded like what he described. That's actually why I answered the door at all. I might not have."

"Was the noise from one of the girls?"

"I don't know. Do you think they have something to do with the body?"

"I have no idea."

"Is it still out there?"

"Yes. Donner secured the scene as best he could, but we need to investigate. I called in some Juneau people. They're on the way."

"How . . . Where is it?"

"After Randy called in what he'd heard, Donner went out to his place and didn't find anything. However, just beyond it, the mudslide you've probably heard about has exposed some land, a road, too. It's not easy to travel, but it was wide enough for Donner's truck to maneuver down. He'd never been out there before. I haven't either. It's been blocked off for years. He went to see what he could see. He came upon a shelter of sorts, and the body was inside." He cleared his throat. "Frozen. I'll see it for the first time when the Juneau crowd gets here."

Thoughts batted around in my mind. Donner must have had to leave the scene because he had no cell phone coverage out there. The idea that the body could be gone by the time anyone else got to it also ran through my mind. It was cold outside, but it wasn't currently freezing. The body might be thawing.

"Deeply frozen? Like it had been in a freezer? It's not cold enough outside to deeply freeze anything, is it?" I asked.

"Donner thought it was frozen. It might have only recently been moved to the shelter. I just don't have the answers yet."

"Jesus. That's terrible. I wonder if it was the girls' mother or something."

"It could be anybody, but so far, none of us knows these girls."

I pulled my eyes from the woods and looked at Gril. "Let me come out there with you."

"What? Are you kidding? No!"

"Gril."

"I was just letting you know, a courtesy as to why people would be in and out around here. It could get busy, and I wanted you to stay out of the way."

"Gril, you know what I can do. Think about it—I might be able to help." I paused. "Do you trust these Juneau people?"

He paused. "Yes."

"Doesn't sound like it."

"I haven't met them."

"See, you trust me. You know I can see things others don't always see right away."

"You're good at math, Beth. You have a knack for understanding distances. Real crime scene investigators have some of those skills, too."

"Yes, some. But maybe I can help. Remember Linda Rafferty? You should have shown me the scene much sooner. I might have . . . understood it better, at least."

Gril was a good police chief. Better than good. But he'd made a mistake at the scene where Linda's body had been found back when I'd first moved to town. She and her husband had moved to Benedict for the same sort of reason I had—tragedy. Unfortunately, their tragedy followed them, and Linda couldn't escape a second time. I was able to help Gril better understand the scene where her body had been found.

I would have worked for my grandfather forever, as a receptionist, a crime scene technician, whatever he'd wanted or needed, if only Gramps had lived. I'd been really good at it, instinctually accurate beyond the numbers. Once Gril had shared all the Linda Rafferty crime scene details with me, I'd been able to notice a measurement mistake and help solve the crime.

He rubbed his hand over his ever-present gray beard. "Donner says it's gruesome."

"I can handle that."

I could. Beyond my own three-day nightmare, I'd seen lots, researched even more. I wrote gruesome, and I wasn't bothered by it when I wasn't a part of it.

I continued, "Maybe it's a terrible thing to admit, but having someone else's problems to solve helps me think less about my own."

He shook his head slowly, inspected my eyes with his, and finally said, "All right. I hope I don't regret this, but all right. Let's call Vi first." He pulled out his phone.

I stepped away as he talked to Viola. The other body crossed my mind again, that white dress shirt, but I wasn't going to ask about it yet. I thought I would have heard if it had been identified, and it seemed a stretch that the new body had anything to do with the one on the shore.

I looked down the road and into the woods again. How far away was the dead woman? Would she still be there? If not, who would have moved her?

I was about to find out.

Five

I went with Gril and the girls back to the Benedict House. Once the girls were introduced to Viola and seemed comfortable enough with her, Gril left, saying he'd be back to pick me up in fifteen minutes. It occurred to me that he could change his mind and not come back.

Viola didn't seem inconvenienced to be given the extra duty of cleaning up the girls. She had help. Her sister, Benny, gathered food and clothing, and Maper, a Tlingit woman I'd met only once at the Glacier Bay Lodge, joined in to help, too. Maper worked at the lodge when the tourist season was going strong, but also had some experience as a nurse. I couldn't understand if that meant she'd been educated as a nurse, or if she'd taken care of someone in particular. Either way, she was gentle and kind, so it would be fine.

"Hello, Annie and Mary," Viola said again as she smiled at them, their still-wide eyes looking up at her. "We'll get you taken care of."

They nodded, but didn't smile back, and continued to remain silent. I was surprised by this other side of Viola. Yes, she was friendly to me most of the time, but I'd never witnessed this much warmth.

"You two okay?" I asked the girls. "I've got to leave, but I'll be back."

For an instant, I thought I saw concern light their eyes, but it didn't last long. They would be fine. I'd gone from freaked out to concerned to pleased that they were out of the elements.

Finally, I nodded at Viola. She told me that Ellen was safe in her room and could fend for herself for a little while. I hoped that was true.

I heard Gril's truck pull up and, with one more smile at Annie and Mary, I left the Benedict House again.

Gril wasn't driving it this time. Donner was. He came to a stop, and I opened the passenger-side door and got in. He was on the phone, so I didn't interrupt as I buckled up and listened.

"Nothing?" he said. "Okay, well, stay in touch. The girls are getting cleaned up. You know Viola, right? Okay. Yes. She'll take care of them. Got it. Bye."

He ended the call and looked at me. "There are still no reports of two girls missing in Alaska. Nothing."

"Maybe their people haven't noticed yet," I offered.

"Maybe. Or maybe they aren't considered missing," he said.

"My mind has conjured a story that connects them with the body we're about to go see," I said.

Donner frowned. "Mine, too. We don't have to be fiction writers to connect those dots, though, do we?"

I looked at him, but he had his eyes on the road. It seemed to have been an offhand comment—he didn't know my secret.

"No, it all seems pretty obvious. The dots are right there," I said.

"But it could be coincidence," he said.

The mud wasn't too challenging as we turned down the road that would take us past the *Petition*, presumably past Randy's, and out to the body.

"What do people do when they live so far out in the woods?" I asked. "Doesn't everybody need civilization sometimes?"

"Some people just want to get away and get off the grid. It's doable, but it isn't an easy life, particularly in the winter. Fishing, hunting, and gardening. Not everyone sees a doctor, takes medicine. But there are ways to make money out here, if you choose not to have a 'real' job. Trapping can bring an income."

"Oh. Well, that sounds terrible," I said.

Donner shrugged. "It's not for me, but it's reality, Beth. I try to be open-minded about it."

"I hear you."

We were silent as we passed the *Petition* and continued down the road for a couple of bumpy miles before we came upon a cabin.

"Randy's?" I asked.

"Yes." Donner put the truck into park.

It wasn't as far away as I might have guessed. I'd never ventured this direction. Doing so had never crossed my mind. It was a jarring trip over ungroomed road, and that was obvious just by looking.

Randy's cabin was a small, simple, square home with a chimney and a peaked roof. There were lots of places just like it in these woods; Randy's seemed to have an upper floor or a windowed alcove or attic. It was stark amid the winter scene. Even though the inside of the truck was warm, a chill ran along my arms. I sensed I was moving out of my comfort zone.

It wasn't until then that I realized how I had assigned mental borders, a perimeter, to my world. The Benedict House, the businesses nearby, the *Petition* shed, the library. Those places and the people in them made up my *perfect* world. I wasn't "over" what had happened to me, but I'd convinced myself that I was getting better, that I was safe, particularly if I stayed inside those lines.

It was ridiculous to feel those borders crumble a little only two miles down the road. I was still in Alaska; I was still far away from Missouri. I was safe.

. I couldn't help it, though. My sense of security wavered.

"Beth?" Donner said. "We're not getting out here."

I looked at him as he nodded at where my fingers were wrapped tightly around the door handle. I pulled my hand away as if the handle were a hot burner on a stove.

"I know," I said.

"You okay?"

"Fine. Sorry about that." I forced my attention to the cabin. "Is that circular window part of a loft, an attic?"

"Yes, a bunk loft. Probably just beds up there. I can't remember the last time I visited Randy at his house."

"Are there other bedrooms?"

Donner thought a moment. "Yeah, one other one on the main level. Why?"

"Just curious."

"We're headed farther down that way." He nodded. "It's even bumpier but not for long. We'll exit out and onto another road."

"What prompted you to explore?"

"It looked different." Donner put the truck back into gear. "The mudslide moved a lot of earth, but I didn't realize it had impacted this area. I thought I should get eyes on it and report back to Gril."

"I guess it's good you listened to your instincts."

"We'll see. Out here, I had no way to let Gril know what I found. I had to leave the body where it was."

"Could it be someone who died of natural causes?"

"Yes, but I don't think so. Even though she was frozen, there was some . . . distortion. Maybe from time. It could be any manner of things, Beth."

"Do people get stranded out here? Die because they have no way out or no way to get help?"

"Sometimes. Usually, though, they know what they're getting into. There's plenty of opportunity to be off the grid, but if you aren't prepared, it's hard not to think your troubles are your own fault. Some people are okay with the idea of dying out here. Civilization, even small Benedict civilization, can be hard for some folks. They'd rather die than face the world. I get it."

"You do?"

"Sure." He sent me a quick look. "I'm not going to live that way, but I understand how the world can be very tiresome for some people."

The road was jutted and rocky and muddy and wet. I would never have tried driving it on my own. I couldn't believe Donner had made it the first time. I was so distracted by holding on that I couldn't focus on talking. A part of me acknowledged, though, that I was glad that I hadn't found the world completely tiresome yet. I wasn't ready to stop hiding, but I wanted to do it on the grid, at least on as much grid as Benedict offered, and I wanted my borders well in place.

A few moments later, the truck pulled onto something still muddy but much easier to maneuver over. My kidneys might have already been bruised, but the scenery was appealing.

"You're not tired of the world yet?" I said, resuming the conversation.

"No. I was, but it's better, well, less awful, I guess." He gestured at the path we were driving on. "This is probably an old logging road. At one time, this whole area was probably cleared out. See how young the trees look?"

"Mother Nature is bringing it back. Is there another way to get to this location?"

"I'm not sure. Maybe back toward the river and then over it somewhere, but I don't know. Gril didn't know of any other way."

I looked behind us and then faced front again and swallowed hard. "It feels like a secret hiding place."

"I thought so, too. Finding the shelter only reinforced that. You'll see."

"Care to tell me what brought you to Alaska? What made you tired?"

"Care to tell me what brought you?" he said.

I looked at him, but he kept his eyes on the road.

"Not today, but maybe someday," I said.

"Same, then." He paused, but I sensed he wanted to say more.

"Actually, my story is pretty simple and not all that interesting. I don't like sharing the details because I don't like it when people feel sorry for me."

"Okay. I promise not to feel sorry for you."

"I lost my family in a plane crash."

"Shit. I'm sorry, Donner." I broke the promise immediately.

"No, don't feel sorry for me."

I looked at his profile. I could see his eyes, but from this angle I especially noticed the pinch beside them. His past would hurt forever.

"Kids?" I said.

"Wife and one kid, a daughter."

"Damn, Donner. Don't ask me not to feel sorry for you. I am sorry, but I won't dwell on it. If you ever need to talk, I can be trusted."

"Thanks, Beth." He took in a deep breath and then let it out. "All right, we're almost there. You know to stay back until you're invited to come closer to the crime scene, right?"

"Yes."

"I wish I knew why Gril thinks it's okay for you to be a part of this, but he must have his reasons."

I hesitated. "You know I used to work for a police chief?"

"Yes, as a secretary." His voice was flat.

I nodded. "It was in a small town in Colorado. The chief was my grandfather. He noticed I was good with numbers, so I became their crime scene measurement expert. When you're the lawman in a small town, you use any resource you can." Other than the Colorado part, I'd just spoken the truth.

"And that's the only reason I won't question Gril too much about this."

I looked forward again and a bluster of activity came into view. Just off the road was a small structure, worn by weather and time, set at the edge of a clearing and surrounded by a truck and a van, and both vehicles I'd seen parked at the small, local airport before. A few official-looking people were walking around.

"We're here," I said.

"Yes, we are." Donner sighed again. "Look, I don't care what you've done and what you've seen—this is going to be shocking, Beth. Keep that in mind."

"Of course," I said.

I suspected he'd spoken the truth, too.

Six

Before we got out of the truck, Donner pointed out who was there from Juneau.

Three people had flown over, two crime scene techs and one medical examiner. Donner assured me this wasn't the same medical examiner who'd been called to Benedict when I'd first arrived, the one who'd overlooked the things I'd discovered at the scene of Linda Rafferty's death.

Christine Gardner, the ME, had recently transferred to Juneau from Homer, where she'd been both the local ME and a halibut fishing boat captain. She was in her seventies, and Donner had heard she was tough and thorough. He hadn't met her yet.

Donner peered out the truck's windshield and told me he thought the names of the two techs were Ben and Jimmy. The three visitors as well as Gril all breathed out small clouds. It was going to be cold out there.

"Just stay back," Donner said after we got out of the truck. "Do whatever Gril says to do."

"I will," I said.

I tucked my chin into my coat collar. Gril didn't behave as if he was cold at all. He stood outside the structure, back from it some, as if he were waiting for something. His jacket was open and he wasn't wearing a hat or gloves.

"Donner, Beth, glad you're here," he said, walking over to meet us at the edge of the road.

Christine frowned deeply when she saw Donner and me. She made a beeline in our direction.

Gril introduced us with only our first names. Donner wore his park ranger gear, and Christine might have heard that he was the one who'd found the body; he looked official. She nodded at him, then looked at me and, without missing a beat, asked, "What do you do with the police, Beth?"

Her still-present frown was weighed down by a face full of ruddy wrinkles. She wore a gray rain hat, but it wasn't currently raining. If anyone pointed that out to her, she'd probably just say what everyone else did: "It will."

I adjusted my own cap, if only to stall a little.

"Beth helps by analyzing some of our paperwork. She's our best proofreader," Gril said.

I tried not to look out of place.

"Yeah?" Christine said. "Never heard of such a thing, but whatever. All right, I gotta get at that body in there, but I want my techs and you all to do your things first. Try not to touch the body. I'll do that when it's time. Gather whatever you need to gather, except for the body. I'd bet a dozen doughnuts that I'll have a good guess at a C.O.D. just by looking at her."

"Body's still there," Donner said quietly and with relief.

"Exactly like the picture you took," Gril said. "I doubt anything was disturbed."

"Well, shit on a shingle," Christine said. "I guess it could have been, though. You didn't tell me that part. I thought you'd been out here waiting for us, Chief."

"No, Christine. There's no cell phone coverage out here. Donner came out earlier. After I contacted you, I came out in the official truck from the airport in case you needed an extra vehicle or driver."

"What the hell were you doing out here?" Christine asked Donner. "Did someone tell you about the body?"

"No. A local resident"—Donner nodded back in the general direction of Randy's cabin—"heard a strange noise last night. He called me first thing this morning and I came out to look around. I explored this way because the mudslide made things seem different. Then, when I found the road, I took it. I'd never been out this far."

"Did you figure out what made the noise?" Christine asked.

"No, ma'am," he said.

No one said a word about the girls. I didn't know why, but I wasn't going to be the one to bring them up.

"Well, I'm pretty sure it wasn't that body that made the noise, but I'll let you know if she might have been alive and screaming or yelling last night." Christine looked at the two techs, who were standing outside the shelter. "Get in there and do a good job. Hear me?"

They both nodded, and Christine turned back to Gril. "You all get in there, too. Now's the time."

Gril looked at me. "Wait out here a minute, Beth."

I nodded. I was suddenly very bothered by the whole scene. I wasn't sure I could handle seeing a dead body, but I didn't want anyone to know that.

"Yes sir," I said.

Christine sniffed and rubbed her hand under her nose as she inspected me. "If you're going to be sick, do it away from the scene, got it?"

I nodded, but Christine had already turned and followed Gril and Donner to the structure. She stayed outside, but looked in through the opening where there should have been a door.

There wasn't a door. The opening was set at an angle that made it look like the frame had been leaned on by wind and snow. The shelter was a quarter the size of the *Petition* shed, and it was bent the same way as the empty doorway. Made of old wood planks, it was even less stable than the tin building I worked inside. Spaces between the bent and rotting planks must have allowed the wind to blow freely through.

A small chimney stood straight up and down on the slanting roof, and I wondered if the chimney was supposed to be the thing slanting but had been moved straight when everything else tilted.

The surrounding landscape was almost like the rest of the Alaska woods I'd come to know, populated with tall spruce trees—except there were fewer trees in these woods, and a good acre around and back from the structure had been cleared. Tree stumps dotted the lightly snow-covered ground, and I thought I saw a miniature Stonehenge set up in the distance on the perimeter of the cleared area. I wanted to walk over and understand the display, but I stayed put, waiting for someone to give me permission to move.

"Jesus H.," Christine said, still at the doorway. "What the hell is that?"

I heard the rumble of an answer from inside, but could only make out the word "clothes."

Christine turned and looked back at me. "You can come up now."

"Okay."

"Only if you're not going to be sick."

"I'm not." I hoped I wasn't.

I tried to keep my feet inside other footprints as I made my way toward the structure. I thought I heard Christine make a noise as she watched me, but I wasn't sure if it was a laugh or an irritated snort.

"She is facedown," she said. "The place is a mess, so it might take a minute or two for everyone to gather what they need. You seen a dead body before?"

"I have."

I'd observed three autopsies, in fact. Research for my novels. They'd been horrible at first, then sad, then interesting in ways I could never have predicted. Back then, I'd moved closer to the tables and peered inside as organs, muscles, bones were pointed out and described. Ultimately, I'd left the last autopsy in a state of complete fascination, only later thinking maybe I should have been more bothered by it.

"All right," Christine said. "Have a look."

I stepped next to her.

At first, and surprisingly, it was difficult to notice the body because of everything else. The four men inside were cramped and had to move carefully around each other. I was surprised that someone didn't decide that only one could go in at a time. The structure didn't seem to be or have been a home, but only a storage shed. Boxes, some spilled and some not, took up much of the space around the walls. I saw lanterns and children's toys, books, magazines, a broken chalkboard still marked with the ghostly outline of a poorly drawn chicken.

"Are all of those things traps?" I asked, gesturing at several items hanging on the walls and piled in a corner.

"Yepper depper," Christine said. "All kinds. Bear and wolf mostly, though."

My eyes continued to take in the sight and landed on a short pile of pelts. Bear, I thought.

But then I steeled myself and focused on the body.

She was along a wall, stuffed up against it, on her stomach, her limbs bent in unlikely directions. She was naked and her white skin was tinged blue, quite obviously stiff and frozen, or that's the impression it made. There were no distinguishing marks on this side of her, no bruises or bullet holes, though considering the blue coloration, maybe that was impossible to know.

"Jesus," I muttered. It was rare that I wished for something more sophisticated than my burner phones, but now was one of those moments. "You guys taking pictures?"

"Of course. She was thrown in here," Christine said. "Probably recently, or it would have thawed much more than it has. I mean, it's cold, but it hasn't gotten down to freezing enough yet for this body to be in this state because of it being here."

"From here, can you tell how long she's been frozen?" I asked as I looked at the long, brown hair, matted and tangled like a giant bird's nest. I tried to memorize the distances between things. It was such a small space full of so much junk that even my ability to see "spatially" probably wouldn't be in any way relevant.

"Nope. Not yet."

"What's been found?" I asked everyone.

Christine answered, "A bunch of junk, but I was particularly bothered by the box of baby clothes that Ben over there found. Where's the baby that goes with them?"

"That's one of the million-dollar questions," Gril said.

"A trapper's shed," Donner added.

"The trapper must live around here somewhere," Gril said. "I know some of those guys, but I've never met one who lives out this way. I didn't think there was anything or anyone out here—but that was shortsighted of me. People are everywhere and nowhere in Alaska."

"Yes, that's true," Christine agreed.

"We need some fingerprints from the body and some around the shed," Gril said to Donner and the techs. "There might be a million, there might be none. Just get me something. Christine and I will see what we can do."

Gril stepped around everything else and then made his way out of the shed. "I need to look for a house. I don't see any reason for your expertise here, Beth. Come with me?"

"Yes," I said, sending Donner a glance.

He was crouched down, inspecting the items strewn everywhere. He didn't look up at me.

Gril and I marched to his truck and got inside. He started it quickly. "You doing okay?"

"I'm fine," I said.

"Good. Though I probably shouldn't have let you come out here, I appreciate you staying out of the way."

"Of course."

"I don't have time to get you back, but I've got to see if I can find someone living out here. Do what I tell you to do, got it?"

"Yes, of course," I said again as I clicked the seat belt into place.

Seven

Gril didn't seem to want to talk as he drove. He was thinking, working, I understood, but I had questions.

"Why didn't you tell Christine about the girls?" I said.

"Oh. That did seem odd, didn't it?"

"A little."

"I've contacted the proper authorities about the girls, but I'm not sure I want Christine involved with that part. She's an ME, but I suspect she would feel a need to get social services from Juneau over here right away. That's probably going to happen at some point, but I want to give the girls' family a chance to find them first."

I nodded. "That makes sense."

"I appreciate you keeping it to yourself, too."

"Do you think someone somehow did something to move the earth to hide the body on purpose, and then Mother Nature recently intervened with the mudslide?"

"I don't know. Hard to pull something like that off, but not impossible," he said.

There was something about the way he suddenly fell silent that got my attention. "What?" I said.

He shook his head. "A lot happened that summer."

"Like?"

Gril hesitated again but then shook his head. "A lot, but the mudslide was a big deal."

"Do people get lost or trapped out here a lot?"

"Shoot, Beth, more than a couple thousand people a year get lost in Alaska. It's a big place. Stuff happens. Sometimes bodies are found, sometimes not. We once found a skull and the rest of a skeleton near it. We tested them and found out they weren't originally attached. The skull belonged to one man who'd come to Alaska to hide, the body to a man who'd come to explore. They'd both been killed by bears and their remaining parts somehow dragged to the same spot. And adding to the strangeness of the whole thing, both of their first names were Dave."

"That is uncanny."

"It is."

"More than two thousand people a year go missing out here?" I said.

Gril nodded solemnly and repeated, "It's a big place."

"Wow."

We were silent as Gril maneuvered over some craters in the road.

"Do you think the two girls are somehow involved with the dead woman?" I said as the road leveled again.

"Not sure. I have no evidence that says that yet, so I need to remain open-minded." He sent me a quick glace before returning his attention to the road. "I didn't mention them to Christine, but I will. She's not a criminal investigator, and I also wanted her and her techs to look at the site with no preconceived notions."

He must have felt guilty about not letting her know about them, but I understood his reasons.

"Do you think the girls were the source of the noise that Randy and I both heard?"

"Maybe, but, again, no evidence of that yet. I didn't hear a sound come from either of them. You didn't either, right? Did the girls do something you forgot to mention, something that might tie them to this?"

"No," I said. "But I did hear the noise."

"We've got two muddy, silent mystery girls and a dead body. It all makes for some real concern."

I nodded as Gril frowned and looked around and out the windows. The road wasn't wide enough to travel down in a truck without moving slowly and carefully, but Gril didn't hesitate as much as I would have. I thought about how safe I felt with him. I trusted him completely, though I couldn't shake the sense that I'd stepped out of the boundaries I was supposed to stay inside. My stomach wouldn't settle, couldn't fill up a hollow feeling growing inside me.

I studied Gril, his determined focus. He was a good cop, a good man. Even if we got lost out here—which we wouldn't—even if we were attacked by a bear—which was always a possibility—Gril would find a way to save the day. The man who had taken me wasn't out here. I was still in my safe zone.

I shifted on the seat and cleared my throat. As I looked away from Gril's profile, something glimmered out in the snowy trees. It was probably just the glass of the snow catching a random ray of sun that had made its way through the clouds.

But it took me someplace else altogether. One second I was with Gril, thinking how safe I felt, and the next I was transported back in time, back to a place I was working so hard to stay away from.

Silver. A silver earring had dangled from my captor's ear. My mind's eye could see it shimmer in the light that came through the van's windshield. It was a silver feather. My captor, still faceless, but with blue eyes that I had, in fact, remembered. He had looked at me and said something, and as I looked over at him, I noticed the flash of light on his ear.

I didn't answer him.

"No," I muttered in the here and now.

"Beth?"

As if I'd been in a tunnel, I was sucked back to the present moment.

"What?" Gril asked.

I shook my head, glad for the quick return to real time and not willing to tell even someone I trusted so completely what had just happened. "Sorry. I just hope we figure out who the girls are."

"We will. Eventually, at least."

A twinge of pain started marching around my scar. I gritted my teeth. Now was not the time. I couldn't close my eyes and meditate the pain away while I was in the truck with Gril. I couldn't talk it out. I swallowed hard and hoped I could stay in the moment.

"Lookee there," Gril said, no amusement in his tone.

I swung my gaze in the direction Gril was looking, glad to have something to take my mind off . . . my mind.

There was an obvious opening in the trees. It was only about four feet wide—a truck couldn't fit through it—but there was no question that it was a purposely made passageway.

Gril turned off the truck and looked in the rearview mirror. Though the road we were on was wide enough for his truck, it was only just wide enough. The only way to go anywhere was either to back up or continue forward and look for a spot where you could do a three-point turn without hitting a tree. It was a tight fit in every direction.

"I have to walk down there," he said as he looked at the opening in the trees. "Lock yourself in the truck, and hightail it out of here if you see anything that doesn't look right. If I don't come back in an hour, get out of here."

"No," I said, the pain in the side of my head still on the move. Not now!

"What do you mean, no?"

"I'm not waiting in the truck and I won't leave without you."

He looked at me. "You have to follow my orders."

"No, Gril, I don't. There's no way I'm sitting in this truck, not knowing what's going on. I'm going with you."

"You said you'd do what I said."

"Well, not this time."

"Beth . . ."

"I don't care what you think. I really don't care at all." I gave him the most level gaze the pain in my head would allow. "Shoot me if you don't want me to go."

"Stay out of my way, then," Gril said angrily as he pulled the door handle and got out of the truck.

"I will," I muttered to myself as I did the same on my side.

Gril wasn't young, nor was he trim and fit, but he could move well, and I had to quicken my pace to keep up with him.

He simmered as he continued to look around. I hoped he was more focused on searching for something that would help him solve the mysteries of the two silent girls and the dead, frozen body than on being angry at me. I followed silently.

These woods were much denser than those by the storage shed, more like the Alaska woods I'd become used to, the trees close together, the foliage under our feet thick and difficult to maneuver—though there *was* less mud here and no real smattering of snow. Gril moved through it better than I did, but I did okay. When he stopped walking and put a hand on the gun holstered at his waist, I was grateful for the rest.

He put his other hand out and told me to stay behind a tree. There were many to choose from, but they were all skinny. I did as he commanded, though, and then peered around a narrow trunk.

A home. A cabin. It wasn't leaning like the storage shed had been; it looked solid and just big enough to be cozy and comfortable, isolated enough to be disturbing. It was set in a clearing, but the trees hugged a close perimeter around it.

"You don't know who lives there?" I said, keeping my voice low.

"I have no idea," Gril said. "I've got no record of *anyone* living out here. This land belongs to the State of Alaska. No one should have built a home on it, but that doesn't stop folks."

The building definitely looked lived in. There was even a rocking chair sitting out on the narrow front porch.

"It looks like a nice home," I said.

"It's illegal," Gril said. He turned to me. "Stay here. I mean it, Beth. I'll shoot you in your leg if you try to come with me. I will signal you if I think it's okay to join me, but stay here or run back to the truck if things get ugly." He reached into his coat pocket, pulled his keys out, and handed them to me.

"I will," I said, taking the keys.

Gril kept his gun holstered as he took a step.

Suddenly, something became very clear. "Gril!" I said in a loud whisper.

He turned around again. "What?"

"I just thought of something. There was a small graveyard near the storage shed. I mean, when I saw it, Stonehenge was the first thing that came to mind. Suddenly, that seems stupid. It was a graveyard, I bet. Did you see it?"

"I did. I think it was a graveyard, too, but I don't know how many people are buried there."

"People have just been living out here on their own, burying their dead. How?"

"I'm going to try to find out." Gril turned again and continued toward the house.

When he stepped out into the clearing, he said, "Hello! Benedict police. I'm Benedict police chief Grilson Samuels. I'm armed, but I haven't drawn my weapon. Come outside."

No one came outside, and I held my breath as Gril started walking forward again, repeating the words.

The pain was still in my head, but I was hyperfocused on Gril and hoped nothing bad would happen. Maybe I could somehow move the pain to another spot, a place where I knew it was still there but not a priority.

Please let him be okay, I thought.

He took another step, and then another, and then one more. He kept repeating the words of warning, each time becoming slightly more adamant.

But then all hell broke loose and Gril went down. I forgot my promise of staying put and ran directly to him. I got there just a moment too late.

Eight

It wasn't Gril's yells that seemed out of place; it was the other noises, the clanging, that didn't fit. If I'd stayed behind the tree a little longer and watched, I would have seen what was causing the cacophony, but when I lost sight of Gril, I took off without thinking.

"I'm okay, Beth. I was trying to look out for some sort of trap, but I missed it." He glanced up at me from the bottom of a dug-out hole in the ground. He was probably about eight feet down. "You can probably just give me a hand up and out, but you might need a rope."

"You're not hurt?"

"No. Didn't even sprain my ankle." He forced a smile up at me. "Did anyone come out of the cabin?"

I'd fallen to the ground on my stomach. I twisted my neck around and looked back at the house. The clanging noise had come from pots and pans strung up on a rope, hidden underneath the awning over the front porch, that had fallen when Gril had tripped a wire or string or something else I couldn't immediately spot. A hillbilly's trap and home. I'd seen one or two even less sophisticated setups in backwoods Missouri. I also knew that guns attached to angry property owners were usually an integral part of this sort of security system. I became hyperfocused again and inspected the house and the woods surrounding it.

I looked down at Gril. "I don't see anyone." My heart was beating so hard that I could feel it bouncing off the ground and back into my chest, but on the positive side, my head didn't hurt as much.

"All right, let's get me out of here. Can you give me your hand? If I can get purchase, I can climb up."

I reached down and our fingers touched, but just barely. I moved closer to the edge of the hole. Gril stood on his toes. It wasn't going to work.

"I have a rope in the truck. Go grab it," Gril said. "Unless you can see something we could use that might have been holding up the pots and pans."

I still didn't see the tripping mechanism. I calculated how far away we were from the truck. It wasn't far, but Gril would be out of my sight when I got there. I didn't like that idea, for either of our sakes.

I moved up to my knees and realized how filthy I'd gotten. The clearing hadn't been as protected by the weather as the walking path had been. I was now covered in mud. But that was the least of my worries. I looked at the house.

"No one came out," I said. "There's no smoke coming from the chimney. I don't think anyone is here. We'd probably both be shot dead if there was."

"Or someone is hiding inside," Gril said.

"I'm going to look." I stood and started toward the front door.

I was scared and angry, and I knew those two emotions were infusing me with a good dose of stupid topped off by some false courage. But I had to get Gril out of that hole, and it wasn't going to happen without a rope or a ladder.

"Beth!" Gril called from the hole. "Don't go in the house!"

"I'll be right back, Gril."

I marched to the house. My boots struggled some in the mud, but I made it to the porch. I climbed the two short steps and kicked away the pots and pans that were in the way. I noticed they were the generic kind, the kind I'd seen sold in Benedict's mercantile. The ropes that had been used to hang them were tied in tight knots around the handles. I could use the ropes if I took the time to free them from the noisemakers. I didn't want to take the time if I didn't have to. The door opened with a latch, not a knob. I lifted it easily and pushed open the door.

"Hello! We need some help. I need a rope or a ladder," I said into the front room. "We'll get out of your way soon."

There was no answer, and the air that reached my face felt cool.

I hadn't considered it much, but any idea that this might be some sort of vacation cabin was squelched. This was not a modernly furnished place, someone's temporary retreat. It was a simple home, made with someone's own hands, as far as I could tell.

"Hello?" I called again.

No answer.

Had it not been a real emergency, I would not have just gone into this unexpected house with the trap out front, but I had to get Gril out of that hole. I stepped inside.

The front room was similar to a great room in that the living, kitchen, and dining areas were all part of one big space. The living room furniture—a couch, two rocking chairs, and a coffee table— were all handmade, but not with any sort of designer flair. They were strictly utilitarian, put together with wood planks and burlap-sack cushions that looked dingy and flat. A long dining table—a picnic table with two benches—was also handmade, as were a kitchen worktable and a few shelves attached to the wall. The large fireplace appeared to serve as the cabin's source of heat as well as where food was cooked. A spit was rigged up over a hanging cauldron, but there wasn't currently a fire underneath. It was cold inside, but there was something about the cold that made me think it hadn't been that way for long. I scanned the shelves on the wall and saw a couple of apples. I walked toward them and grabbed one. They were fresh. Whoever lived here shopped at a grocery store. The mercantile had apples; so did Tochco's, a store supplied by frequent ferry trips to the Juneau Costco. I put the apple back.

I scanned two doors on a side wall. They were closed, but I walked over and opened both of them. Two bedrooms, again with furniture someone had made.

Inside one bedroom was an almost full-size bed and some shelves that held folded items of clothing. There were also pegs on the wall where other clothes hung. The clothes were as utilitarian as all the furniture, and I thought they probably belonged to a man. I didn't take a closer look.

In the other bedroom were two beds, almost twin-size. That was it. There were no bed linens, just two burlap-sack-covered mattresses atop ragged frames. There were no clothes inside the room, no personal items, nothing to hint at who the room belonged to. Still, I couldn't help but think of the two girls.

I closed both doors and made my way around to the back of the house, where a short hallway led farther back and to another door.

I lifted that door's latch and went inside.

From the front of the house, you would never know there was a room like this attached to the back. It was the size of the front room, but filled with lots more stuff.

Traps of all shapes and sizes hung on pegs on the walls or were stacked on shelves. I saw two brown pelts, but I didn't know from which animals they came. Knives were lined up on one shelf. A steel worktable sat in the middle of the room, with a drain system underneath. It might have been interesting if I didn't know what really went on in there.

The good news was that there were no animals inside, no blood anywhere, but it didn't take real-life experience to know what this room had seen. No matter what Donner said, I wasn't sure I could ever be open-minded about such a thing. I could try to ignore it, though.

My eyes landed on a rope on one of the many packed shelves. I grabbed it and hurriedly left the room of horrors, running back outside. I was glad to find Gril still in the hole and no worse for wear.

"I found a rope," I said.

"Good." Relief lined that one word. "What else?"

I told him about the interior of the house as I threw one end of the rope down into the hole.

"No one inside? Dead or alive?" he asked.

"No."

"Okay, haul me out."

It wasn't easy, but I wrapped the rope around me and then a sturdy tree, and I levered Gril up. He went into the house, following the same route I had taken inside, but didn't say a word, then stood on the porch inspecting the tripped alarm.

"Want to try to re-rig it?" I said.

"There's not enough time, and it's getting too dark. I need more people on this. Whoever lives here will notice the tripped alarm, the exposed trap, and the mud we left in the house. I don't much care, but it would be better to have more official folks with me."

Gril stood back from the house and rubbed his chin as he looked up at the chimney and around the clearing.

"Do you have to have licenses to trap?" I asked.

"You're supposed to. There are also trap seasons. Something tells me whoever lives here might not pay attention to such things."

"No, probably not."

Something moved in the woods to the side of the house. I noticed it out of the corner of my eye just as Gril said, "Hey, who's there?"

He took careful but hurried steps to the perimeter. I followed behind.

Twilight was beginning to settle in again, and the dense forest made it difficult to distinguish shapes, but there was no question that there was something out there. Not too big, but a shade darker than the other dark all around.

"A bear cub, teenager?" I said as we watched the dark spot move farther away.

"I don't know." Gril crouched as if he could get a better line of sight.

I did the same, but couldn't make out anything. A moment later, there was no movement to see.

"It left?" I said.

"I think so, but . . ."

"What?" We stood straight.

"It didn't move right."

"Right?"

"Like an animal."

"A person watching us?"

"I don't know." Gril looked into the woods again and then turned around. "Let's go."

We hiked back across the property, toward the truck.

Just as Gril and I made it to the edge of the clearing and the entrance to the walking path, we were halted in our steps. I flung my hand up to my mouth to keep myself from screaming; a squeak still came from my throat.

In the deepening gloom we were met by a beast of a man—both in size and in the clothes that covered his body. He appeared before us like something from a Viking-themed video game, tall and wide, covered in a coat of animal pelts and wearing a hat with hooked horns. A gun was slung over his shoulder, and he carried a staff. I wouldn't have been surprised to see a human skull atop the staff, but there wasn't one.

Gril and I froze as the man filled the width of the walking path about ten feet in front of us. We stared at him for a good long moment before Gril put his hand back on his still-holstered gun and took a step to one side so he was standing all the way in front of me.

"Can I help you?" the man said.

I was pleased to hear that he was only a man, not something unexplainable.

"I'm the Benedict police chief . . ." Gril started.

"I know who you are," the man said.

"I need to ask you some questions," Gril said.

"All right." He bent over slightly to remove the horned hat. He moved as if it was heavy but he held it as if it was light. "Come in, please."

"I need you to come with me," Gril said, but he removed his hand from the gun.

"Why?"

"I'd like to talk to you at my office. Would you come with us, please?"

"Do I need an attorney?"

Ah, yes, definitely human.

"Honestly, I don't know yet. I have some questions. If you want an attorney, we'll get you one," Gril said.

He might have been in his forties, but it was difficult to tell in the dark. I could, however, recognize that he was glaring at Gril. "I don't want to come with you, but I will."

"That would be good."

"I don't want any trouble. I don't bother anybody."

Gril nodded. "That's good, too, but some things have come up and we need to talk."

"May I change clothes?" he said.

Gril paused, but then said, "Yes."

"I'll be right back," he said.

He walked toward us. Gril and I took a couple of steps backward. The man stepped around us and made his way to the house. Gril followed him, so I followed Gril. The man stopped when he noticed his alarm had been tripped. He investigated the exposed hole and then looked up at the porch. He hesitated as if considering what to say or do, but ultimately, he just kept moving, stepping around the stuff on the porch before he went into the house.

"You think he'll come back out?" I asked.

"I don't know, Beth," Gril said. "I hope so. I'd have gone with him, but I didn't want you to either come, too, or wait out here alone."

"I'd be okay."

"Not worth the risk."

"Do you know him?"

"Maybe."

I looked at him. "What does that mean?"

"It means maybe."

"Who is he, maybe?"

"I'll tell you when I know for sure."

Nine

Gril's truck didn't have a back seat, just a front bench. We had to crowd together. I sat in the middle. The entire idea bothered Gril to his core. He was not pleased that I was there, but our company didn't behave in a threatening manner.

"If you pull forward about a hundred feet, there's a place where you can turn around," the man said as Gril started the truck.

Gril nodded. "What's your name?"

"Lane," he said.

"That your first or last name?" Gril said.

"That's my only name." Lane kept his eyes forward and then pointed when we came to the spot where Gril could turn the truck around. "There. Pull in there."

It was dark now, but the truck's lights were good. Gril did as instructed, and when the truck was headed in the other direction, he pushed harder on the accelerator than he had when we'd traveled in.

The light from the dashboard radio illuminated us all with an unforgiving starkness, but I was able to see more of what Lane looked like. He *was* probably in his forties, but his icy blue eyes seemed older than that, probably because they were pinched with what I could only guess was concern about being asked to talk to the police. His skin was dark, and I guessed he was Tlingit, but he would be the first I'd met who had blue eyes. His messy brown hair was cut with almost the same amount of skill I'd displayed when I cut mine in that hospital bathroom.

"This is an old logging road," Lane said. "I didn't clear it. Loggers did a long time ago. A mudslide covered it years ago, and a recent one exposed it."

He was answering questions he hadn't been asked yet. Gril hadn't arrested him, though. I was silent, as I was crammed in between the two big men.

"How long have you been out here?" Gril asked.

"Awhile."

"Why the trap in the front yard? You get a lot of company?"

"Used to, years ago. Old habits die hard, I guess. Any company is too much."

Gril didn't comment further.

Lane sat up in the seat as we came close to the curve that would take us by the storage shed. Gril didn't say anything, but I was sure he noticed Lane's attention was directed out the window, perhaps in anticipation.

Unfortunately, after the turn around the curve, the shed and the people still investigating it shone in Gril's truck's lights and stirred up a whole new set of turmoil.

As the truck kept moving, Lane reached for the door handle. "What's going on there?"

With lightning speed, Gril reached over me and grabbed Lane's arm. "Stay in the vehicle."

Gril's grip must have been viselike; the bigger, younger, probably stronger man couldn't seem to wrest his arm away.

"What's going on?" Lane said.

"That your shed?"

"Yes."

"I'll tell you what's going on when we get to the police station."

"What? No!"

I was elbowed in the stomach hard enough to take my breath away as Lane pried himself free. Gril had slowed the truck. Lane got the door open and propelled himself out. He started running toward the shed.

"Shit." Gril threw the truck into park and hurried out, too.

I couldn't quite catch my breath enough to follow right away, but I managed to a few seconds later, just as Gril finally made good on the promise of drawing his gun.

"I will shoot, Lane. Stop!" he yelled, his gun leveled at the man.

The scene played out in the light from the truck and a battery-powered lantern that had been placed next to the shed. I hadn't noticed that Donner didn't have his gun today, but I did now. Unarmed, he stepped in front of Christine, Ben, and Jimmy as if to shield them. Christine didn't like that, so she stepped around Donner. She put her thumbs into her waistband and sent Lane a tight glare from under her steely gray eyebrows.

"I need to know what's going on here." Lane, smarter than he might have seemed when he jumped out of the truck, stopped and raised his hands as he spoke back over his shoulder to Gril.

"This your shed? Your property?" Gril asked.

Lane didn't answer for the longest moment. "Yes. I already told you."

"Donner, handcuff him," Gril said, keeping his gun aimed.

"I'm under arrest?" Lane said.

"Yes," Gril said.

"For what?"

Gril looked at me as I approached. He glanced to where I had placed my hand, the spot I'd been elbowed. He might have had a few things he could charge Lane with, but he didn't have answers on many of them yet. "Assault," he finally said.

Once Donner had Lane handcuffed and in the truck, Gril turned to me. "You okay?" he asked as he holstered the gun.

"I'm fine," I said.

"Want Powder to look at you?"

"No, I'm fine," I repeated.

"You'll be going back with them," Gril said. He nodded at Christine.

"I figured," I said. "Hope I didn't mess things up."

Gril looked at me and I could see him work to look less policelike. "Not at all. You being here gave me a good reason to arrest him. I'll get the rest of his story."

"Okay. Be careful," I said.

"Except when I said you could come out here today, I always am."

I nodded, and we all watched them drive away.

"Who the hell was that?" Christine said as we watched Gril's truck bump over the road.

"Said his name was Lane," I said. "There's a house out there, too."

"Goodness, this is getting more and more interesting by the minute," Christine said.

Donner took off right away in one of the vehicles from the airport to meet Gril back at the station. Christine told everyone else what to do—I was instructed to stay back as the boys loaded the van, and then I hopped in the van with them.

And the body.

It had been bagged and put in the back, still frozen. Christine drove; per another one of her instructions, I got in the only other seat, the front passenger seat, and Ben and Jimmy sat right behind us, closer to the bagged body than I thought would be comfortable. They weren't fazed.

"Did you determine the cause of death?" I asked Christine.

"I need to confirm a little more in the lab, but I think she was strangled."

"I couldn't tell for sure how old she was. Could you when you rolled her over?"

"I think she was somewhere in her forties, probably late," Christine said, after giving me a quick frown.

"How long has she been . . . frozen?" I asked.

"Not sure about that yet, either. She has a tattoo on the inside of her wrist, two intertwined hearts. Sound familiar?"

I shook my head. "I've only lived here a few months."

"What brought you here? Wait! No, don't tell me. Let me guess. You wanted to get away from it all?"

"That's right."

"I've heard that story a time or two. I was in Homer and moved to Juneau. I guess I wanted to be around it all."

"Donner told me you were the Homer medical examiner as well as a fishing boat captain."

Christine laughed. "That's right." She paused. "It was because a previous medical examiner screwed up a Benedict case that I'm here. Benedict sees more action than I would have predicted."

I nodded, but didn't add that "action" seemed to be following me lately. Besides, that would only have made me sound paranoid.

"You know your police chief well?" Christine asked.

"He's been very helpful."

"Your scar. What happened?"

"I fell off a horse and had to have a subdural hematoma removed."

"Brain surgery from falling off a horse? Must have been some fall," Christine said.

"It was."

"You know Chief Samuels came from Chicago?"

"I do."

"He and his wife. I heard she died."

"I heard that, too, but I don't know the details. I didn't know her." I looked at Christine. Her profile was lit by the van's dashboard radio's blue light—a more forgiving light than in Gril's truck. The radio was on, the volume turned down. There was no signal out here.

She nodded and bit her lip like she wanted to say something more.

"What?" I said.

"His wife died of cancer?" she asked.

"I think that's what I heard," I said.

"Okay." She looked in the rearview mirror at Jimmy and Ben.

I looked back at them, too. They hadn't said much of anything.

"What's going on?" I asked everyone.

"Nothing," Christine said just as we passed the *Petition* building.

Had Donner told her about the two girls? As we passed by my shed, it seemed like eons instead of hours ago that the girls had knocked on my door.

I was glad when Christine continued.

"I just like to get the lay of the land of the folks I'll be working with. If all goes as planned, and if Benedict needs another ME, I'll probably be the one to do the job. That's all," she said.

I looked back at Ben and Jimmy again. They both nodded in confirmation.

"I see," I said.

"Where am I dropping you?" Christine asked. We've got a plane waiting for us, and I'll leave the van at the airport."

"Just downtown."

"Can do."

Christine let me out in front of the Benedict House, and I watched her steer the van back out to the road that would take her to the airport. The sky was thick with clouds, but it was neither raining nor snowing. A cold wind bit at my nose, but it calmed quickly. My headache was all but gone, the pain in my side lessening, too.

I looked around. The only sound was some leftover ringing in my ear next to the scar. I'd become accustomed to the ringing, but it was a little louder today. I turned and made my way into the Benedict House.

"Hello?" I said as I peered down the hallway toward Viola's room.

There was no answer, but that wasn't a surprise. I didn't usually call down the hallway or feel required to check in with Viola, but today was different.

I walked to her room and knocked on her door, but there was no answer. I continued to the end of the hallway and glanced up the stairway. I didn't hear anything there, either, and I didn't walk up to check on Ellen. I wondered where everyone was, most particularly the girls, and how they were doing.

I could use the phone in Viola's office to try to call someone, but I'd never entered the room on my own. I didn't really know who to call, either. I didn't want to bother Gril or Donner.

I was tired; that much I knew. Maybe I could get some writing done in my room, at least some notes for the book I'd been working on, but I'd have to get my equipment from the *Petition*.

Since being in Benedict, I'd learned how to enjoy my own quiet. I'd used some of that quiet to work on meditation, relaxation, and self-improvement, but today I determined I was too tired to do much of anything.

Maybe I'll lie down, I thought, *rest my eyes a little.*

Ten

The next morning began with the duo of a ringing phone and someone pounding on my door. I sat up in bed and tried to get my bearings.

"Beth, open up!" Viola said from the hallway.

I grabbed the burner phone I'd hidden under my pillow. "Be there in a sec, Viola." I unfolded the phone. "Hello?"

"It's me, Beth," Detective Majors from St. Louis said. "I have news."

"Shoot. There's someone at my door. Can I call you back in a bit?"

"Yes, as soon as possible."

"Will do." I folded the phone and jumped out of bed.

I opened the door just after Viola knocked again. "Sorry, what's up? What time is it?"

"It's early, but your presence is requested."

"Where?"

"Community center. Let's go."

"I need a minute to get dressed."

"I'll wait for you in the lobby. Just slip some stuff on. No time for prissy."

I was never prissy. "I'll be right there."

I closed the door and gathered the phone again. I tried to ring back Detective Majors, but my burner couldn't find a signal—I tried holding it under the pillow, but it couldn't even find that small signal Detective Majors had called in on. Frustration zipped through me.

Primitive is what I wanted, I silently reminded myself.

I glanced at the clock on my nightstand. It was only five a.m. I was frequently up early, but not quite this early. It was later in St. Louis, but Detective Majors knew how early she'd called; she must have something good.

I was going to have to accept that I wasn't going to learn her news right away.

I threw on some clothes, pulled the moose hat I'd purchased from the mercantile over my unruly hair, and brushed my teeth. I hoped someone had coffee somewhere as I exited and locked my room.

"Here," Viola said as she handed me a cup.

"You read my mind."

"I don't have anything to eat, so we'll have to have breakfast later. Let's go."

She already had her mud boots on. I slipped into mine and hurried to follow her out to her truck.

"What's going on?" I asked as she started the engine. It was cold outside, and I could see my breath again.

"The girls still aren't talking. One of them drew a picture that looks like you, so I've been commanded to bring you to the community center. That's where we set them up. I was there late, but Maper stayed with them overnight."

"Did it look like they were hurt after they were cleaned up?"

Viola shook her head. "It doesn't appear so. Dr. Powder examined them again, and he said they look skinny, but not too, and not malnourished. They seem about the same age—maybe eight or nine—but there's no resemblance between them. They still aren't talking."

I nodded. "Either they can't, or there's a reason they're silent."

Viola shook her head. "I hope it's not a bad reason, but I can't imagine there's any other."

"Does Dr. Powder think they *can* talk?"

"He says they have the equipment."

"Psychological reason."

"Best guess. We're not experts here, Beth, and the girls are going to have to go to Juneau. Social services will have to step in. Gril would really like to find out what he can about them before they're carted away, though."

I nodded. "What about the man Gril arrested yesterday?"

"I don't know anything about the man Gril arrested yesterday. Tell me more."

I told her the entire story, from beginning to end. We had to sit out in front of the community center for a few minutes so she could hear all the details.

"Goddamn, a body? That's . . . terrible. Do we know of a missing woman?"

"I don't know. I didn't see the body when it was turned over, but the ME said there was a tattoo on the inside of her wrist. Linking hearts. Gril didn't mention knowing about any missing women, but he said lots of people go missing in Alaska."

"Any tie to the body from a few months ago?"

"Crossed my mind, too. Not that I know. I wanted to ask Gril if it had been identified yet, but there wasn't a good moment."

"It hasn't been identified. I would know." Viola paused. "Linking-hearts tattoo, huh?"

"It sounds like a common tattoo, but I can't remember seeing one on anyone."

"Me either. No wonder Gril wants the girls to talk. He probably thinks everything is connected," Viola said.

"I think that's possible."

I followed her inside the community center. It served the exact purpose it was named for; many meetings, gatherings, and classes were conducted inside. I'd joined a knitting class a few times, and the *Petition* had recently published a notice about an upcoming potluck honoring the late Bobby Reardon, the man who'd originally begun the *Petition*. But today, the center was set up as a bedroom. I didn't know where the two twin beds had come from; they were headboard to headboard in the center of the big main shared space. Tables held piles of folded clothes and snack foods and drinks. There was a small kitchenette in the back of the center, and I smelled a lingering scent that made me think bacon had been cooked recently.

"Hello, Beth, Viola," Gril said as he greeted us inside the door. The two girls and Maper sat on one of the beds. She was reading to them from what looked like a children's book, something I would think would be too young for them, but their attention was rapt. I couldn't get a good look at them, just that one had light hair, the other dark. Gril stood in front of me, seeming to want to block my view.

"Hey," I said.

He lowered his voice. "One of the girls drew a picture of you about an hour ago. They woke up really early. Maper called me right away, saying they made their beds as if it was something they did every morning. She fixed them some breakfast, and then Annie took a piece of paper and a pencil and drew this." He held up the picture.

"I see," I said.

It was a drawing of a woman with short, white, messy hair and a scar on her head. It wasn't a terrible picture, a little better than a stick-figure drawing, but it didn't show the promise of a special artistic talent. But the scar told the story. It was unquestionably me.

"When Maper asked her if she wanted to talk to you, she nodded adamantly," Gril said.

"Okay. I'll see if I can get anything out of them."

"Thanks. Whatever you can. Last names, places, other people in their lives. I know absolutely nothing. We think they can write other words besides their names, but they haven't volunteered."

I stepped around him and walked slowly to the bed. In tandem, the girls looked up and noticed me. I remembered their eyes, but now that they were cleaned up, their differences were apparent. Annie was unquestionably Tlingit, and Mary was unquestionably a white girl. They looked like two normal little girls; cute, both with expressions that made me think they were intelligent and fully aware.

They blinked at me for a long moment. I didn't look much different than I had the day before. I took off the hat. My hair was bedhead crazy, but the scar was my most memorable feature. Mary smiled with recognition, but Annie jumped from the bed and ran to me, wrapping her arms around me tightly.

"Hello," I said as I hugged her back. I looked at Mary. "Hello."

Mary didn't continue to smile, but she didn't seem bothered, either. Annie hugged me tighter. I let her hug until she was done.

When she finally pulled away, almost a full minute later, I said, "How are you?"

She smiled and nodded, and pointed at me. The girls were much less . . . in a state of shock? I'd thought that's what they were yesterday—shocked. Today, their bright eyes didn't have that same flat gleam. They seemed fine.

"Oh, I'm fine, too," I said. "It's good to see you again."

Annie nodded and then took my hand. She guided me back to the bed and patted the mattress on her other side as she sidled up next to Maper again. Annie pointed at the book and looked up at Maper. Maper smiled at her and then looked at me. It would be great to enjoy a day of being read to, but I knew we had more serious things to consider.

"Annie," I said, and put my hand on her arm, "I would love to sit and hear the story, but can I ask you some questions first?"

Annie and Mary looked at each other over Maper's lap. Their silent conversation made me think they'd known each other a long time and were very skilled at communicating with each other with their eyes.

"Girls, I'm going to run and check on some things in the kitchen," Maper said. "Spend some time with Beth, okay?" Maper closed the book and stood, walking away from the bed before anyone could stop her.

The girls scooted closer to each other. I made myself comfortable on the bed, folding my legs and facing them. A card table had been set up nearby, where more paper and colored pencils had been placed. I reached over and grabbed some of each.

"Have you had enough to eat?" I asked them.

They nodded, but were clearly unsettled that Maper had left. Mary kept looking toward the direction the older woman had gone. I hoped we were doing the right thing for these children, but I knew we also needed some solid answers.

"Good. It's nice to see your smiles," I said.

They weren't smiling, but I smiled at them as I spoke. They sent me a couple of weak ones in return.

"Everyone here wants to make sure you're okay," I said. "Do you feel okay?"

They both nodded, but their eye contact was now spottier than my room's cell phone coverage. They'd quickly become attached to Maper. I reached out and gently grabbed one of each of their hands. They were okay with the touch; they didn't flinch. In fact, they relaxed a little as their fingers curled around mine.

"Good," I said. "Everyone wants to find out where you live. Do you want to help me understand where that is? Could you maybe tell me or show me?"

They frowned and shook their heads.

"Why not?" I said. "Are you scared to go home? If you are, you just need to let me know. I promise you both, we will keep you safe and we'll never let anyone hurt you." I hoped that was true. I hoped these two girls were going to be safe forever.

Mary shook her head, but Annie looked at me with earnest brown eyes. She neither nodded nor shook her head.

"Is there something you want me to understand?" I said to Annie.

She frowned.

"You know, it's okay to talk if you want to. No one is going to be mad at you for talking. But you can also draw if you want."

Annie let go of my hand and pinched her fingers around her lips, but I wasn't sure if she meant she couldn't talk or she wasn't allowed to.

I handed her some paper and a colored pencil. "That's okay. Can you maybe draw something? That picture of me is great. Can you draw a picture of someone else, maybe someone you know or someone you live with?"

Annie blinked at me.

"How about where you live?" I said. "Here, let me show you where I live."

I had zero drawing ability, but the Russian dome wasn't too challenging. I finished quickly and held the picture toward the girls.

They smiled at each other.

"I know, I'm a pretty bad artist. You're good, though. Your turn. Show me where you live."

Annie took the offered paper and pencil. She looked at Mary, who thought a long moment before she nodded her okay.

Annie got to work drawing a house. I watched with almost breathless anticipation. At first, I thought she might be drawing Lane's house, but that wasn't it. Then I wondered if she was drawing the dilapidated shed, but that wasn't it, either.

Gril had made his way to a spot behind my right shoulder and was watching as Annie drew.

"That's great," I said when Annie handed me the picture. "Really great." I still didn't recognize it, but I heard Gril's breathing change pace. "Can you tell me where your rooms are?"

Annie looked surprised for a second, but then pointed at the top window.

"Is your room at the top of the house?" Gril asked.

Annie looked at him and flinched. It was one of the most upsetting things I'd ever witnessed.

"Annie, it's okay. Chief Gril would never, ever hurt you. I promise," I said.

It didn't matter. Even though Gril stepped away, Annie had shut down. She dropped the paper and pencil and turned to Mary. They hugged, holding on to each other tightly as one of them made a noise like the one I'd heard on the other side of my door, except quieter this time.

I looked toward Gril. Had he heard, too? He stopped and faced us again. I mouthed the words, *Did you hear that?*

Gril nodded.

I'm sure that's the noise I heard, I mouthed again.

But I wasn't sure I was being as clear as I wanted to be. I stood and went to him. I spoke in a whisper. "There is no doubt in my mind that these girls made the noises both Randy and I heard. I am one hundred percent sure."

Gril nodded again and resumed his exit from the community center. He must have recognized the structure. I went back to the girls and looked at the picture again. It suddenly became clear. It was Randy's house.

Annie's interpretation was squatter than it was in real life, and that's probably why I didn't recognize it at first. Besides, I'd only seen it the one time.

Maper came out from the kitchen and beelined to the bed. I got out of her way as she sat by the girls. They glommed on to her for dear life. I felt terrible for upsetting them, but it looked like Gril had something now, which was surely better than nothing. I stepped away from the bed as Maper's presence comforted the girls and hurried to catch Gril.

"That Randy's house?" I said as I reached him by the front door.

"Sure looks like it might be," Gril said. "I'll find out."

"Do you know who the dead woman is yet?" I asked.

"No idea. We're working on it."

"What about Lane?" I said.

"What about him?"

"What have you learned?"

"He's waiting for an attorney before he talks. I was going to bring him here to see if the girls recognized him, but I didn't want to scare them with another possible stranger. I need some official help here. You did great with them, but we could use a therapist or a social worker or something. I'm ready to get some help."

"What about the name you gave me?" I said, just as something ran into my legs.

It was Annie. She was upset, and held on tight to me. I held on to her, too.

"It's okay," I said, because I didn't know what else to say.

"What name?" Gril asked me.

I pointed to my head and kept my voice low. "The therapist in Juneau who specializes in recovery from assault. You gave me the name a while ago. I haven't called her yet, but maybe she could help the girls."

"I'll look her up when I get back to the office. Right now, I think I need to talk to Randy."

"Makes sense." I looked down at Annie. "Hey, sweetheart, does the name Randy mean anything to you?"

She looked up at me and shook her head, her eyes so very earnest again. It was almost too much to take, and I felt tears burn behind my own eyes.

"I'll be in touch soon," Gril said as he turned to leave the center.

I looked down again at the girl wrapped around me. What in the world was going on in the woods of Benedict, Alaska?

Eleven

Maper and Viola asked me to leave; the girls needed less stimulation for a while, they thought. I gave each girl one more hug and told them I'd check in with them again later. Viola ran me back to the Benedict House, where I got into my own truck and drove it as fast as the muddy elements would allow toward the *Petition*. Once there, I jumped out of the truck and, burner phone in hand, hurried to get inside.

Unfortunately, the call to Detective Majors was destined to be further delayed.

"Beth?" Orin said, coming around the corner of the building when I was almost to the door.

My hand went to my heart and I made a noise that was somewhere between a gasp and a scream.

"I'm sorry, I didn't mean to startle you. I was just walking around the building at the wrong time," Orin said, overexplaining. "I was coming around to knock. If I'd known you were out here, I would have announced myself sooner. Sorry."

He and I had already discussed his seemingly sneaky ways, but I had become convinced he was just naturally stealthy.

Orin looked like a somewhat younger version of Willie Nelson, with long gray braids and faded jeans. He always smelled like weed, but I'd never seen him smoking. He had a thing for peace signs, both saluting with them as well as displaying artwork and pictures of them. Our friendship had grown over the past few months, turning into something siblings might have, and we'd skated over his hints that made me think he might know my secrets.

If I were to make a list of the people I'd thought about sharing my secrets with, Orin would be in either second or third place. Viola was first. I was split between Donner and Orin coming in next. Donner because he was law enforcement and it was good for law enforcement to know about possible threats, no matter how remote. Orin had a secretive past in government work and dark web research, from what I could glean, at least. While I enjoyed our friendship, my real reason for wanting to share with him was that I wondered if his skills might help me figure out who my abductor was, and maybe even where he was hiding.

"It's okay, Orin, what's up?" I tried to sound like I had it together, wasn't in a crazy rush.

"What's going on?" He looked in the direction of Randy's house. "What's with all the travel down there yesterday? Do you know?"

The library Orin ran wasn't directly on the road we'd traveled yesterday, but off it a little, behind the *Petition*. He must have noticed the traffic from the library's back windows.

I suddenly saw an opportunity. "Come in. If Gril hasn't had the chance to ask you to look up some things yet, I'm going to."

"I haven't talked to Gril. I tried to call him, but no answer. What's going on?"

"Let's get inside."

I knew I was overstepping. In fact, I told Orin as much. But I also knew that Gril had trusted Orin with many things he wouldn't have trusted other people with. Maybe Orin could help by answering some obvious questions.

Every day before I left the shed, I made sure I put all my writing away just in case I was surprised by a visitor, as I'd been today. As we went inside, I noticed the piece of paper I'd threaded into my type-writer the day before. Not one word had been written. It wouldn't do to miss many days of writing; I'd write today, or tonight, whenever I could.

I told Orin everything I knew about yesterday's strange happen-ings. He listened with such intensity, it made me slightly uncomfort-able. It was like he was waiting to pounce on a lie.

"A body, and two silent girls?" he said when I finished.

"And a mysterious man," I said.

"Well, there are lots of mysterious men out here. And another body, the one from a few months ago. I can't imagine there's any con-nection to all the new stuff, but who knows. Stuff just happens out here, Beth."

"I've heard."

"I can't think of anyone missing. Winter hasn't hit hard enough for us all to hide away in our homes. Sometimes when spring comes, we find bodies. Old or sick people who can't get out to seek help."

"That's awful."

"It's a way of life."

"I've heard that, too. What do you know about Randy?" I asked. "Have you been to his place?"

"I've never been to his cabin," Orin said. "He's run the mercan-tile for a while, came here from—I can't remember. I think we both moved here around the same time, so I probably didn't pay him much attention."

"But he came *here*," I said. "And he's living in a house far away from everyone else."

"As you know, he's not the only one, and most everyone living that way hasn't had trouble with the law; well, with local law. Most aren't the type to keep young girls hidden in their homes, though I admit, it wouldn't be difficult to do out here. Some folks just like it here."

"I know." I paused. "Can you think of anyone who might have visited him, friends or someone? Could someone else have noticed something strange?"

"See there, that's the interesting question." Orin leaned back in the chair he'd come to claim as his when he visited. Today, he hadn't wanted a whiskey. It *was* early. "Who is Randy friends with?"

"Who?" I said.

"Everyone." Orin smiled. "Or at least, he's friendly with every-one, but I don't know of anyone with whom he has a close relation-ship. He's not dated that I've seen. We're not old-fashioned around here—as long as it's legal, consenting adults, we don't care who's sleeping with who. No one tries very hard to hide those things, but I don't know of anyone Randy has had a romantic relationship with. No one."

"Does he hang out at the bar after work? Attend community cen-ter classes?"

"Not that I know. I can't say I've seen him anywhere but the mer-cantile. I've never given it much thought. He's great at running his business, and those are some long hours. *If* I've ever thought about it, which, again, I can't say I have, I've probably just thought he wanted to get home, get away from everyone."

Away from the rat race.

"Okay, so that might still be the case, and maybe the girls, the body, have nothing to do with him. There are lots of cabins in these woods. But what *about* the girls? There has to be some information about them somewhere, right?"

"I don't know," Orin said. "Babies get born out in the wild and no record is ever made. It happens."

Before I'd moved to Benedict, a place where I had to hurry to an-other location just to have cell phone and internet coverage, I hadn't given much thought to the still-primitive places in my very own country. Even the Missouri woods I was familiar with had been more connected to the rest of the world than Benedict.

But it wasn't just Benedict. Alaska was different than anywhere else.

"Laptop?" Orin asked as he righted the chair. "I'll need my own computer for anything deep, but yours will give me a good start."

I quickly made sure my email was closed and then handed him the laptop. "What specifically are you going to search?" I pulled my chair around to sit next to him.

"I'll start with missing people, women and girls, and go from there." His fingers flew over the keyboard.

I watched in silent awe as his typing took us to places I might never understand how to reach.

"Were you educated as a librarian?" I'd asked Orin a lot of questions before, but not that one.

The corner of his mouth quirked. "Sort of. Not officially, but I was taught those sorts of skills, along with others. Librarians are the only ones who can keep up with me." He typed some more. "No recent local reports of missing women, but you said she was frozen. She might have been for some time."

"That was the impression I got."

"I know. Okay, what about this?" He opened a page. The headline read "Benedict, Alaska: Twin Two-Year-Old Girls Perish in Fire, Only One Body Recovered."

"Oh, no. That's terrible."

"I remember this," Orin said distractedly as we both read. "It was right before I moved here, like a month or so. I lived in Anchorage at the time, but I remember this."

The short article, dated six and a half years earlier, was from the *Empire*, Juneau's daily newspaper.

During the summer that year, a house on the edge of Benedict had burned down. This wasn't a completely uncommon occurrence because of lightning as well as the frequent use of fire for heat and light. And Alaska had wildfires. The focus of the article was, oddly, on the fact that the fire was contained to the house and didn't spread, but mentioned, almost as an afterthought, that only one child's body had been recovered. There was no indication of where the other child had gone.

"Could the body have burned . . . away?" I asked Orin.

"I guess, maybe," Orin said. "But it's suspicious. It seems like they would have found some remains. I don't know, Beth, sometimes our authorities aren't all that qualified. It could just be uneducated or lazy investigating."

"Gril?"

"Well, I guess maybe. Others who come over to help us out. It's just the way it is—we aren't a priority, and, again, you have to understand that some people move here for that reason. And I wasn't here until right after, so I don't know the details."

I heard the insinuation in his voice, but I kept my eyes on the screen instead of letting him see them. "That's it? That's the only article about a fire where a child perished and another's body wasn't found? It seems like there should be more than that."

"Also, Juneau's paper doesn't always send someone over to dig for more information, for a few reasons. It's a different world than Juneau out here, and sometimes the weather doesn't cooperate." Orin's fingers were flying over the keyboard again. "And news changes every day, always something shinier to pursue. I'm not finding any follow-up."

"What else are you looking for?"

"Names aren't listed in the article. I'm looking for a death notice."

"I didn't see obituaries in any old *Petition* files."

"Bobby posted notices sometimes, but not all the time. Here. This is an official state record of death. This was probably the girl they found."

It listed the date and read: "Two-year-old Jenny Horton. Cause of death: injuries sustained during a house fire."

"That's it?"

Orin shrugged. "It gives the official cause of death; that's all it's supposed to do."

"Do you know the Hortons?" I asked.

Orin shook his head. "Don't think so. They must have left before I got here, maybe shortly after the fire."

"Can you find where they went? Where the house was located?" I said.

Orin typed and clicked. "I don't know where they went, but their house was close to where Randy's is. I don't quite understand the property lines. I can figure it out in time."

"This sounds like another possible mystery to add to our growing list," I said. "Maybe all part of the same one, or maybe not." I blinked. "What the hell is going on, Orin?"

He closed the laptop. "I'm heading back to the library. I'll do some searching there and give Gril a call."

"Wait," I said as he set the laptop back on the desk.

"What?"

"What about Lane? The guy out in the woods, the guy who seemed to be living way off the grid?"

Orin shook his head. "I don't know him. Maybe I'd recognize him if he's visited the library, but I don't know the name."

"He knew who Gril was."

"Okay. Lots of people know who the police chief is."

"How does that work?" I asked. "How does someone manage to live without electricity, without anyone knowing about them? Can trapping animals and selling their pelts *really* make someone enough money to live on?"

"Yes, if it's living simply," Orin said. "I've met some trappers. They are a unique bunch, but honestly, they could be anyone. I've met some who couldn't string together proper English and others who seemed well educated. It's a lifestyle choice, I suppose."

"And you never explored out that far?"

"No, I'm not much for exploring unless a computer is involved. I used to be more adventurous, but haven't been in a long time. The mudslide opening an old logging road, though, I've heard of stuff like that happening. I'll search for information about Lane, too."

"I think there were some gravestones out by the storage shed, and inside the shed, among other things, were baby clothes," I said. I'd forgotten those details in my first telling.

"Ugh. Maybe we're making all of this creepy, Beth. I mean, our imaginations are forcing the connections, but they could all be separate things, easily explainable."

"Where did those girls come from?"

"Gril will get the answer. He's good."

"I hope so."

"He will."

I nodded.

"All right. I will get back to you," Orin said. "I really appreciate you sharing the information. I promise Gril won't be mad, particularly if I find something to help him."

I said, "I'll let him know I talked to you."

Orin sent me a quick peace sign. I closed and locked the door behind him and finally called Detective Majors. I was very glad when she picked up.

Twelve

eth, you okay?" she said as she answered.

"I'm sorry. Yes, I'm fine. I lost phone service and had to wait to get in a better spot to call you."

Detective Majors knew I'd gone to Benedict, Alaska. She knew about the spotty coverage, but we hadn't talked on the phone in a few weeks.

She was the one I had called to pick me up at the hospital and take me to the airport. She was the only one in the Lower 48 who knew where I'd gone.

"Well, I'm glad you're all right," she said a long moment later.

"What's up?"

"Are you sitting down?"

"Yes." I was.

"We have a name. A real one."

Swiftly, my hands turned ice cold, my breaths came short. I reminded myself that, yes, I'd been out of my comfort zone yesterday, but I was back inside it, back where I belonged. I was safe.

Since the day he'd taken me, it had become hard for me to explain or understand my emotions. They weren't right, weren't correct, if you considered how people were supposed to feel. My feelings were over-the-top, swayed to the side, backward. But they were real. Tears suddenly flooded from my eyes.

"Who is he?" I said. The tide of emotion roiling through me hadn't hit my voice, and the words sounded so normal under the flowing tears.

"Based on the DNA we found on the blanket, his name is Travis Walker."

"Travis Walker?" I sniffed and wiped a hand over my cheeks just as both my hands started to shake. *No!* I silently commanded them.

"I know, it's so common. Does the name sound familiar?"

"No, not at all. How do you know? What happened?" I curled my shaking, icy fingers into a fist. *Travis Walker* sounded so harmless. Maybe Detective Majors was wrong. Maybe there had been a mistake.

"The blanket," she repeated. "The pink blanket we found. It had all kinds of trace evidence on it. Not just from you and him, but others, too. We've been testing all the DNA, and it's taken this long to figure out that one person on that blanket is Travis Walker, a fifty-six-year-old man who is registered as living in St. Louis, Missouri, and drives an old brown van."

"Travis Walker," I said his name aloud again, but this time the shaking hit my voice.

"Beth?"

"I'm okay. How can you be so sure? What about the other DNA?"

"It was the only male DNA we found." She cleared her throat. "There were five different DNA panels on the blanket. Yours, two women we were able to identify, his, and one other woman. Unless your kidnapper was actually a female, we're pretty sure it was Travis Walker."

I heard the question in her voice. She wondered if I had made a mistake and my kidnapper had, indeed, been female. I'd already led everyone down one false path, but I was sure I had this right.

"No, my kidnapper was definitely male."

"I believe you."

"But what if my kidnapper didn't leave trace DNA on the blanket?"

"We're confident."

"What about the other women?"

She was silent. I thought we'd lost the connection.

"Detective Majors?" I said.

"Beth, the two women we identified are deceased."

"Jesus. Did he kill them?"

Detective Majors sighed. "We're not sure, but we're investigating."

"Goddamn. What about the woman you haven't identified? How will you try to figure it out?"

"We're at a dead end . . . that sounds bad. Sorry. We're at a standstill until something shows up in the system. We're investigating."

I had suspected my unsub—Travis—would have killed me at some point, but as I'd remembered bits and pieces of his years of stalking and then the kidnapping, I'd speculated that he'd wanted to keep me around for a while, keep me as his. My stomach churned; my limbs still shook.

"What else do you know about Travis?" I asked.

"He's been in some trouble all his life, which isn't surprising." She paused again. I could hear her steeling herself. A new wave of dread came over me. There was more. "Beth, he was born in Milton, Missouri."

"My Milton?" *The town I was born and raised in?*

"Yes, but we think he left when he was just a kid, long before you were born. We are working on figuring out all the places he's lived; we don't have all that information yet."

"But . . . shit, Detective, he knows who I am, then. He knows I'm Beth."

"Not necessarily," she said, unconvincingly.

I'd assumed that my kidnapper had thought I was Elizabeth Fairchild, thriller author from Missouri—no specific town had ever been noted publicly. Elizabeth Fairchild was the name on all my books. My mother had suggested I use a pen name because she knew I would not only be famous, but that I would be writing things that delved into the darker sides of life. I hadn't even noticed my writing was that dark until Mom and my agent had told me it was. Mill had said that my father's disappearance had set my writing destiny on its path and there would be no denying it. She'd said that's the one thing my father and his disappearing act could take credit for—the darkness I'd internalized and brought to my books, to my readers.

"Of course he knows who I am," I said. "It's not a coincidence that he was born there. Shit, he knows everything. He knows who my grandfather was, he knows who my mother is. She's not safe!"

"Beth," Detective Majors said. "I need to you breathe. Come on, take some deep breaths."

I hadn't realized, but my breathing had become ragged. "I'm not sure I can."

"Come on, take a minute. You're fine. No one is going to find you. No one."

I nodded.

"Beth, you there?"

A second later, I was in the van again, looking over at my captor—Travis—and that silver feather earring.

Those blue eyes. How did someone so evil have such pretty blue eyes? I still couldn't quite see the rest of his face.

"You think you're such a smart thing, don't you?" he said.

I looked away from him.

"Huh?" he said as he shoved on my shoulder, propelling my other shoulder into the passenger-side door.

I cringed, but I wasn't going to tell him he'd hurt me. I wasn't going to talk to him ever again.

"You know me, don'tcha? Remember me?"

I didn't know him. After he kidnapped me, I started to have flashbacks of him stalking me for a couple of years, but I didn't know him before that.

"Come on, you should remember me." As he drove down the road,

he leaned over and said in my ear, "Think about it, you just might know me."

"Beth!"

I blinked back to the present moment. "He said I might know him." I choked out the words.

"Calm down. What do you mean?"

"I just remembered that he taunted me. Detective Majors, I think Travis knew me, he knows who I am."

"Okay, so what if he does? You are far, far away. See, you did the right thing by running. You got away. You are safe. Now, enough. You were doing better. You can't let this information get the best of you. Shape up, right this minute. Do you hear me? Beth, do you hear me?"

I blinked some more. The tears had stopped, and my body wasn't shaking as much. "I think I just had to remember. Maybe . . . maybe I just needed to remember."

Detective Majors sighed. "Oh, Beth, I don't know what you need, but you need something. You still need help."

I nodded again.

"Beth?"

"I hear you. I'm through whatever that was. I will get help." I didn't promise her as much, but I would try to figure something out—try *harder* to figure something out.

"Good. Look, I'm sorry to drop these bombs on you, but the media, and frankly your mom, is bound to get ahold of this stuff, and the last thing I want is for you to hear about it from someone other than me."

"I appreciate that."

Detective Majors sighed again. "Listen, there's more, and I can't hang up this phone without you having everything from me first. Are you ready?"

"Yes." I was.

"We also have a current address, outside St. Louis, but from all indications Walker hasn't been at his apartment for months. No one has called in spotting his van since the calls shortly after you left. But, as you know, he got away that time when he was spotted near Geneva Spooner's house in Weyford. Your mother didn't help, but that's for another day. We think he's dumped the van at this point, so we're working other angles."

"Outside St. Louis? Where?"

"Chesterfield."

"What other angles?"

"Looking for and talking to people from his life before all this. We'll find him, Beth. He's spent his life screwing up, and he'll do it again. People like him can't help themselves. We will catch him."

"My mom needs to know," I said. "Just in case he really does know who I am, who we are, my mom needs to know. She needs to be aware."

"I will tell her, but again, I wanted you to know first."

"Thanks . . . Detective Majors, do you have a picture?"

Detective Majors was silent for a long few seconds. "Yes, Beth, I do. It's a booking photo from about five years ago, when he was picked up and then shortly thereafter released for armed robbery. He's been in and out of the system for a lot of things."

"Send it to me?"

"Only if you really think I should."

"I think you should."

"I'm going to send it to you now. Okay?"

"Yes. Okay. I'm at my computer."

I heard a few keystrokes before she said, "Sent. Give it a look when you're ready."

"I'm ready now." I hoped that was true. She probably did, too.

Her message took only seconds to reach my inbox. When it was there, I held the cursor over the attachment.

"Hang on, Beth. Maybe you want someone there with you. Can you call over the police chief?" Detective Majors said.

Cool-as-a-cucumber Detective Majors was rattled. Most of the time she hid it well, but I'd just heard it in her voice.

"Gril's probably pretty busy, but I'm okay. I really am."

"Gril. I like that you're calling him by his first name. You're making friends."

"I guess I am."

"That's great news," she said. I heard the forced optimism. "All right. I'm right here, and remember, it's just a picture."

It was more than that, but I appreciated her assurance.

I clicked.

And it opened immediately, flashed and filled the screen.

There he was. Travis Walker. I didn't recognize him—at first. He seemed so very common looking, with no distinguishing features. No feather earrings.

"It's not in this picture, but I remembered a silver feather earring in his left ear," I said into the phone.

"Good to know," Detective Majors said. "How are you doing?"

"I'm fine. He looks so normal." His eyes *were* blue, but they weren't as vivid as they'd been in my mind when I'd *seen* them a few moments ago. His face was round, but not because he was overweight. That was just its shape. His nose did nothing special and his mouth made a straight line. He had a full head of hair but in this picture it was cut short. He looked emotionless, except for those eyes. Irritation, probably at being booked for a crime, showed in a purposeful squint.

"I think I remember longer hair, but I can't be sure," I said. "Maybe some gray at the temples, but I'm not sure about that, either."

"Okay, that's good. Does he look familiar?"

"The more I look at the picture, the more I think he does. But . . . I can't be sure, and I'm not bothered. At all. I feel . . . detached from this picture."

"Well, that's good."

"I think I'll be okay." But I knew this conversation had set me back some. I would have to work on getting to where I'd been before I saw it, and then getting even better than that. "Detective Majors, now I know who to look for. I mean, I've been wondering if he's here, watching me, thinking, 'Is he that guy, someone clearly from out of town, who just came out of the restaurant?' Now I'll be able to know for sure. This is actually a very good thing, Detective. I'm happy to have this."

"Good."

I closed my eyes, just to see what my mind might do. Yes, that picture was there now, yet it wasn't terrifying. But though it didn't immediately conjure other memories, it did promise there were probably more to come. I opened my eyes.

"Good work, Detective," I said.

"Well, thank you, Beth, but now we have to find him, and frankly, we have to find him before your mother does."

"She's distracted. She might have a line on my father. She will probably talk to you about it."

"She called, wants to talk to me. I'll see if I can help."

"Oh, Detective Majors, she's asked many police officers and detectives to help her. Some have tried, others she's managed to offend before they're even done saying hello. My mother thinks she knows how to do all police work better than anyone else."

"Because your grandfather was a police chief?"

"No, because my mother is my mother, a unique blend of intelligent, narcissistic, and pissed off about what life has done to her."

"Well, I might do some looking into things regarding your father. I'll let you know what I find. I'll tell her about Walker myself, though. I just got this information today, and you were my first call."

"Thank you."

"All right. I'm going to get back to work. You sure you're okay?"

I looked at the picture on the screen. "I'm good. I'm really good."

"Excellent. Talk to you later, Beth."

I ended the call. I knew I needed to get to work, but I couldn't help but spend a few long minutes looking at the picture of the man who'd taken me. I wondered if I would ever feel the hatred I should feel for him. I didn't feel it at that moment. I didn't feel anything warm and cozy, either. I felt nothing, which was better than fear, better than anxiety or panic. But those things were sure to come back. Travis Walker and I weren't done with each other yet.

The one thing Detective Majors and I didn't talk about was the fact that if, indeed, Walker knew me, my mother, and my grandfather, he probably knew my father, too. It had crossed my mind that maybe my father's disappearance and my kidnapper were somehow tied together. I hadn't given much credence to that idea, but now I wondered if I should. I knew my mother would.

Oh boy. I couldn't let myself dwell on those ideas.

It was time to get to work.

Thirteen

I sat in my chair, told myself to forget everything except my work. Not only did I have deadlines, I needed to get my head back in a better space, and ironically, writing about fictional characters' terror sometimes helped me forget my own.

For two hours, as rain fell on the tin roof above, I fell into a writing well. I loved writing wells, their rarity making them precious. The days my fingers flew over the keyboard, struggling to keep up with the story playing out in my mind, were few and far between. Those two hours were one of those times.

Of course, I had no way of knowing if the words were any good. I'd have to read them again in a few weeks. I could hope, though.

Just as the well began to run dry, a knock sounded on the door, startling me back to reality, moving my heart rate up again.

"Who's there?" I said with way too much hostility.

"It's me, Beth. Open up," Viola said from the other side.

I stuck the stack of papers I'd filled with potentially good words into a top drawer and locked it with a small key. I put the key into my pocket and went to the door.

I unlocked the door, but as I pulled it open wide and my eyes landed on Viola, something went wrong. Instead of Viola standing there in the rain, her hat drooping on one side like it sometimes did, Travis Walker was there, his generic features slack as he looked at me, his silver earring catching light from somewhere.

I gasped, blinked, and just before I screamed and maybe fainted, the vision disappeared. Popped away. Viola came back into view, hat included.

"What the hell?" Viola said, and pushed her way inside. "You okay?"

My hand was over my mouth. Shit. This wasn't good. *Get a grip. Get a grip.* "I'm fine. Sorry, I thought I saw something out there."

"What?"

"Nothing." I closed the door and hoped Viola couldn't hear my heart pounding in my chest. I worked to stabilize my voice. "What's going on?"

"Some weird shit, let me tell you."

Oh good. Somebody else's weird shit. "I'm listening."

Viola knew where the whiskey was kept. She pulled the bottle and a glass from the bottom desk drawer and poured herself a shot. She didn't offer me one, which was unusual.

"Ah," she said after she downed the shot and sat. She grabbed the bottle again but didn't pour another, just held it on her lap.

I sat in my chair. "You okay?"

"I don't know. I'm stressed, Beth. What the hell is going on in my town?"

"What's happened since this morning?"

"Everything, and not nearly enough."

I nodded. She'd continue.

"The girls," she finally said after a few moments. "They still aren't talking, but their father came to get them."

"What?" I sat up in the chair. "Who's their father?"

"His name is Tex Southern."

"Is that his real name?"

"So he says. He had identification."

"What happened? Clearly, you're not happy about this."

"He marched into town looking for Gril. He'd come to report that his girls were missing, said he'd tracked them in this direction. Gril asked him a million questions and then gave him the girls. I wasn't in on the questions or how Gril determined it was okay for the girls to go with him, but Gril said he'd tell me later."

"They're gone?" I said. "What about social services?"

"Social services folks never even left Juneau. Now that Dad is found, they aren't going to bother."

"But the girls aren't talking. They might need help."

Viola frowned. "I agree, Beth, but that's not how it's done."

"Not how what's done? Making sure that children are okay? No, I can't accept that."

Viola poured another shot into the glass. She looked at me. "You're going to have to. We're all going to have to."

"Wait. He marched into town. Where was he from?"

"He's a native. He lives in a village not far from here."

"He's a Tlingit?" I said.

"Yes."

I paused. The world was a delicate place. "Viola, I'm only asking this because whatever is the right thing is what needs to happen. Annie is obviously Tlingit. But Mary isn't. What's up?"

Viola nodded slowly. "It's an unavoidable question. Apparently, Gril was okay with however Tex explained it."

"Is this all legal?"

"If they're his daughters, it is."

"Did you see the girls with him?"

"I did. I think they were scared they were in trouble at first, but then they were happy to see him. I witnessed Gril asking them if Tex was their father, and they both nodded."

"Did Gril ask him why the girls don't talk?"

"Not in front of me."

I pondered, and wished I could have seen Tex. "Did he . . . look okay?"

Viola shrugged. "He's a big guy."

"Okay. How does he or Gril think the girls got lost in the woods?"

"The village is on the other side of the mudslide and a narrow river passage. It is thought that the girls got lost while they were out checking traps."

That got my attention. "Traps?"

"Yeah."

I told Viola more about what I'd seen at Lane's house, this time elaborating on the traps and the back room.

She listened intently, her eyes calming even more. Something came clear to me as I spoke, and it was the same something Viola said aloud.

"This is all because of the mudslide," she said.

"It's had quite the ripple effect."

"Yes, but . . ."

"I know. There's more. There's a body. If the girls really are okay, the body is the real problem here."

Viola sat forward, balancing the whiskey bottle on her knee. "What if the girls saw something out there? What if they know something about the body?"

"I'm sure Gril has considered that."

"I don't know," Viola said. "I just don't know."

"You can ask him."

"I can and I will." She paused. "But they weren't hurt. No injuries whatsoever on either of them."

I thought a long minute and then grabbed the bottle from Viola. I found my own shot glass and poured. I wasn't much of a drinker, but now seemed like a good time for a shot. And there was that vision of Travis. I pushed it away.

"Am I bothered because one of the girls is white? Am I that kind of a person?" I finally said to Viola.

She shook her head slowly. "I don't think so, Beth. I wondered the same thing about myself and then I realized I'd feel the same way if he was a white man and he was taking Annie away with him."

I was embarrassed by another sense of relief washing through me. Yes, I would have been bothered by that, too. I wasn't racist, but still maybe too race aware.

"Where's their mother?" I asked.

"Long gone, that's all Gril said about that."

"Oh boy, any chance she's the body?"

"I'm sure Gril is looking at that, too."

It made sense. In my mind, I'd solved the mysteries. The answers were right there. Well, sort of. We still didn't know who'd killed the woman, or why. Tex was probably involved, though I couldn't pinpoint how. So was Lane. And the girls would be able to talk once everything was figured out. There was a happy ending coming, I was sure.

"I bet. I talked to Orin about all of this. He's searching for something that might help."

"That's good. That's very good. No one better than Orin."

"Who did he used to be?" I'd asked Viola before, but she'd never answered.

Viola quirked an eyebrow. "If I told you, I'd have to shoot you." She patted the gun holstered at her hip.

I didn't think Viola would ever shoot me, but we still hadn't known each other long enough for me to be one hundred percent sure.

We could go around and around on the details, the facts as we knew them to be, but bottom line, it didn't matter what I thought, didn't matter if I'd solved any mystery in my imagination. It was all up to Gril. The girls were presumably safe now; that was the most important thing of all.

Besides, I had my own problems, and I wasn't going to let Travis Walker become a part of this new life of mine.

I poured myself another shot.

Fourteen

Baby girl—Wish me luck. I'm going to the principal's office.
Detective Majors called and I think she wants to see me even
more than I want to see her. What's the skinny on this?

I don't trust her, and I sense . . . something's up.

I read my mother's short email a few times and silently debated
with myself about what I wanted to tell her. I hit reply and wrote a
first draft.

I talked to Detective Majors.

The police know who he is, Mom. I still feel terrible for the wild-goose
chase I sent everyone on when I had the wrong name, but now they
know for sure. DNA on that damn pink blanket has confirmed it. Detective Majors even has a picture of him. She'll show you. Be on the
lookout. That DOESN'T mean I want you to look for him.

His name is Travis Walker, and he was born in Milton, Mom. He might know who I really am. He might know who Gramps was, who you are. Be careful, be aware.

Also, I wonder if he might have known Dad.

I read my own words over again. If I sent this email to my mother, she would have the information before she met with Detective Majors. I wasn't exactly sure how that would affect their face-to-face, but my gut told me it wouldn't be good. At least for Detective Majors.

I didn't delete the message, but I didn't send it, either. Mill hadn't mentioned when she was going into the police station. Maybe my note would just have to be a little too late.

I turned away from my laptop and switched gears.

Before my escape to Alaska, I would have wondered how someone could go missing, especially for as long as the woman seemed to have been without alarms being sounded. But even in the few months I'd been here, I'd seen how it was not only possible, but easy. In fact, if I hadn't found a room at the Benedict House—if I'd found a cabin to rent—my social interactions probably would have been near nil. If something had gone wrong for me, few people would even know who I was or how to figure out what had happened to me.

A chill ran up my spine. I was lucky to have the Benedict House.

I wondered if Gril had heard back from Christine, the ME. I thought about calling him but decided not to. Maybe the woman hadn't been killed. Maybe a murder hadn't occurred. It seemed that most things that had appeared alarming over the last couple of days weren't as outrageous as first assumed. A dead body was always alarming, though.

Something else had occurred to me when I'd seen Mill's email. An idea sparked at the back of my mind. I grabbed the burner phone from my pocket and dialed a number I hadn't called for years until recently, but had known all my life. It was even more ingrained in my memory than any of my own phone numbers.

"Milton Police," the female voice said. "Do you have an emergency?"

"I don't. I was hoping to talk to Chief Graystone."

"May I ask who's calling?"

"Sure. This is Beth Rivers."

The pause became more and more pregnant. I was surprised that my name was still known. No, I wasn't surprised it was known by some people in the place my grandfather had run, a place I'd worked, but I was surprised the woman who answered, who sounded young, seemed to recognize it.

She finally spoke. "One minute, please."

I wasn't on hold long.

"Beth? That you?" Chief Stellan Graystone picked up quickly.

"Hey, Chief. It's me."

"Prove it. What did you carve into the corner of your grandfather's desk?" I heard the smile in his voice.

"SuperGramps," I said with my own smile. Maybe someday, memories of my grandfather wouldn't be mixed with so much pain, but I missed him terribly.

"It is you." I could hear his chair squeak through the phone line. "How are you? Where are you?"

"I can't tell you where I am, but I'm doing well. Healed completely from everything."

"That's great news. You're still hiding?"

"I am. The guy who took me hasn't been caught yet."

"Shoot, Beth, I hoped he'd been found by now. What can I do to help?"

"Well, I have a name now. Has Detective Majors called you yet?" I knew Detective Majors had worked a little with Stellan on the search for my captor.

"No. Who is it?"

"Travis Walker, and he was born in Milton."

"Holy moly," Stellan said. "Give me all the details you can."

While I was sharing the few facts I knew, Stellan got an email from Detective Majors with Travis's picture attached. I'd thought she might be in touch with him soon. I'd timed my call about right.

"I don't recognize him at all, Beth," he said after looking at the picture.

"I remember some Walker families in town, but I don't remember any problems with them," I said.

"No, no problems that I'm aware of. I'll do some research, though, look into things. If he still has family around, he might be in touch with them."

"That's what I was thinking. Detective Majors is probably thinking the same thing, but she and I didn't discuss that specifically. I'm calling for another reason, too. I'm just going to be blunt. If my mom comes around, that means there could be more trouble. I guess I just want to send fair warning."

"Well, I do appreciate that, and it is something I'm aware of. She's a woman with a mission."

"Two missions. My father, and now Travis Walker."

"Two missions. That could get messy."

"Yes."

"I'll be on the lookout, Beth. My staff, most of us around town, are doing a good job of keeping your secret. I can't control everyone, but I've got an officer scouring social media for any locals posting anything that gives away who Elizabeth Fairchild really is. Something might be slipping somewhere, but we're working to catch things and shut them down."

"Thank you," I said, but I knew how impossible it would be to catch everything. The truth would all be out in the world someday, and I suspected Travis Walker knew my real identity already. I wasn't going to discourage Stellan's diligence, though.

"You are welcome. How can I get ahold of you?"

"I'll get back to you, Stellan."

"I understand. I guess. I can help with protection," he said.

"I appreciate that, but I'm my own protection, and I like it that way."

"Got it. Be safe."

"Will do."

We ended the call and I packed up my stuff. It was time to work on exactly what I'd told Stellan I was working on: me.

However, I decided it was also time to destroy this phone. I still had another one, but I'd talked to too many people, said too many things using this phone. It was time for it to go. I'd figure out a way to order more.

I only had to stomp down hard once and the phone exploded into a million pieces. It was one of the most satisfying things I'd done in this new life of mine.

Fifteen

Serena looked at me. "Are you sure?"

"Yes. Hit me!"

"All right." She pulled her fist back and swung it at my head, the side without the scar.

I put my arm up defensively, a pose our instructor had first shown us at last week's class. My arm stopped hers. I twisted it just right so that Serena's came down. I turned my body, held tight to her arm, now around my waist, and found some power in my core as I flipped her over my back. She landed on the mat.

"You okay?" I asked her.

"Great. But I wouldn't be if there wasn't a mat there. Nice job," Serena said with a smile up at me.

I helped her stand.

If Annie and Mary had still been in town, the self-defense class would have been canceled. But the beds and table and piles of clothes had been cleared away, making way for thick mats that were used for everything from yoga to gymnastics to this class, Benedict's newest: self-defense training.

Serena had come to Benedict years earlier to escape an abusive husband and had thrived here; she was now our local knitting instructor. When the sign-up sheet had been posted for this class, both of us had put our names under about five others, and we'd ended up as sparring partners. Though we'd both learned a lot and improved, we'd managed a few bumps and bruises, too.

Her husband was now deceased, had died before their divorce was finalized, leaving her to inherit a good chunk of money. She hadn't gone back to Washington State because she'd grown fond of Benedict. I envied almost everything about her situation and hoped mine ended as happily, though I still hoped to go back to St. Louis.

Our instructor was named Cecile Throckmorton. The first time I saw her, I'd been looking out the *Petition*'s window and watched her make her way into the library. She was hard to miss. Just over six feet tall, she was thickly muscled everywhere. I'd asked Orin who she was. He'd told me her name and her past experience as one of the first women to attempt to become a Navy SEAL. She hadn't succeeded, which had been the biggest blow of her life. She'd escaped to Benedict from Oklahoma after that and two years later was still licking her wounds—those were the words Orin had used. He'd said she didn't want to go home because she only wanted to find ways to keep moving forward.

I'd asked him if he thought she might be willing to teach me a thing or two about self-defense. His eyes had lit up at the idea, and the next thing I knew, he was knocking on the *Petition*'s door to inform me about the sign-up sheet that would be taped to the community center's door that day.

Orin told me Cecile wished she'd thought of giving the classes a long time ago. He'd said she was getting her groove back, her mojo— again, his words. He gave me credit for making her life better. I didn't want credit; I was just grateful for the things she'd taught Serena, me, and the other five locals—one man and four women—who'd been there for class every week for the last four. We were only at the beginning of our "training," but flipping Serena onto her back was a big step for me.

"Nice," Cecile said to me now. "But you're going to tweak your back if you don't plant your feet better. You have to be quick, though. Keep at it and it will become instinctual."

"Okay," I said.

Cecile began and ended every class with tai chi, and it had helped me just as much as the defensive training had. My need to breathe deeply and calm down had been better handled since I'd started Cecile's classes. I wished I'd had all these experiences and skills years earlier, and over the last couple of days I'd needed them even more. I needed to get back on track. I hadn't even realized how much better I'd been doing until the visions of my captor—of Travis Walker—had started nudging their way back into my life. I not only *wanted* this class to help me. I *needed* it to.

"All right, everyone. Good job tonight," Cecile said.

I wiped some sweat off my forehead.

"You all need to work on your cardio," Cecile continued. "I know it's difficult to be outside when it's getting colder and we don't have a gym around here. I'm having a treadmill and a stationary bike ferried over from Juneau. I got approval to have them set up in the back, by the kitchen. I need promises that you'll all come use them."

We all nodded with as much enthusiasm as we could muster at the end of one of Cecile's exhausting classes. I would do my best to use the equipment, but I was glad it wasn't something I needed to find energy for that evening.

"Drink?" Serena asked.

"Yes please," I said.

We each drove our own vehicle back downtown. I parked my truck on the side of the Benedict House, and Serena parked her car on the road in front of the shops. As I passed the mercantile on my way to the bar, I peered into the windows. I couldn't make out anything behind the drawn shade. *Maybe I'll stop by and see Randy tomorrow*, I thought.

Just then, the door was flung open, and I started. I moved out of the way, thinking that Randy would notice me in the dark space under the awning, but when the man in the doorway turned around, it wasn't Randy at all.

It was Lane.

"Evening," he said, sending me a quick glance.

I'd opened my mouth to say something, though I'm not sure what greeting would have come out, when he did a double take.

"You," he said. He turned and faced me. "I never got your name, but you work with the chief."

I couldn't see his face well, and the tone in his voice was more critical than curious.

"Beth Rivers," I said, jutting my chin out a little. I didn't think he noticed, but I wasn't going to back down.

He nodded but didn't approach. With the same critical tone, he said, "I'm sorry if I hurt you, Beth. I didn't mean to. I was just reacting."

"Apology accepted." I kept my hand from going to the spot he'd elbowed.

"I asked Gril to tell you."

I nodded, but didn't want him to know that Gril hadn't mentioned the apology.

"I don't know what you do with him, but I hope you've heard by now that I didn't know the . . . woman who was found in my shed. I'm sorry for whatever happened to her."

"You and Randy are friends?" I asked, noting to myself the odd timing of my question.

Lane paused. "This is where most of us around here get our supplies."

"Right. Of course."

"Well, again, I apologize if I hurt you. Good night."

"Good night."

I watched him walk toward the dark woods. A part of me wanted to offer him a ride, but it was only a small part. I calculated that he was going to walk about three miles, in the dark, to get back to his house. Maybe that just wasn't a big deal to him, or to anyone who lived out there.

"Beth?" Serena said as she approached. "Who's that?"

"His name is Lane, but I don't know him. I do know he lives a few miles away. I think he's going to walk."

Serena shrugged. "It's a nice night."

It was cold, but maybe not cold enough to be concerned.

"Still want a drink?" Serena asked.

"Sure Just a sec."

I watched another moment as Lane's figure was absorbed by the darkness. I reached for the mercantile' s doorknob, but it wouldn't turn. Sometime in the last few moments, the door had been locked. I debated knocking, but decided I'd talk to Randy later. Besides, I wasn't quite sure why I wanted to talk to him anyway, other than to satisfy my curiosity about . . . everything.

Finally, I followed Serena into the bar.

The space was crowded, but Serena made her way to one of the five booths. Mostly, locals met there for conversation, and during the winter people would stop by just so everyone knew they were still alive. Apparently, the night after a stretch of stormy days was pretty busy.

> *I survived just fine.*
> *It was touch and go there for a while.*
> *I about lost my mind. I never thought the weather would get better.*

I'd already heard versions of such stories. Tonight, I overheard folks talking about recent challenges—the landscape could cause problems in other seasons, too, as we'd all now seen with the mudslide. But many times, previous winters' storms were discussed. The part about someone losing their mind was a real thing; mental health was a challenge when people got cooped up. It was another reason I liked the Benedict House and hoped not to have to leave it any time soon—unless I got to go home, of course.

Benny, Viola's sister, ran the bar, and had poured beers into cold mugs for us when she spotted us walking through the door. She passed the drinks over the bar as I handed her some cash.

"Keep the change," I said.

"Need to talk to you later, if possible," Benny said.

I nodded and sent her a question with my eyes. She was too busy to notice. I carried the beers over to the booth and sat across from Serena.

"You heard what's been going on around here?" I said.

"No. Tell me."

I told her most everything, as best as I could remember.

"A body? A frozen woman?" Serena said. She hadn't even blinked about the girls. "How interesting."

I inspected her and nodded.

"And that guy we just saw was the one who elbowed you?"

"It doesn't hurt anymore," I lied.

"Well, of course it's awful and tragic, but I'm more interested in what or who put her there."

I nodded again.

"I mean, I know all about a life where being murdered is a real possibility. If she lived that sort of life, I can picture myself in similar situations, and I know her opportunities for leaving were probably small and brief. I wouldn't be surprised if this is all about domestic violence. Too much of that everywhere, particularly here."

"Alaska?" I took a drink of foamy, cold beer.

"It's all part of the whole picture, per capita, you know, and our capita is smaller than most places. And since people move here to get away, hide, some are hiding their cruelty." Serena shrugged. "Then you never know what the winter will do to a person. If it's a particularly bad one, it can be rough."

I'd just been thinking about all she was saying; maybe there *was* a tenuous connection we could sense but were missing at the moment. "But it's sad."

Serena shrugged again. "It's not all of us. I moved here to get away from it." Her eyes unfocused as she fell into thought. "It's a place of peace for me, for many people. I can't imagine living anywhere else."

I held up my mug. "Cheers to that."

We clinked.

"What do you know about Randy?" I said.

"He runs the mercantile. Never missed a day, from what I can tell. He ordered me a special coat I wanted last year. I like him."

I realized I had left out the part about Annie's drawing of his house, but I still didn't mention it.

"He's the one who heard the girls first," I repeated from my first telling. "I'm certain they made the noises we both heard."

"Right. So?"

"I don't know."

"You think he has something to do with the girls?"

"No, not really, but I wonder if anyone knows him well enough to have been inside his house, to see if anyone else might live there."

I was sure Gril would have asked the girls' father if he knew Randy, particularly after Annie drew a picture that looked like Randy's house. But I wondered if connections might have been noticed by others.

Serena fell into thought again. "I haven't, but I don't know about anyone else. I've never known him to be associated with little girls. From your description, they don't sound familiar to me." Serena paused. Her eyebrows came together, and she sat up straighter. "I just remembered something. He was married when he first moved here."

I swallowed a gulp of beer. "I hadn't heard that."

"His wife hated it. She tried to knit, but hated that, too. She left. I bet that's why I remember her; she came to one knitting class but didn't stay long."

"Really?"

Serena frowned. "She was so upset. You know, asking people

how they could possibly live here without real phones and internet, couldn't believe animals just walked around on their own."

"I can't believe no one has mentioned her to me before this."

"They might not remember her. She was only here for a short time, and she made quite the scene at the knitting class. Also, I have a good memory. Not everyone else does."

Orin does, I thought, but didn't say it out loud. But he had mentioned that he'd moved here shortly after Randy had.

"Do you remember what she looked like?" I asked.

"Kind of. Pretty, long brown hair. Quite a bit younger than Randy, if I remember correctly."

Lots of women are pretty and have long brown hair. There was no need to immediately jump to the conclusion that the frozen woman might be Randy's wife.

"Thin, heavy?"

"Normal, I guess, not noticeably thin or fat."

If I were to describe the body I'd seen, I would have said something similar. *Average weight and height*.

Jesus.

No.

That couldn't be it.

I shook it off. "Any idea where she went?"

"No, none at all. Beth, I just now realized she hasn't been around, but I'm not very social. I remember being glad when she didn't show up to another knitting class, but then didn't give her any thought until right now."

I needed to research Randy's wife and where she'd gone.

I could try my satellite hot spot or just talk to Orin, use the library's internet. I was anxious to do something productive. This new mystery needed attention. But it was late; too late to bother Orin and too dark to venture back to the *Petition*. A chill ran up my spine as I remembered seeing Lane disappear into the woods.

I'd wait until tomorrow. Tonight, I'd try to enjoy the evening and find out what Benny needed to talk to me about.

Serena and I only had one beer each but managed to make it last through a detailed conversation about fishing. Serena said I was a fool for not heading out on a fishing boat yet. I didn't explain to her that I was afraid of open water and that Ruke, a local Tlingit, had told me his intuition was that I should stay out of the bay. I was living near Glacier Bay National Park, and I had yet to see a glacier. I'd even missed the big one in Juneau on my way here.

Serena went home, and the bar cleared enough after she left that I sidled up to a stool and waited for Benny to have a moment to talk. I didn't have to wait long.

"How's my sister?" she asked.

"Fine, I think," I said. "Why?"

"She got a new client, an addict, I hear."

"Yes, she's not in good shape." I had all but forgotten about Ellen.

"Damn. That's so unfair."

"I don't understand."

"After all the mess a few months ago, they told Vi she wasn't going to get to do her job anymore," Benny said.

"I might have heard something about that, but you make it sound much more serious."

"This one is her test. She's got to prove herself," Benny said.

"What? She has to get an addict clean? That's her test? That seems both unfair and immoral."

"She told them to send her a challenge. She'd prove she was up for it and earn her way back into the job."

"She's been busy with other things, too," I said. "I don't know how much attention she's been able to give Ellen."

"I know. She helped take care of those girls."

"You both did, I hear. What can I do to help Viola?" I asked.

"Nothing. She won't let anyone help. I offered to close the bar and sit with the woman so Viola could have a break. She wouldn't hear of it, and now the girls are gone, so that's . . . at least helpful. I just wondered if you knew if she was doing okay."

"Honestly, I don't know. She's pretty good at multitasking, though."

I didn't mention Viola's time venting at the *Petition* because though she'd arrived in a concerned state, by the time she left, she was back to her level self. She hadn't even downed the second shot she'd poured. I'd ended up throwing it out, which I suspect would have bothered Bobby Reardon.

"Yeah." Benny grabbed a towel and wiped the bar in front of me. "Just keep an eye on her. Let me know if I need to intervene."

"Can I ask you what your impression was of the girls?"

"No impression. I just gathered clothes and toys and dropped them off. I didn't even meet them—Viola and Maper had it handled. They didn't want another person to cause confusion. Glad their dad found them."

"Me too." I paused, not adding that I was only glad if he was a good man, a good dad. "Hey, what do you know about Randy?"

"Mercantile Randy?"

"Yes."

"He's a great guy. Does his job well."

"Do you remember his wife?"

"He's not . . . oh, wait, he *was* married when he first moved here. I had forgotten about her. I think she was pretty unhappy, left shortly after they moved here. Happens every now and then."

"I have many questions about that, Benny. Why would someone move here without knowing for sure they want to live here?"

"Oh. Happens all the time. They have an idea of what they want, but when they get here, it's not exactly what they expected, or it's too much of what they expected. How did you decide to move here?"

I smiled. "A fifteen-minute internet search."

"And you're still here? If that's how you found Benedict, I would have only given you about a thirty percent chance of staying. If you're not hiding."

"No, not hiding," I lied.

I really did like it here. I missed home, but for the first time, I wondered if maybe this place would eventually rub off on me like it had on Serena.

"Well, we're glad you're here. Want another beer?"

"No, I'm good. Time to call it a night. I'll check on Viola."

"Appreciate it."

As I left, Benny moved to the other end of the bar to wait on another customer, someone I didn't know. I was surprised that even in a community of about five hundred people, I still didn't know or recognize every single person.

I'd now met and seen Lane twice, though I'd never noticed him before. Randy must have. Gril must have asked Randy about the trapper shopping at the mercantile. Gril had mentioned that he *maybe* thought he knew who Lane was. I wondered if he just thought he'd seen him around or if it was something else.

I stepped outside into the cold, quiet night. It wasn't raining. In fact, it wasn't even cloudy. A blanket of stars lit the sky. There wasn't enough light in Benedict to dull the stars, so when it wasn't cloudy, the sight above was stunning. I considered taking a short walk. I looked out toward the woods again. But I wasn't made of the same stuff as Lane. It was cold, and I still didn't feel prepared to handle all the Alaskan night might offer. I noticed the lights were now off in the mercantile before I hurried over to the Benedict's front door.

As I pulled it wide, I immediately heard a ruckus coming from the dining room. I ran down the short hallway and peered in.

"Get out of here, Beth," Viola said. "Now!"

I froze in place. I was finally witnessing Viola with her gun drawn.

Sixteen

The furniture had been upturned. Though there were only tables and chairs in the dining area, none of them were upright or in their normal places. I couldn't see into the kitchen on the other side of the far wall, but I hoped it hadn't also been in the path of destruction.

"Viola, what's going on?" I said, though it was pretty easy to figure out.

"Get out of here, Beth," she repeated.

The gun was aimed at Ellen. She was curled into a ball on the floor but held a lamp as if she wanted to throw it at Viola. I had a lamp just like it in my room.

"No, no," I said as I registered a scratch on the side of Viola's face. I stepped toward Ellen. She turned the lamp my direction.

"I'll shoot her," Viola said. "She's out of control."

Ellen snarled, just like any junkie coming down, probably.

"Why don't we call Dr. Powder," I said. "Or I'll go get him if he's hard to reach by phone. Don't shoot her, Viola. No matter what she does, don't shoot her."

Truthfully, I didn't think she would. She was just using the gun as a threat to stop Ellen from continuing the destruction she'd begun.

Still, though, I knew you were never supposed to aim a gun unless you truly thought you would use it. It was a Mill rule, one I'd learned when she showed me the gun she kept holstered at her ankle. Unfortunately, Mill always thought she might need to use her gun, or maybe wanted to.

"I don't know who you are," Ellen said. "I don't know who either of you are! I need help. I need . . . something. Help me! Get me out of here!"

I put my hand up, signaling her to stop.

"I tried all that," Viola said. "She's not listening."

"Maybe if two people tell her, she won't be afraid?" I said as I looked at Viola.

Viola sighed as a drip of blood from the scratch on her face rolled down over her jaw to her neck. "Go for it."

"Ellen, you're in Benedict, Alaska, a halfway house. You were convicted of . . ." I looked at Viola, but she was only glaring at the scared woman in the corner, gun still pointed, so I punted. "Drug possession and a slew of other things. Does that part make sense to you?"

She squinted hard my direction. "I don't remember that."

"Of course you don't, you were strung out, big-time. But that's what happened. You were sent to Benedict to get straightened out."

"Not a recovery facility?" Ellen said. "That doesn't make sense."

"Viola?" I said. "Why is she here and not somewhere else?"

"Because she failed too many times in Anchorage. They booted her out of town. She can only go back if I give permission or if she swims. And it's a cold, cold swim."

"Okay, Ellen, if you have any memory left, does this make sense?"

She shook her head hard.

"Are you sure?" I said.

She snarled again. It was worse than some of the wild bear noises I'd heard.

"Ellen?" I said.

"I'm dying here. I need a fix, bad."

It was my turn to shake my head. I wasn't going to lie. "No fixes here. This is Benedict. We don't have anything like that close by. You're going to have to do this the hard way, I'm afraid."

I did wonder where Orin got his weed.

"Then I'm going to die," Ellen said. "I'm going to die."

I shrugged. "Then so be it." She shot me a look with wild eyes. I continued. "Or you can battle like you've never battled before and finally get yourself cleaned up. Your choice." I looked at Viola and back at Ellen. "Or she can just shoot you—and she will if you continue to mess with her stuff. You want Viola to just put you out of your misery?"

I really hoped she wouldn't say yes, but for the longest moment, I thought she might.

"No" was all she said.

"Then you have to get up to your room and stay there until you're through it. Worse women than you have made it. You will, too, if you want to," I said.

Tears started rolling down her gray face. "I don't think I can walk."

"We'll help you," I said. "But you have to behave."

She bit her bottom lip so hard that tiny blood bubbles formed around her teeth.

It took more convincing—we had to get her to put the lamp down and let us lift her up. But we did get her upstairs and into the shower. Viola got her cleaned up and I changed her bedding and aired out her room. I filled a few water bottles and grabbed a couple of apples from the kitchen, which seemed to have been spared from damage.

We put Ellen, her eyes still big and terrified, into bed, though sitting up. I didn't know if she'd decided to obey us or was just too tired to fight anymore. She had calmed down enough to stay on the bed, but it was going to be a rough night.

"Should we lock her in?" I asked Viola.

"Nah. If she gets out and tries to run, she'll die of exposure. Problem will be solved for all of us." Viola paused, noticing my questioning eyes. "Don't worry, Beth, I'll check on her through the night," she continued as she closed Ellen's door. "We're past the worst of it. Now that she knows where she is and what's going on, she's still going to struggle, but maybe she'll stay in her room. She knows she's safe and at some point she might realize that others care about her."

"How long before she can function?"

"Not sure. Couple more days, maybe. I've seen it happen sooner. Maybe tomorrow."

I debated my next words, but then went for it. "Viola, Benny told me that Ellen is a test."

Viola rolled her eyes. She still had a streak of blood on her face, but it had dried. "Of course she did. None of her business, none of your business, but there we are."

We made our way toward the stairs.

"I'm sorry you're going through this," I said as I took the first step.

Viola laughed once. "Beth, this is nothing. Absolutely nothing. The girls who have come through here have given me hundreds of challenges. I screwed up a few months ago. I understand why the powers that be felt like they needed to 'test' me. But they aren't going to take this job from me. This is a great place to send troublemakers. They don't want to lose it, and no one else will run this place. It's all going to be fine. My goal is to get Ellen clean and then convince her to stay that way, but not because it's a test—because it's what needs to be done. It will take some time, but I'm the one to do it. If she fails, then at least I gave it my best."

We stopped outside Viola's room.

"You've worked with other junkies?"

"So many, I couldn't even count." Viola frowned. "Ellen was particularly messed up, though. Honestly, I wasn't sure she would survive, but I think she will now. At least until she uses again. I'm going to work hard to make sure that never happens."

"You're not just a babysitter. You do good."

Viola smirked. "Let's keep that between the two of us. Want to help me a little more? I need to get the dining room put back together."

"Sure," I said. "But I have to know, Viola. Would you have shot her?"

"If I thought I needed to." Viola didn't hesitate.

"Were you close?"

She smirked again. "Gun wasn't loaded tonight, Beth, but don't get me wrong, most of the time it is. I've had to fire it before, but I'm not giving you those details. Don't bother asking me if I've killed anyone. I won't answer, and anyone who would brag about such a thing shouldn't carry a weapon. Anyway, let's get the dining room cleaned up."

As we worked, I asked about Randy's wife. Viola had no memory of her at all, nothing. I asked her about the girls and their father again, but she wanted to talk about that less than she did about who she might have shot.

She did ease my mind one way. She said she had asked Donner to check on the girls, and he was going to drive out to Tex's home the next day or so to make sure they were okay.

I was relieved that someone was going to do that. I wanted to go with Donner. As I told Viola good night, I tried to figure out how to ask him, how to word the question the right way so he would say yes.

But by the time I crawled under the covers and closed my eyes, I was too tired to think about anything else.

Seventeen

was again awakened by a knock at the door. At least this time, it wasn't an anxious pounding.

"Beth, you've got a call. Wake up, you've got a call," she said from the other side.

I slipped out of bed and went to the door. I opened it without touching my bedhead hair. "I do?"

"Hey, good morning," Viola said. She was dressed, and the cut on her face had been cleaned up. She wasn't wearing the Indiana Jones hat, and her hair was pulled back in a neat ponytail. I'd never seen it pulled back before. "You have a call in my office."

"Who?"

"It's someone calling herself Mill."

I caught the word before it made its way out of my mouth—*Mom*?

"Okay," I said. I reached over to the small table where I kept my room key and grabbed it. I closed the door and followed Viola to her office.

She didn't ask if I wanted privacy, just let me go in by myself and closed the door after I was inside.

My heart was racing in my chest. How did my mother find me? What did she want? Was she okay?

There was only one way to find out. I picked up the landline handset.

"Mill?"

"Hey, girlie," she said.

"How? What's going on?" I said.

Mill sighed, then took a sizzling pull on one of her ever-present cigarettes and blew out the smoke. "I had to talk to you."

"Text me?"

"I tried. You didn't respond."

Shit. I had destroyed the burner phone tied to the number she'd last used. I hadn't used the new phone yet. I should have fired it up immediately and let her know the new number.

"Jesus, Mom, how in the world did you get this number?"

"I went to talk to Detective Majors. Saw a note on her desk that said 'B.R.' and this phone number. Figured it was her code for you. Here we are."

"Shit. That's . . ."

"Brilliant on my part, idiotic on her part? Yep. Couldn't agree more. Don't worry. I won't tell anyone."

"I know, but . . ."

"I memorized the number and then destroyed the note. Mostly just to mess with her. I had her go grab me a water and I ate it."

"You ate it?"

Mill snorted. "Not really. But I took it and destroyed it good."

"Thanks."

"Of course. You always got me, kid, you know that."

"I do." My heart rate started to slow, and I blinked back tears I hadn't even noticed had welled in my eyes.

The note had been a careless oversight. Why hadn't Detective Majors known that? Even if it hadn't specifically included my name, just the letters were enough for someone like my mom to figure out or make a good guess. Why had she kept it—out in the open?

I sighed. "How did it go?"

"Never got around to bringing up the reason I wanted to talk to her, but I have a name and a picture of our other problem."

"She told you, showed you?"

"That she did, and I gotta give her a little credit. It takes a million years to test DNA, but I think they got a solid answer in about half the time. Now we just have to find him. And I will. I think . . ."

"What?"

"I think I've seen him, girlie."

"Where? Recently?"

"Listen, this is going to upset you and I don't want it to. It is what it fucking is, right? Knowledge is power. Blah, blah, blah."

"Okay."

"I think I know him from Milton, but I can't place how or when, and I thought that before the good detective told me that's where he'd been hatched. I'm going to work on it. I'll get Stellan the stud involved."

I didn't tell her I'd talked to him because she'd be upset I hadn't told her first, that I'd let Detective Majors give her the news. Frankly, from this vantage point, as I now knew about the note, I wasn't sure I'd made the right decision not to send the email I'd drafted to Mill. So often since my abduction, nothing seemed completely clear or understandable.

"You need to be careful," I said.

"Always. You know that. Don't tell Majors. I didn't tell her I thought he looked familiar. None of her beeswax, you know. Once I was there, I decided not to mention that you-know-who might be alive, too. It just all felt like too much info."

In fact, it *was* the police's beeswax, but I wouldn't point that out right now. Mill was speaking in code, just in case someone was listening. No one was, probably, but on the phone Mill always spoke as if someone might be listening. "All right. She might figure it out on her own. And why do you think he might be alive?"

"You know how our subconscious sometimes picks up on things that our conscious selves don't?"

"Sure."

"That name you saw on the envelope, the one you thought was attached to the man who took you?"

"Levi Brooks?"

"Jesus, darlin', let's not say it out loud. Anyway, even though I do think there's a chance you really did see it on an envelope, I think it struck a bell with you for another reason. I think that since that was the name of the man who burned down a barn, you glommed on to it, because your subconscious remembered that fire from when you were little. I wouldn't be surprised if it was somehow discussed in that . . . van. I hate thinking of you in that vile thing."

"Right, but . . ."

"I found Brooks, girlie. Shit, now *I* said it. Oh well. I talked to him. He knew your dad back in the day. Shit. I mean, he knew you-know-who, your dad. Crap, I'm just gonna say it—he knew Eddy."

"What?"

"He told me that . . . he saw Eddy a couple years ago."

"What?" I said, louder this time. My mind tried to make sense of what she was saying. "Come on, Mill. If you found the same Levi Brooks, who we *know* is a bad guy because he burned down a barn, he's probably lying to you." I didn't much care about being careful with names now. We needed clarity.

"I don't think so, but that's what I'm looking into. He told me stories about him and your dad, things they did when we were all younger. They were friends. Brooks said he met me, met you when you were a little girl. I don't remember that. Do you?"

"No."

"Hold tight, I'm not ready to believe him all the way. I'm looking at it, that's all. It . . . it just feels more solid than other things. I really need you not to tell Majors about any of this; this time it's extra important. Please."

My head was swimming. I had questions, but I also knew Mill would do whatever she wanted to do. And maybe she really was onto something.

Mill and I were a team. A strange team, one that had stayed together maybe only because my grandfather had had vision enough
to know that even though my mother had all but abandoned me like
my father had, she still loved me, and she would come back to me
every time she went away. She'd proved that much. And she'd been
there for me when I'd needed her the most.

After a few moments of digging deep inside myself to try to pre-
dict ramifications I couldn't possibly yet understand, I said, "Okay.
I promise."

"Atta girl. Gotta go. Got work to do. Send me a different number
if you don't want me to use this one."

"I will do that. Love you, Mill."

"More than Cheerios with extra sugar, baby girl. Later."

She disconnected the call, and I sat there a long moment, holding
the handset, my head still swimming.

The part we hadn't discussed but was making its way up to the top
of my thoughts now was that her call to me meant that, really, anyone could find me if they wanted to badly enough. Anyone.

But "anyone" wasn't Mill Rivers, and I had to remember that too.

I hung up the handset and sat back in Viola's chair. I glanced at the
old digital clock on the edge of Viola's desk; it was only five thirty in
the morning. My people in St. Louis needed a better understanding
of the time difference between here and there. I smiled to myself, but
I was still riddled with shaky nerves.

How could Detective Majors have left that note out when she knew
my mother was coming in? She should have known Mill was always
looking for clues.

My eyes were absently wandering over Viola's desk when they
landed on almost the exact thing I'd been thinking about: a note with
an address, a handwritten scribble in a notebook on the corner. It
read: "Girls' address—end of village. Brayn." Pretty easy to memorize.

It seemed the universe might be trying to tell me something.

I pushed away the overload of information Mill had shared and left
the office with only the Brayn address on my mind.

Viola wasn't in the hallway, but I thought I heard activity coming from the dining room again. It sounded less violent than the noises the night before, but I hurried toward it anyway. The scents of breakfast hit me before I turned the corner.

"Eat your eggs," Viola said to Ellen.

They sat next to each other at a table overflowing with food.

"Hey, Beth, since you're awake, you might as well come on in and join us. We've got plenty," Viola said.

Ellen didn't look like the same woman she'd been only about seven hours earlier. Her still-blemished face wasn't gray anymore; her eyes weren't sunk as deep in their sockets. She still had an unhealthy waxiness to her skin, but she seemed to be on the mend.

I joined them, sitting across the table and serving myself some scrambled eggs.

"Are you feeling better?" I asked Ellen.

"Better than I was," she said. "Still not good, but better."

"I understand."

Ellen pushed the food around on her plate. It was only a guess, but I would have bet that Viola made her prepare all this food just so she would get up and get moving, have something to focus on other than her situation.

"I remember last night, and I'm sorry," she said as she looked at me. She rushed to add, "I wasn't always like this."

I nodded and didn't ask for further clarification.

"I got in trouble, got into the bad stuff when I was thirty-five. Before that, I was a teetotaler. Really."

"Happens. Unfortunately," I said. My heart wanted to go out to her, but my head told me not to be too quick with my sympathy.

"I hurt my back. That's all it was, a pulled muscle in my back. A doctor gave me some pills, and that was the end of me. I can't believe it happened," Ellen said.

"Do you have a family?" I asked. I wasn't sure if I was allowed to ask personal questions, but Viola didn't send me a sideways glare.

Ellen nodded. "Well, I did. I doubt I'll ever get them back. My husband left me, took our eleven-year-old daughter." Tears filled her eyes. "I didn't much care. I care today and it hurts more than you can imagine."

"You'll care tomorrow then, too. Care one day at a time, don't try to dilute your feelings with the bad stuff, and maybe you'll get them back," I said.

"I doubt it," she said again.

"They're worth a try, right?" Viola said.

"Yes. Of course." Ellen sniffed.

"Eat your eggs," Viola said again.

Ellen blinked. I sent her a quick smile before I put my attention back to my food.

I hoped she'd find it in herself to stay clean, but her one-day-at-a-times were only just the beginning. I realized how perfect Benedict was for her situation, but the rest of the world would work against her. I didn't know her, but I wanted to believe in her. Maybe I would in another few days.

She scooped up some eggs and took a bite.

"Your call go okay?" Viola asked me.

"It did. Thanks for that."

"Beth runs our local paper," Viola said to Ellen. "She puts in notices about some of the classes offered at our community center. Knitting tonight. Any desire to go?"

"I've never been a knitter," Ellen said.

"Me either," I said. "The instructor is Serena, and she's patient. Viola's sister, Benny, sometimes attends. The town's best knitter is a young blind woman named Janell who attends with her mother, Larrie. Some guys come, too—when they're in town between shifts on an oil rig up north. It's a great group of people. I'll go with you, if you want."

"Really?" Ellen said.

"Sure. Want to?"

"Is that okay?" she asked Viola.

"Sure, if you think you can handle it. If you run away, you'll just die of exposure. Keep that in mind."

Ellen nodded, her fork in midair. "All right. I'll go."

In those few moments, I saw glimpses of the woman she used to be. She'd never be that person again, but she might find a roughed-up version. Who of us wasn't like that? Life was way too full of opportunities to take some hits, make some scars.

I finished breakfast, and with the address from Viola's desk on my mind, I offered to help clean up. I was glad when Viola sent me away, saying that was Ellen's job now and she'd start cooking all breakfasts and dinners as of the next day. Ellen seemed surprised by her new duties, but she didn't argue.

I made my way back to my room, ready to conquer a new mission.

Eighteen

had a whole day in front of me, filled with many possibilities. Writing should've been my first priority, but I had that address and I couldn't stop thinking about it.

I stepped outside to find a thin blanket of newly fallen snow. I should have put my snowshoes on and tried to go for a walk, but I didn't do that, either.

Work and exercise would have to wait.

I looked toward the mercantile. The light was still on in the window, but the door would probably be unlocked. I noticed Randy's truck out front, not remembering if I'd seen it there the night before.

I made my way over the boardwalk. Someone had cleared away the snow and mud. It was twilight-dark and cold outside, enough so that the chill seeped into my bones before I made it all the way to the mercantile doors, which was less than a thirty-second walk. It must have been well below freezing.

I sensed there would be more wet weather today; I hoped for snow over rain.

A bell jingled above the door as I opened it. Randy was in the back of the small space, stacking some blue enamel camping dishes.

"Beth, hello, come in," he said, just like he always did. "What are you looking for today?"

I got no sense that he was bothered by anything. Of course, even if Gril had wanted to talk to him about the picture that Annie drew, it might not have mattered once the girls' father showed up.

The space inside was old-fashioned, made of simple wood planks and old barrels full of goods—Donner had referred to it all as "gear" when I first arrived in town with only a T-shirt and a flimsy jacket, in need of some serious re-outfitting. Now almost my entire wardrobe consisted of gear from the mercantile, including the jeans I'd donned this morning. When I first purchased them, I'd wondered if I would ever be able to bend my knees again, but they'd finally softened some.

"I need some more of those thick socks," I said.

"White ones or the gray wool ones?" Randy said as he put down the dishes and walked toward the barrels of socks.

"The wool ones."

"That's easy. How many?"

"Two pairs."

He grabbed them. "Anything else? Want to look around a bit?"

"No, that's good."

I followed him to the cash register.

"On your account?"

"No, I'll pay. I think I owe a payment, too." I pulled some cash from my pocket.

He reached under the cash register and grabbed the notebook where he kept a handwritten list of what everyone had charged. He let anyone charge anything, and from what I could tell, he never pushed for payment. I could pay for everything I purchased, but the first time I'd come in, I hadn't wanted to flash all the cash I had hidden on me from my escape from St. Louis.

"All righty. How much would you like to pay?"

"What do I owe?"

"Total, with the socks, of two hundred sixty-two dollars."

"I can pay it all today."

Randy looked at me with raised eyebrows. "You sure? You don't have to."

I laughed. "I'm sure. You let everyone charge. How do you do it?"

He shrugged. "I like being able to do it. I have the money."

"Well, I can't help but ask, and it's okay if it's none of my business, but did you get an inheritance or something?"

"Nah, before I moved here, I managed a hedge fund, got out right before the economy fell apart. I have more money than I should."

"I'm surprised. I keep forgetting that most people here had significantly different lives before moving to Benedict. You shouldn't feel guilty about your money. You earned it."

"Yes ma'am."

I handed him the cash.

"Where'd you live?" I asked.

"New York City," he said, just like that old salsa commercial.

"Wow, what a difference—NYC to here. That had to be rough," I said.

"It wasn't rough on me," he said with a sad smile.

"Ah, I hear something in your voice. It was hard on someone else. Did you leave someone or bring someone here who didn't like it?"

He waved off the question, but then surprised me and answered it. "I was married back then."

"Oh. Was? I'm sorry. Sounds like she wasn't happy here. That would be a tough transition, though. Some people like it, but I can understand why some wouldn't. Did she just go back to New York?"

Doubt crossed his features, but he probably didn't think I was watching him closely. "Yes."

I opened my mouth to ask another question, but closed it again. *Enough*, I thought. Anything I asked now would only make me seem way too nosy. I just smiled and nodded. But, I admit, I was pleasantly surprised when he continued on his own.

"Divorce. Still waiting on the papers," he said with a shrug.

I blinked. "Haven't you been here awhile?"

"Six and a half or so years."

"She hasn't signed the papers?" So much for no more questions. I couldn't help myself now.

"Not yet."

"Geez, come on, Mrs. Randy, get your act together," I said, trying to make him smile. It worked for a second. "Hard to move on if that tie still binds, right?"

"Wanda. Her name was . . . is Wanda. And yes, being married to someone who truly doesn't want to be married to you does make moving on difficult."

"What does she say about not signing?"

"Nothing." His eyebrows came together as he looked down at the counter. He was smiling by the time he looked up again. "Goodness, Beth, I'm sorry to bother you with that old, boring story. I haven't talked about her in a long time. Forget I said anything."

I picked up the bag with the socks. "Forget what?" I smiled again.

"Thanks."

"Hey, I'm here if you ever need to talk. Well, if I'm not here, I'm at the *Petition* shed or the Benedict House, but I promise to keep anything off the record, if that's what you want."

"Very good." He pulled in a deep breath. "I'm okay, though. Business to run and everything."

"Oh! You did a good job reporting that sound you heard. You know what's been going on the last couple of days, don't you?"

"The girls? You heard it, too, right?"

"Yes, and I'm sure it was them who made that noise outside the *Petition*. It was just like you described. Did you know I was the one who brought them into town?"

"I've heard a few different stories, but that makes sense."

"It was all so eerie. They weren't talking. Their father picked them up, thankfully. They'd gotten lost after the mudslide moved things around a bit."

"That can happen sometimes," he said absently.

"Which part?"

"Oh, the mudslide."

"I thought you might mean the not talking."

"That too, I suppose."

"That's freaky to me," I said. "Why would two girls not talk? And then they drew a picture of your house."

"They did. Gril and I figured they'd just seen it, passed by and it made an impression. They must have been close when they made that noise."

It was the first thing he'd said that sounded . . . not like a lie, but not completely truthful.

"Probably," I said. "You built it, didn't you? It's really great."

"I had it built," he said, looking up again with a modest smile, his tone back to normal. "I'm not a builder, not handy at all."

"Really? I'm thinking of building something, too—well, like you, having something built, but I want a good design. I've looked at stuff on the internet, but I can't find the right thing. I would hate to intrude, but is there any way I could have a tour of your place?"

"Sure," he said. "How about tonight, after I close?"

"That would be perfect! Thanks, Randy."

"You're welcome." He hesitated. "Come on over about seven."

"Will do. See you then." I picked up the socks and made my way to the door. I turned back around when I got there. "You were open late last night?"

"I don't know if it was late. I just stay open until it feels like it's time to close."

"I saw that trapper leaving last night. Lane."

"Yes. Why?"

"I'd never seen him in town before."

"He comes in about every other month. A good enough guy. Not the friendliest. A loner; lots of those out there. Came in last night to pick up a sharpening stone he ordered a while back."

I'd told everyone I'd talked to about the body on Lane's property, but I suddenly realized there was a chance I wasn't supposed to be sharing that news. Did Randy know about the body?

"His property became more exposed after the mudslide," I said.

If Randy wondered how I knew that, he didn't ask.

"He mentioned that. Told me he could get here easier now, might come in more. It took him a while to pick up his order. Honestly, I think he's worried about the legality of living there. He said that Gril told him that land belongs to the state."

"I heard that, too."

"Gril will take care of everything. He's gone to bat for folks before. He knows how to convince the state to change a policy or a rule. I've seen him work his magic. Are you concerned for Lane?"

"No. Until a few days ago, he was a stranger, that's all. I thought I'd seen almost everyone who lives around here by now."

Randy laughed once. "Nope. You'll constantly be surprised by who emerges from the woods when they need something. We're small in population, but spread over lots of land."

Gril must not have suspected either Randy or Lane of doing anything wrong, or they wouldn't be free. I decided I needed to be done asking questions for a while, if only to keep myself from further oversharing, if, in fact, that's what I'd done with others.

I laughed, too. "I'll keep an eye out. Thanks for helping with the socks, Randy."

"My pleasure. Thanks for paying off your account." He looked down at the notebook on the counter. "I'm used to seeing mostly red ink on this page. You added some black."

I left the mercantile and walked back toward the Benedict House. I was going to put the socks in my room and then see if I could track down the address from Viola's desk. Instead, I walked directly to my truck. Another change of plans. I decided to swing by Randy's house now. I couldn't pinpoint what felt off about our conversation, what wasn't the complete truth, but I knew he wasn't there right now. It would be a good time to have a look.

A close look.

Nineteen

My ancient truck had both four-wheel drive and four good tires. As I drove along the snow-covered road surrounded by the freshly snow-covered trees and then past the *Petition*, I felt almost invincible.

It took parking in front of Randy's house for me to realize I wasn't going to be able to do anything secretly. Unless it snowed some more by the end of his work shift, my tire tracks would be obvious and easy to identify.

I looked out my windshield up to the patch of gray sky above the tall spruces and willed the snow to come down—just as soon as I finished my reconnaissance mission, that was.

I stepped out of the truck and made my way to the front door. The wide porch was welcoming, though there wasn't any furniture on it. I noticed hooks in the wood plank roof above and thought a swing must sometimes hang there. It was the perfect spot for one. I looked at the view it would offer and could envision myself swinging the day away.

Two big windows framed a wide front door. I walked to one window and peered in. A bedroom. Something right out of a woodsy home decorator magazine. A big bed filled the center of the space. The chunky log frame matched the wood used for the other furniture—two nightstands and a dresser set. The bedspread was red-and-brown zigzag, and cut-out moose marched all the way around the brown lampshades.

The bed wasn't perfectly made, and there were some familiar-looking clothes—gear—here and there. It was a comfortable and well-used room.

I walked to the other window. This side was the kitchen and dining area. More wood was used for the long dining table, the island counter, and the cabinets. The appliances were stainless, top of the line five years ago, I thought. They must have ferried them over from Juneau.

I went to the door and turned the knob. It wasn't a surprise to find it unlocked and easy to open. Why would Randy lock the door way out here? I hesitated, not because I'd never gone into someone else's house uninvited, but because I hadn't done it in a long time, and it wasn't . . . who I thought I was. Though Mill had left me with my grandfather when she'd done most of her "investigating," she'd also taken me with her a few times.

"Stick close to me and don't touch anything, girlie."

"Do you think Dad is in this house?"

"Dunno what we'll find, but according to his log sheet, this was his last sale. The police haven't done anything. We're just going to look. Hush now, and stick with me."

We hadn't found anything leading us to Dad, but it had been . . . fun. It was exhilarating to be somewhere we shouldn't be, but only because we weren't caught. My grandfather had lost his mind when he heard my mother had taken me with her.

"Mill, what in the hell were you thinking?" he'd yelled.

"That that house needed to be looked through and I was the only one to do it the right way. Beth wasn't in any danger. Take a chill, Pops."

"You will never, ever do that again. If you do, I'll turn you in myself."

"Whatever."

She *had* done it again, but my grandfather, the police chief, never knew. Mill always was extraordinary at being sneaky.

Was that why it was so easy to consider walking into Randy's house—because I'd talked to my ballsy mother today? Had that call infused me with her inclinations, reminded me of them, or just brought my own inherited tendencies to the surface?

I wanted answers—even if I wasn't quite sure what the exact questions were, and dammit, I didn't trust anyone else to get them as well as I could. Boy, that was typical Mill. Was it typical me, too? I didn't want it to be, but here I was, and I didn't seem to be able to stop myself from pushing the door open.

"Shit," I muttered, and went inside.

I walked into the dining area on one side and then glanced in the bedroom on the other. I peered inside a full bathroom as I made my way down the short hallway and into the living room. It took up the whole back half of the house and was decorated with so many animal pelts, I couldn't count them quickly. I lifted the brown rug at my feet, searching for a tag that would tell me it was fake. No tags. How many dead animals were in this place?

It didn't turn my stomach, but I didn't like it. I would never use animal pelts to decorate my living spaces. But I also knew my attitude was hypocritical. I had my share of leather shoes, coats, and handbags, though never a fur coat.

A long couch sat in the middle of the room, facing a large fireplace with a big-screen television above. If there was a satellite on the roof, I'd missed it, but that was probably the only way to watch anything other than DVDs, and even satellite feeds might not reach through some of the thicker clouds. Two chairs at angles flanked the couch, and more moose lamps sat on end tables.

A sleek black modern stereo system, the likes of which I had never seen, had been placed on a shelf on the wall opposite the television.

I stepped farther into the room and looked around. I didn't touch anything, and I hoped I wouldn't see something more bothersome than a bunch of animal pelts. But I didn't notice anything strange at all. Even on a small desk in the corner, where Randy kept some pieces of mail—I didn't look closely at any of the mail—nothing was unusual. It all seemed very Spartan.

A loft took up the front part of the house, the space above the kitchen and front bedroom. The loft area on Annie's sketch had been where she pointed when asked where her and Mary's bedroom was. The only way to get up there was via a ladder that had been nailed to the wall. I didn't see a stairway.

I'd come this far. I climbed the ladder.

The loft was less neat than the rest of the house, seemingly lived in—maybe.

There were three beds, all twins, all messy and unmade. A few piles of clothes were sprinkled throughout, and two pine dressers had clothes peeking out of the tops of closed drawers.

Without going all the way up the ladder and into the space, I searched for girls' clothing, anything feminine or childlike, but nothing stood out. All the clothing seemed like it could be worn by anyone.

But that was the nature of the gear at the mercantile, wasn't it? Unisex, to a point, generic, utilitarian. The rest of the house seemed designer, but the loft was all about the necessities. There were even two electric heaters, one at each end, though they weren't turned on.

It struck me as a space where people might sleep, or maybe it was just a place where extra stuff was stored. There were no knickknacks, nothing personal, nothing that told me about the age or sex of the person or persons who might spend time there.

I really wanted to look closely at everything, but something told me not to. That same something told me that *if* Randy was guilty of things I couldn't quite define but that bothered me nonetheless, this was the place that would contain the evidence.

I had a hard time believing he'd ever done anything wrong, but some of the best bad guys knew how to hide behind good-guy disguises.

I should never have let myself in for a personal tour. I didn't regret it quite yet, but I knew without a doubt that I should not go into that loft.

I lifted a foot and started to move it down a rung. I'd turned my head to look down when something moved in my peripheral vision. I gasped and turned more fully to look out the windowed back doors. Amid the trees, I was sure I caught sight of a dark spot moving away from the house.

It could have been an animal, but I remembered what Gril had said about the dark shadow behind Lane's house—that it didn't quite move like an animal. This dark spot was moving quickly.

I was probably six or seven rungs up. I twisted a little more, keeping my eyes aimed outside, and took a quick step—too quick.

I went down, landing hard on my back on the floor. I hit my head.

Dr. Genero had told me I would be able to live a normal life but that I should stay away from contact sports like football and hockey, and to wear a helmet if I ever rode a bike. She made it clear that hitting my head was a very bad idea.

At the very least this time I'd knocked myself silly—at the most, knocked myself out. Whatever it was, the result was a scene playing out in my mind's eye.

I was sitting in the back of the van, on top of piles of clothes. They stank. I could smell them. I'd been with him just over a day, but I smelled, too—like fear and sweat. A bandanna had been stuck into my mouth to gag me. I couldn't talk, but I could make noise. He'd turned and looked at me from the driver's seat.

"I'm going to get something to eat. If you so much as whimper, I'll kill you dead."

I was crying as he talked to me, tears fogging my vision, making my nose run. My ankles were zip-tied together, my wrists zip-tied behind my back. He left the van. I started rocking and mewling, sounding so much like the noise the girls had made outside the Petition's door.

He came back only a few minutes later. He got into the van, into the driver's seat, smelling like greasy food. My stomach lurched. He turned and sent me a smile.

"Want some?" he said as he extended a burger my direction, then pulled it back. "Psych. No food for you."

I came to, or the stars stopped spinning, or something. The vision cleared and I was on the floor in Randy's cabin, flat on my back, watching the beamed ceiling waver before coming into focus.

I'd just seen something I hadn't remembered before, something that had happened in the van, but while that memory was something that might take me down under other circumstances, it was currently the least of my worries.

I'd hit my head. That was not good, worse even than the terrifying scene from the van.

I had to get out of there.

I had to get help.

I hoped there was time.

Twenty

took inventory. My head seared with pain and my eyes watered.
What time was it? How long had I been out?

I looked around. The light outside wasn't much different than when I'd arrived—still gray. There was no dark figure out there anymore, so far as I could see. Maybe there hadn't ever been one.

My eyes landed on a clock on one of the end tables. I did some silent calculations and decided I'd only been out for a few minutes. My hand went to my head. I'd hit the side opposite the scar. I blinked and checked my vision. It was fine; well, not too bad. I focused on the pain. Yes, it hurt, but did it hurt bad enough that I really did need to see a doctor? *My pupils, I need to look at my pupils.* I didn't know why that idea came to me—no one had told me to do such a thing if I hit my head—but I made my way to the bathroom and looked in the mirror over the medicine cabinet door.

My pupils looked fine, and they reacted to the light appropriately. I opened the medicine cabinet door, but didn't see anything inside that might help me; in fact, I wasn't even sure what I was looking for.

Did I have a concussion? I needed to find Dr. Powder.

I hurried out of the house, pulling the front door shut behind me.

As I reached the truck, I looked back toward the house again, and then up at the loft window.

I hadn't noticed it before, but there, attached to the glass, was what looked like a small, green piece of paper. Even with my throbbing head, I couldn't leave before I understood what I was seeing.

Following the footsteps I'd made the first time, I walked back toward the house again and looked up. Yes, there was something taped to the glass, like green construction paper. I couldn't make it out exactly, but I thought I knew what the material was.

I debated going back inside and climbing the ladder again, but I knew I still couldn't go into that loft, and I didn't want to risk another misstep. I didn't have a camera on my burner phone, so I had no way to take a picture.

I would remember it. For now, I just needed to find Dr. Powder.

I stopped at the *Petition* to try to see if I could figure out how to find the doctor. Two notes had been stuck under the door. One was a winter ferry schedule. That note had been written on some stationery emblazoned with the Alaska Marine Highway logo along the top of the page.

The other note was from Orin. "Come see me" was all it said.

I was torn. I wanted to talk to Orin, find out what information he'd uncovered, but Dr. Powder came first.

He sometimes met patients in a back room at the bar, but I thought I'd heard that people sometimes saw him at his home. I tried to call Viola, and then Gril and Donner, but no one answered. Not uncommon. None of us hung out around the landlines much. I even tried Orin, but he didn't answer, either. I thought I'd seen a possible address once in some files of back issues of the *Petition*. I opened a drawer and started looking. Yes, there it was—a notice from Dr. Powder, listing a change in his office hours. His address was listed, too—west side of the West Coordinate, State Road 63. A Benedict address that I could find.

I locked up and made my way back to the truck. Snow had started to fall again.

I was still confident in my truck and its tires, but I didn't feel quite as invincible anymore. My head hurt enough that I slowed as I made my way toward the West Coordinate.

Not for the first time since I'd moved to Benedict, I wondered if maybe I shouldn't have chosen a place with more modern technology. The closest hospital was either a plane or ferry ride away. Never mind the spotty cell phone coverage. I was currently experiencing Benedict's "emergency services," glad that at least I still wasn't unconscious on Randy's living room floor.

I traveled past downtown, past Tochco's, and turned onto what I thought was the West Coordinate's main "road." It was covered in new snow and, just like so many of the roads around town, framed by tall spruces. I hadn't seen one other vehicle on the roads. I hoped I'd picked the right turn. I passed a couple of small cabins, but didn't think they were lived in during the winter months. I counted the state roads aloud as I passed them: 61, 62, and then, finally, 63.

If the trip had taken much longer, the amount of snow coming down might have scared me away from turning, but I plowed forward.

For a few more long minutes, I saw no houses or cabins along the narrow lane. I wondered how I would manage turning around if I had to.

If Donner knew I'd ventured out in a snowstorm without anyone else knowing—though I'd tried!—he would be angry. I would probably agree with him this time, but the pain in my head hadn't lessened—though it hadn't worsened, either—and I'd become hyperfocused on finding the doctor.

Relief washed through me when I finally came upon a house. It was most definitely a house, not a cabin. Made of brick, it reminded me of a smaller version of a southern plantation. It didn't fit with much of anything else I'd seen in Benedict, but the only thing that mattered was the sign that hung from the front porch overhang: "Dr. Powder."

Two trucks and one car were parked on a circular drive in front of the house. I found a place behind the car and made a space that would keep my truck out of everyone else's way.

As I walked inside, someone was coming out. A woman I'd seen at the restaurant, whose name I didn't know. She had a tissue to her nose.

"Who says cold weather doesn't make you sick?" she said as we passed on the porch.

"I know," I said. "I hope you feel better."

"You too." She stepped carefully toward one of the trucks.

I opened the front door to find a comfortable but undecorated waiting room. One person not looking well sat in a chair against the wall. A woman sat behind a desk.

"Can I help you?" she said, her southern drawl thick.

There would be no privacy. I walked to her, took off my hat, and spoke as quietly as I could. "I hit my head."

Her eyes flicked over my scar as she frowned and stood. "Well, then, come with me now."

She led me down a short hallway and opened a door to what must have once been a home office or a small bedroom, but was now an exam room. Dr. Powder was inside with a patient. Fortunately, the patient's most exposed body part was her mouth. It was open wide as the doctor peered inside with a tongue depressor.

"Excuse me?" the doctor said.

"Hun, this gal's hit her head. Not for the first time, apparently."

Dr. Powder peered at us over the glasses perched on the tip of his nose. "All right. Let me have a look."

He cleared out everyone else and had me sit up on the exam table. He looked at my eyes, made the pupils do what they were supposed to do, and then we talked about the pain I felt. I told him I just slipped outside and hit my head on the ground. That seemed to be good enough for him. He asked other specific questions and I gave specific answers, my nerves calming and the pain lessening as we spoke, his slow, confident tone a salve.

Finally, he said, "I think you're fine, but do you want me to call the Harvingtons to get a plane ready? If you were in Juneau, they'd probably do a CT scan."

"I don't really want to do that unless you think it's absolutely necessary."

He looked at me a long time. I didn't know how good a doctor he was, but I hoped for the best.

He finally said, "I don't think it is. You are showing no signs of a concussion." He sat down on an old folding chair that had been next to the wall. "What happened that you needed the surgery? Did you really fall off a horse?"

I gauged if he was suspecting me of being the liar I was or just wanted to be able to treat me appropriately.

"I fell off a horse onto some gravel. I had road rash on the side of my face, as well as my arm. It wasn't pretty."

"You were helped quickly," he stated.

"I was. I was in surgery within two hours of the fall."

"Lucky girl," he said.

"Yes."

He crossed his legs, folded his fingers together, and placed them on his knee. "Anything else you want to talk about? Despite my wife's interruption because she thought we had an emergency—and she was correct, it was best to check—doctor-patient privilege applies here. Are you okay?"

I got no sense that he was in any hurry to see his other patients. Dr. Genero had never seemed in a rush, either, but I couldn't imagine her or any of the doctors I'd met in St. Louis asking me questions as they relaxed on a chair, their folded hands over a knee.

Everyone kept telling me I needed someone to talk to. I wouldn't mind having someone I could trust completely.

I came close to spilling the story, but ultimately, I didn't, not really.

"I'm still having some headaches, but they aren't as frequent. I have flashback memories from when I was a child. My father disappeared when I was young, and though I thought about him all the time before I hurt myself, I don't remember ever remembering the things I have lately."

Dr. Powder nodded. "Are the memories scary? Did you have bad times with your dad?"

"No, not at all. They were great times. After he left, my mother fell apart. For the most part, my grandfather raised me, but he died when I was sixteen."

"That had to be tough."

"It was." It *still* was sometimes.

"I'm sorry." He paused. "I think your memories are the product of the recent trauma. If I were you, I would look at them as your get-well gifts."

I lifted my eyebrows.

"You said they were good memories. You wouldn't have them if you hadn't hit your head the first time, I bet. They are there to help you get well." He tapped the side of his head with a finger. "Some of us think this is where God lives. If you're religious, maybe just think of your good memories as angels. You are fine, as far as I can tell. Enjoy the good memories. If you have some bad ones, too, just file those away, tell them they can't hurt you."

I'd heard some version of what he was saying from a few people, but he spoke with a little more awe of the divine than any of the others had. He was an interesting man. I wouldn't tell him I wasn't religious.

"Thank you, Dr. Powder," I said.

"You're welcome. Come back anytime. I do full physicals for everyone during April, but you don't have to wait until then if you have any concerns. And, of course, I see everything from colds to STDs, so don't be shy."

I blinked, but then smiled. "Good to know."

"Winter does strange things around this place. Keep that in mind."

"Will do."

He escorted me out to the waiting room, where three patients

and his wife were sitting patiently, then walked me outside and instructed me on the best way to get out of the driveway as I hopped
into the truck.

Something occurred to me, and I stopped. The original mission I'd
had after talking to Mill, after I'd seen the address on Viola's desk.

"Brayn Village? Am I far from there?" I had to open the door to
ask the question because I didn't want to risk the window crank in
temperatures this cold.

"Way west. You really can't miss it if you're out on the main road,
but if you get to the ocean, turn around. It's an old village along a
river." He looked up at the cloudy sky. It had stopped snowing. "Who
are you looking for?"

I hesitated. "Well, I thought I'd check on those two girls."

Seemingly unsurprised by my answer, Dr. Powder put his hands
in his jeans pockets and looked at me a long time again. He was not a
man in a hurry. A gust of wind blew his hair sideways, but he didn't
seem bothered in the least. I thought he might ask me why or tell me
I shouldn't try the trip on my own. He surprised me.

"Turn left out on the main road. I think you'll need to travel about
twenty minutes, but you should find it. Be careful. And, Beth, report
back to me if you feel concerned, about yourself or the girls."

"I will. Thanks again." I shut the truck door.

Dr. Powder watched me leave. I saw him in my rearview mirror
until the trees hid him from view.

Maybe I'd talk to him soon about all my issues.

Or maybe not.

Twenty-One

did as Dr. Powder instructed and turned left onto the main road. The snowpack still wasn't daunting, but it could get to be. I told myself that if it started coming down again, I would turn around and go home, talk to Orin. Do some writing.

I was so relieved Dr. Powder didn't think I'd done further damage to my head that a sense of freedom relaxed my limbs and infused me with new confidence. I even managed to tell myself that I might never have strange Travis Walker visions again. I was over all that. That was the last one. I was going to beat this . . . haunting, or whatever it was.

About twenty minutes later, I came upon a speck of civilization. On a stretch of snow-covered ground between me and the river were some old houses. There were no trees; just open land stretching toward the river on one side and a mountain range on the other. Houses dotted the foothills, too. Some of them reminded me of the smaller postwar clapboard-and-brick styles down in my neck of the Lower 48—the smaller Missouri Ozark towns. Some were cute, well taken care of; some weren't. Trailers were interspersed here and there as well. There was no consistent pattern, other than that each home was allotted a good acre of land. I didn't see any log cabins like the kind common around Benedict.

I spotted a couple of paved driveways, but old cars and trucks were mostly parked willy-nilly. I even saw one old truck that had sunk halfway into the ground.

In another blink I came upon what was probably the downtown. Most of the six small brick buildings looked empty, but two showed signs of life and activity: the post office and one with a sign that simply read "Brayn."

I parked off the road, but not in any sort of designated parking spot, and stepped through the snow to the doors. The first one was locked, but the other wasn't. I entered the tiniest post office I'd ever seen.

There was barely room to stand inside and close the door behind me, but I managed. Inside was a narrow counter with one stool behind it. Stamp posters decorated the walls, but the only other item I could see was a bell on the counter. I rang it.

A moment later, a back door swung open.

"Hello, are you lost?" A woman came through.

"No, I just have some questions," I said.

"All right." She pushed up her glasses and smiled. Her gray hair was pulled back into a long ponytail and she and I might have purchased our clothes from the same place. We were both dressed in jeans and matching jackets, though I thought the blue color looked better on her darker skin than my paler version. She reminded me of Maper, but with more gray than dark brown hair.

"I'm looking for Tex Southern. Can you tell me where he lives?" I said.

She squinted. "Why?"

There was no reason to lie. There were no believable lies, anyway.

"His girls got lost over by Benedict. I found them and took them into town. I didn't get a chance to meet Tex or say goodbye to the girls. I was hoping to see them."

She frowned. "You were hoping to check on them." It wasn't a question.

"Well. That's part of it. Yes."

She nodded. "Tex is quite an imposing figure, but he's a good father. He takes care of the girls."

"I'm glad to hear that. They don't . . . didn't talk. Is that . . . just them?"

I wondered if she'd be surprised to hear they hadn't spoken; maybe their silence had been an anomaly, something temporary that had happened because they'd been lost. But she wasn't surprised.

She shrugged, and in that gesture, I heard the words she *didn't* speak: it was none of my business.

It *wasn't* any of my business, except that maybe it was. Wasn't children's welfare supposed to be everybody's business?

Granted, this land was not my native land, and maybe things were different, but children were children. They had to be everybody's business. I didn't much care if I was stepping out of bounds.

"I really would like to see them," I said. "They . . . trusted me, and I didn't say goodbye. It's been bothering me."

I didn't think she would tell me. I was prepared to leave and start knocking on doors until I either found the Southern family or someone who'd tell me where they were. There were fewer than a hundred houses in town. I could search, if it didn't start snowing again.

"Keep going the direction you were going." She pointed and I nodded. "They're on the river side, a yellow house. You didn't meet Tex?"

"I didn't."

A smile pulled at the corner of her mouth. "He won't like you stopping by."

"I won't intrude."

"You'll be stopping by—that's intruding."

"I'll be friendly."

"Do what you need to do, but there's no reason to bother Tex and the girls. They are well cared for. You might make him angry, and he is . . . imposing."

That word again.

"Then I'll leave if I have to."

She nodded. "All right. Good luck to you."

She remained on the stool as I maneuvered the front door open and myself back outside. I noticed electrical poles and wires and wondered if the cell phone coverage was better here than in Benedict. If it was, or if Tex Southern had a landline, he was probably receiving a phone call right about now.

Couldn't be helped. At least the weather was still cooperating.

On the edge of town, there was only one yellow house on the river side. I pulled off the road and found a spot next to another truck. Smoke came from the chimney of the small two-story house, but I didn't see anyone.

Though the house was cute—one of the well-taken-care-of ones— stacked along the outside wall angled toward the river was a small mountain of rusted old appliances. I saw everything from a toilet to a porcelain sink, a couple of stoves, a few refrigerators and freezers. The appliances were covered in snow, but just a smattering.

I scanned the area around the house and finally saw someone beside the river. Someone watching me. Tex Southern, I presumed.

Imposing was putting it mildly. He wore a bearskin coat. His long brown hair and long brown beard matched the coat. He was probably fifty yards away as he worked on a table made of two-by-fours set up next to the river. He *was* large—somewhat round, but mostly just tall and wide-shouldered.

I swallowed. I was beyond intimidated, but I wasn't going to stop now. I wanted to check on the girls, and not even a big guy in bearskin was going to stop me. I got out of the truck.

Tex turned so that I could see the large knife he held. With an irritated stab, he stuck the tip into the table before he gave me his full attention. His long strides toward me made me feel like my legs scissored funny as I worked to meet him halfway.

"Help you?" he said, from somewhere under the beard, his voice appropriately deep.

"Hi, I'm Beth Rivers from Benedict."

"Okay."

"Your daughters knocked on the door of where I work. I took them into town."

"And?"

He wasn't going to invite me in.

"I didn't get to tell them goodbye. I was hoping to see them."

"You were hoping to check on them," he said.

"I was," I said as boldly as I could manage.

His brown eyes flared with something I might have defined as anger, but he didn't behave as if he was going to send me away, knock me down, or threaten me with another knife he might have had hidden under that coat.

I looked at him closely. There was something else that struck me. A warmth. Despite every impression he'd made in the last couple of minutes, I sensed something so unexpected that I almost gasped. I felt drawn to him.

Silently, I checked myself. What the hell? I didn't even know the man, and yet something in me wanted to move closer to him.

I was messed up. That's all I could think—that my time with Travis Walker had messed me up so badly that my senses, my signals, were way far off. I'd hit my head again earlier today. I was worried about the girls. There were so many reasons that the unreal sensation of attraction had happened. It couldn't be normal.

"Please," I said as I took a small step away from him. "I really would just like to say hello."

His brown eyes didn't become friendlier as he studied me for another long moment. I wanted to look away, and I didn't want to look away.

Oh boy.

"All right. Come in. They're okay, but they were scared. Leave if seeing you upsets them."

"Absolutely."

Without further ado or invitation, Tex turned and marched toward the house. He pushed through the door and went inside. He didn't hold the door or wait for me. I kept up.

The house wasn't cozy. It was warm, but sparse, reminding me of Lane's house but with furniture that had come from a store, not homemade things. The upholstery on the couch was worn through in a couple of spots but the few things in the room were in good shape.

"Girls!" Tex called up a narrow stairway. "You have company."

The small front room was crowded. Any room that Tex stood in probably felt immediately filled up.

He swung out of his massive coat and dropped it on the couch. Tex didn't take up much less space without the coat.

"Girls!" he exclaimed up the stairs again. "Now!"

The thumps of their feet came through the ceiling and then down the stairs. Tex hadn't looked at me again, let alone asked me if I wanted to sit or wanted something to drink. Not that I expected him to.

The girls noticed me the second they came down the stairs. They both smiled and ran to me, throwing their arms around me.

"Hey, it's great to see you two," I said.

They looked up and smiled. They didn't speak.

"I didn't get to say goodbye. I wanted to let you know it was good to meet you."

Annie stepped back and signed something. They hadn't spoken with sign language while they were in Benedict, at least as far as I knew.

I looked at Tex.

"Annie says thank you for helping them," he said.

"I didn't know they knew sign language," I said.

"You understand any of it?" Tex asked.

"No, I'm afraid not," I said.

"That's why. What's the point if no one can understand? They shut down when others don't understand them."

"They can hear?" I said, even though I already knew they could.

"Of course," Tex said suspiciously.

"Oh yes, I did know that." I looked at them. "I'm sorry we didn't understand you. I'm glad your dad found you." I looked at Tex. "I asked them for a parent's name. I would have just found you, but they didn't give me any information."

Tex nodded. "I think they were afraid of getting in trouble, but I'm not sure I understand that completely myself yet. I've told them they shouldn't have been afraid to tell people where they live. I guess it's something we need to work on."

I nodded.

Annie grabbed my hand and led me toward the stairs. I looked at Tex again.

Annie signed something and he sighed as he looked at the girls. "I have work to get done, but if you hurry, you can show her around. Make it quick." He looked at me. "They'd like to show you their room."

Annie and Mary nodded.

It had been the briefest of exchanges, but it had told me a lot. The girls weren't afraid of their father. He might be brusque and to the point, but he didn't seem mean. If they were mistreated, they wouldn't have just grabbed my hand to show me their room. They would have either waited for their father to answer them, or not even tried.

"I would love to."

I followed them up the stairs and into the attic. It was unquestionably their room, their space. Still furnished and decorated in old furniture, it was all very girly, with pink and girl things everywhere. Their wardrobe wasn't too different than mine, but I spotted a couple of dresses hanging in the closet, which didn't have a door.

Annie led me to a dollhouse. This was the first homemade thing I'd seen in the Southern household. Someone had crafted something beyond a Barbie house, creating a simple but wonderful mansion for their collection of dolls.

"This is wonderful!" I said.

They smiled proudly.

"Girls," I said, "I'm so sorry you got lost and that you were afraid. I'm glad you're back home. It all ended well, didn't it?"

They nodded.

I reached into the dollhouse and grabbed one of the chairs. It was store-bought and seemed fairly new.

"You drew a picture of a different house," I said with a light laugh. "I was looking around Brayn for that house. I'm glad I found you anyway."

They shared a silent look before they both nodded again, their smiles fading some.

"That house you drew," I said to Annie. "Have you ever been inside it?"

She shook her head and then pointed at Mary, who slapped down her sister's hand and made a frustrated noise.

I grabbed one of each of their hands. "No big deal. I'm sorry I asked. This house is much better than that one anyway, because your dad is here. He'd glad to have you home. I bet you're glad to be home, too."

The smiles came back as they nodded.

"Enough up there. Time for our company to go. I've got to get back to work," Tex called up the stairs.

They were fine. There was a reason Annie had drawn Randy's house, something that might need to be answered or might not, I wasn't sure. But these two girls were perfectly fine, and were well taken care of, from all indications.

They walked me back down the stairs and hugged me one more time before their father, without his giant coat on, walked me out to my truck. I was sure he had to go outside anyway. I doubt he would have gone out just to escort me.

"What happened to your head?" he asked as I put my hand on the truck's door handle.

"Oh," I said, once again having forgotten the scar, and forgotten to put a cap back on. "I fell off a horse."

He looked at me, brows knitted together. "I'm sorry."

I blinked at his sympathetic tone. "Thank you. I'm okay." I got into the truck, and since he hadn't walked away yet, risked rolling down the window. It worked okay. "Tex, may I ask you about their mom?"

"No mom." He stood steely still, his eyes locked on mine in what might have been a challenge.

I blinked, but he didn't say anything else. Finally, I nodded. I wondered if he'd told Gril who their mother, or mothers were. Were they fraternal twins?

"Thanks for letting me see them. They really . . . I don't know, touched my heart maybe. That sounds silly, but that's the best I can explain it."

"You're welcome, and I understand completely."

I frowned. "They got pretty far away from here."

"I tracked them, through the woods, on the other side of the river. Found their footprints out back, crossed the river, and continued to follow them." It was the most he'd said to me.

"Did they explore because of the mudslide?"

"I don't know. They'd never gone that way before, though." He crossed his thick arms over his wide chest.

He wasn't a body-builder type. He was just a large human being whose life included a lot of physical activity that gave him muscles.

I pulled my wandering eyes away. What was wrong with me?

"Thanks again," I said.

"You're welcome. If we come by Benedict and the girls want to say hello, where can we find you?"

"A room at the Benedict House."

His eyebrows moved even closer.

"No." I laughed. "I'm not a felon. I accidentally booked a room there, and it stuck. That's all."

He nodded doubtfully. Snow started to fall again. "You better get back to Benedict."

"I better," I said.

He turned and marched back to the table by the river, still not retrieving his coat. I watched him for way too long. He pulled the knife out and reached into a bucket, grabbing a fish. He dropped the fish on the table and then started chopping with the knife. I couldn't see the gore, but I could imagine it.

He looked back over his shoulder. I hoped he couldn't see my cheeks turn red. I waved and backed out onto the road. It would probably be a good thing if I never saw him again.

It was as I listened to the quiet of the snow falling that I remembered something. I'd been so worried about my head when I'd gone into Randy's bathroom to check my pupils that I hadn't registered everything I'd seen inside the medicine cabinet.

But now it came to me. Maybe my subconscious just needed the time to process it. Maybe all the girl stuff I'd just seen had jarred the memory.

In a cup in Randy's medicine cabinet, there had been three toothbrushes. One adult-sized—a blue one. And two smaller ones, both pink.

"What the hell was that?" I said aloud to myself.

I couldn't wait to look in that medicine cabinet again.

Twenty-Two

It wasn't quite time for me to head to Randy's, but I decided to be a little early. It had snowed some since I'd last been at his house, but only barely enough to cover my tracks. Though twilight was coming, casting deeper and darker shadows everywhere, I was slightly concerned that Randy would know he'd had an earlier visitor. His truck hadn't been in front of the mercantile, so I predicted I would find him already at home. My concern transformed and deepened as the house came fully into sight. Something was very wrong.

Two trucks and the van that was kept at the airport were parked there, with their lights illuminating the front of the house. The trucks belonged to Gril and Donner, but I didn't immediately know who'd driven the van.

"Shit," I said as I pulled up next to Gril's vehicle. I couldn't figure out how any of this had anything to do with me, but it was impossible not to think I might have somehow been behind this gathering. Had I disturbed something to criminal proportions?

Gril walked out of the house and noticed me.

"What are you doing here?" he asked as I stepped out of my truck.

"I asked for a tour of Randy's house. He invited me over."

"Invitation's been rescinded. Go home, Beth," Gril said.

"What's going on?"

"Nothing that's any of your business."

I stood beside my truck, thinking about confessing my earlier trespassing.

"Gril . . ." I began.

But I was interrupted as Donner and Randy came out of the house together. Randy wasn't handcuffed, but there was no mistaking the terrified and confused look on his face as Donner held on to his arm. Randy didn't want to go with Donner; he had no choice. I didn't think he even noticed I was there.

"Gril?" I said again.

He looked at me, hesitated a moment, and then said, "You'll hear soon enough anyway. The dead body might be Randy's wife, and Christine confirmed that the woman was murdered, strangled."

"Oh no," I said. "Might be his wife?"

"Fits her description. We need Randy to . . . confirm. Christine came to get him; she's taking him back to Juneau."

Christine followed the others out of Randy's house. She pulled the door closed and then stood on the porch, her hands on her hips as she surveyed the scene. She hiked up her snow pants and sent me a distinct frown.

My earlier trespassing didn't matter. They weren't here for that.

"He lives alone?" I said.

"As far as I know, he's been alone since his wife 'left.'" Gril didn't make finger quotes in the air, but I heard them in his voice.

"That's horrible. But wasn't the body frozen? Has it been that way for six years?"

"How do you know how long his wife has been gone?" Gril asked.

"Believe it or not, just this morning I was talking to Randy about her. She came up in conversation."

"Maybe she's been on his mind."

"You think he killed her?" I asked.

"Unknown at this time." Gril turned away.

I interjected, "Where has the body been? Where was it frozen?"

"We're working on that," he said over his shoulder.

"So, he put her body in Lane's storage shed recently?" I hurried to catch up to him.

"Again, working on that."

"You let Lane go."

Gril shrugged. "No choice right now, but he's not going anywhere."

"He was coming out of the mercantile late last night."

"Yeah?" Gril stopped walking.

"Yes."

"Good to know. Thanks." He looked back toward where Lane lived, bit his bottom lip, and then turned back to me.

"Why do you think it's Randy's wife?" I asked.

"The tattoo." He looked toward Christine, still observing the scene from the porch. "Christine did some research."

"She researched tattoos?"

"I believe so."

"I don't get it."

Christine stepped off the porch and walked toward us as Donner deposited Randy into the passenger side of the van and then stood next to it. He crossed his arms in front of himself and waited.

I didn't mention my visit to Brayn. I thought about my conversation with Randy in front of the mercantile, when he'd first told me about the strange noise he'd heard, the one I was now sure had come from the girls. He'd seemed bothered by it. Maybe upset, but mostly just bothered. In my mind, now I superimposed a different concern over the one he'd claimed he'd had. Instead of being worried about the strange noise he'd simply heard, maybe he was worried that the person or persons who made it might have seen him moving his wife's body. My imagination was certainly cranking on high.

"May I ask why you're here, young proofreader?" Christine said as she approached.

"I told Randy I was considering building a home. He said I could look at his floorplan."

Christine turned and looked at the house and then back at me. "Well, well, well, of all the cabins in all the woods . . . You'll have to have a gander another time."

"So I understand."

Christine squinted at me. "No, really, who are you?"

"She's a new resident, Christine. She has nothing to do with this. Yes, she's done some work for me, but she used to work for her grandfather, a longtime and well-respected police chief."

"Oh? That's interesting. His name?"

I suddenly realized that no one had asked that question before. Donner knew I'd worked for my grandfather. So did Orin. Neither of them had asked for my grandfather's name. I hadn't prepared a lie.

I opened my mouth to say something, though it wasn't going to be the truth.

"I hate to break this up, Christine, but you need to get to the airport before the storm keeps the Harvingtons from flying tonight. Unless you want to stay?" Gril said.

Christine rocked on her bootheels and then puckered her lips as she looked at me. I felt guilty just being in her line of vision.

"No, as much as I love your little hamlet, Chief, duty calls and I must get myself and Mr. Phillips back to Juneau," she said. "We've a body to identify, after all, perhaps a murder confession to take, you just never know. It could be a lucky night. Well, for everyone but the dead woman, I suppose."

Christine turned and made her way to the van. She got into the driver's side and started the engine.

"She scares me," I said.

Gril laughed once. "She's smart and strong-willed, but you have nothing to fear." He put his hands in his pockets as we watched the van leave. "You might want to be ready with a name next time."

"I will be. Is there anyone else with them? Is she in charge of Randy by herself?"

"Yes. She wouldn't let anyone join her. I tried."

The light had dimmed some with one less vehicle's lights. Donner joined us, but it was impossible to see his face.

"Do we know when last he spoke with his wife, Gril?" Donner asked.

"Unfortunately, they haven't spoken for years. He doesn't have a working number for her, either. When she left, she didn't want to ever speak to him again, or so he says that's what he concluded. He hadn't realized it would be so literally, but she never returned his calls, and then her number quit working. He didn't think it meant she might be in trouble. He claims she's had divorce papers for years, too, but just never signed them. He said he didn't much care, thinking she was just ignoring him to irritate him. He just went about living his life, says he hadn't really thought about her for a long time."

"So bizarre," I said.

"That can happen out here sometimes," Donner said. "You forget there's another world out there. Benedict can insulate you, in bad ways as well as good."

"We'll do our due diligence. I will know more later tonight," Gril said. "Go home, Beth. Get out of the cold."

There would be no rechecking the toothbrushes tonight. I hopped into my truck, watching Gril and Donner as they walked back to each of theirs. I led the way away from Randy's house, but the two of them followed close behind. I slowed and came to a stop outside the *Petition* shed. I stepped out of my truck and waved as they each passed by. It was reasonable to think I'd stopped at the shed to get some work done.

However, after their taillights were no longer visible, I jumped into my truck and headed back toward Randy's. But I didn't stop there—the toothbrush questions would definitely have to wait to be answered.

I'd been around killers before. My grandfather had arrested two brutal serial killers in Missouri. I'd been in the same police station where they were being held inside a cell, locked up, but not muzzled. I'd heard them, watched them, observed them. I'd used some of their words, chunks of their personalities in some of my books.

They behaved like killers, said things that killers would say. They were obviously evil.

I also knew some killers could fake it. I wasn't oblivious to their skills or that impressed by my intuition, particularly in its new incarnation, the one that had been influenced by Travis Walker.

But Randy wasn't a killer. I was almost one hundred percent sure he wasn't.

Someone was, though.

I was drawn back out to the scene where the body was found, not because I suspected Lane (though I didn't *not* suspect him), and not because I didn't think Christine and her crew had done a good job, but because I'd helped my grandfather enough to know that, yes, I did have something—a way of seeing things that few people had. The first time at the shed, I'd only glanced in briefly and neither Gril nor Christine had shared any pictures with me. I just wanted a look inside, a chance to take my time and see if anything struck me.

My headlights glimmered off the wood planks, seemingly even more dilapidated than they'd been before. I stopped and looked at the shed through my windshield for a few minutes.

I left the truck running but threw it into park. The light from my headlights would help but wouldn't be enough. Fortunately, I had a flashlight in the glove box. I grabbed it and was grateful to find it still had battery power.

Thankful again for all my winter gear, I high-stepped in my boots through the snow. I swung the flashlight out toward the gravestones. They were far enough away from the road that I didn't think I'd explore them tonight.

I stood in the shed's open doorway and shone my flashlight inside. Things, boxes, traps were still there, but better organized. The boxes had been lined up, some of them stacked. I didn't understand what steps had been taken to gather evidence, but my grandfather would have had everything taken in for closer looks. Where would this stuff go here in Benedict? Or would it be shipped back to Juneau? Maybe that's what was going to happen at some point. Is that why everything had been semi-organized?

Nevertheless, I carefully stepped inside and looked for the box of baby clothes. It wasn't hard to find; it had been placed on top of three other boxes. My glove-stiff fingers lifted the flaps.

I stuck the flashlight under my chin and aimed it inside the box. The baby clothes were clean and folded. I saw lots of blues and yellows. There was no way to know what gender of child these clothes might have covered, but I got the impression they'd been for a boy. I looked for sets of matching things, similar items, but didn't find any. If these clothes had been used for fraternal twin girls, the parents hadn't cared that the clothes weren't feminine or that the girls wouldn't be dressed to match each other.

I packed the box up again and closed the flaps. I shone the flashlight around the shed. Nothing else struck a chord. There was nothing unusual or special about the size of the space. There was no indication that a body had been on the floor, stuck up against the wall. The light from my flashlight didn't glimmer off even one strand of hair.

I had to come to the realization that my trip out to the shed had been only for me, something to satisfy a curiosity even I didn't understand completely. There was nothing new to see here.

I sighed and shook my head at myself.

And then the world fell apart.

Cracks and crashes, too-loud booms sounded as the shed fell in and on me. Instinctually, I covered my head; and a good thing I had, I thought, as a plank came down hard on the forearm that covered the scar. The pain seared up through my elbow and all the way to my ear, but my head hadn't been hit. I yelled.

But no one would hear me out here. I was pinned in place. I couldn't move any part of my body, except the toes in my boots.

I was completely trapped.

Twenty-Three

Once I got past the initial shock, I decided I probably wasn't badly injured, except possibly for my forearm. I didn't immediately know if I'd broken it or just bruised it badly, but I couldn't move my fingers—maybe they were just immobilized from the debris. I couldn't tell if I was bleeding from anywhere, but I didn't sense that I was.

I was pinned to the floor of the shed, which was made of the same old wooden planks that had fallen on top of me. It was cold on that floor, but thankfully not as cold as the bare ground would have been. I couldn't turn my head enough to see exactly what was on top of me—every time I tried, something sharp stabbed into my neck. It didn't seem that any of the heavy metal traps had either landed on me or jabbed into me; I had enough sense to realize that was lucky.

I wasn't dead, I wasn't badly hurt, but this wasn't good.

"Help?" I tried. My voice was muffled by all the elements of this disastrous equation. No one would hear me, even if there had been someone around *to* hear me.

I was a good quarter mile from Lane's house, and as far as I knew, no one else lived out here. But then again, maybe someone did. Maybe that someone would come save me.

"Help?" I tried again.

I wasn't freaking out yet, but I knew that was coming. For a moment I held still, listening to the quiet, noticing the sounds of the falling snow. Snowflakes made the tiniest crunching noises when they landed. Was it the weight of the snow or a big gust of wind that had taken down the shed? Had I done something to help the elements along? Either I had, or my timing was spectacularly bad.

I was going to have to make some moves, but I was very aware of sharp edges and splinters, of the teeth on traps.

I forced one foot. I could move it a little; I tried more force. It ran into an immovable object. At least there was another foot. Unfortunately, not much good there, either.

Then it quickly became time to freak out, maybe just to flail and hope for the best.

I was scared; I could feel tears start to burn at the back of my eyes. *Come on, Beth Rivers, you're still you, just with a few more layers. Figure this out.*

"Hello?" a man's voice said from outside.

"What?" I exclaimed, wondering if my silent pep talk had conjured an auditory hallucination. "Hello! I'm here, under all the wood. Can you help?" Those tears I'd been holding back started to pour out of my eyes.

"Yes, I can help. Be still. It will only take a minute."

"No problem. I can't move." I still wasn't convinced I was hearing something real.

"All right, here we go."

It was a puzzle being dismantled. The weight on my body released a little with each plank. Light came through; I'd forgotten I'd left my truck lights on.

"How did you find me?" I asked.

"Hang on."

I waited as the man continued to clear the wood away. He was quick and efficient, but it still seemed to take too long. Because of the way my headlights were angled, I couldn't make out his facial features even once my view was cleared and he was looking down at me.

He extended his hand. "If you're not hurt, just grab my hand and I can probably pull you up."

I wiggled the fingers that wouldn't wiggle before. They moved. My arm was sore, but not broken.

"Deal," I said as I reached upward. "Whoa. Hang on, my toe is caught."

He turned and lifted another piece of wood. My foot came free as he reached for me again. I grabbed on and he heaved, and a few clatters of wood later, I was out. The man was covered in bearskin. He held tight to my hand as he led me to flat ground.

He turned and looked at me, the light from my headlights now illuminating more than backlighting him.

I let go of his hand as my insides crumbled just like the shed had. A scream made its way up my throat, but I was so hollowed out, I couldn't find my voice.

Travis Walker had pulled me out of the rubble.

Finally, I managed a scream mixed with a yell. And I swung my fist. I wasn't aware that I was swinging toward his face, but my punch landed firmly. He was so caught off guard that he stumbled backward a step or two as his hand went up to his jaw.

I thought hard, trying to remember what Cecile Throckmorton had taught us. I could get away from him. I could flip him. I could hurt him. I just had to remember what to do, but I couldn't remember a thing.

"What the hell?" he said as he looked at me.

I blinked hard. Yes, it was snowing, and yes, it was dark outside, but the lights from my truck were bright. As I looked at Travis Walker, he transformed. He wasn't Travis Walker at all; he was Lane, the man with the kill room in the back of his house. He'd saved me.

"Oh no," I said. "I'm so sorry. I . . . oh, shit."

I don't know if I looked crazed or afraid, but whatever my expression was, Lane's face relaxed from anger into disbelief. He kept his distance.

"Are you okay?" he asked. "Are you hurt?"

I shook my head and collapsed onto the snow-covered ground. I wasn't hurt, but I wasn't okay. All I could do—again—was cry, and cry hard.

I hated it when that happened.

Twenty-Four

ere, drink this." Lane handed me a cup of hot chocolate.

I sat on his homemade couch, wrapped in a crocheted quilt, in front of the large fireplace. The fire had already been blazing when he brought me inside.

"Thank you." I took the mug, but not without noticing the bruise spreading up from his jawline. "Oh, Jesus, I can't believe I hit you. I don't even know what to say."

His eyebrows came together. He didn't attempt a smile. "It's okay. You must have had your reasons."

He turned and went back toward the kitchen area. He poured more hot water from a kettle into a mug and then opened a bag of hot chocolate mix. He dumped it into the water and stirred.

I'd stopped crying shortly after I'd started. Lane had made it clear that it was important for us to get out of the elements. He guided me to the passenger side of my truck and then drove us back to his house. He said he'd found me because he'd heard the truck's engine. He had waited for the vehicle attached to it to pass his house. When it didn't and the engine rumble didn't seem to move away in the other direction, he thought someone might have gotten stuck. He set out on a search.

I'd wiped my cheeks, snorted once, and told him that "stuck" was putting it lightly. He wasn't much of a talker and didn't laugh at my poor attempt at dark humor.

His house was warm and comfortable, the fire and lantern light cozy, but primitive beyond anything even in Benedict.

He must have read my mind. "I have a generator and some powered lighting, but I like to save it for when I'm working."

I took a sip of my hot chocolate. It was very good. "You make a living from animal pelts?"

"It's not for everyone, I know, but, yes, it's what I do."

I took another sip, afraid that if I said anything else, I would sound stupid, patronizing, judgmental, or simply off my rocker.

He brought his own mug over and sat in a chair facing me. He didn't make small talk, but didn't seem uncomfortable with the silence. I tried not to be.

"You shop at the mercantile frequently?" I finally asked.

He nodded. "Every few weeks or so. There's another small shop up in Flynn. Sometimes I go there."

I had no idea where Flynn was.

He continued, "There's also a Tlingit village the other way and across the river. There's a low-water area where you can cross sometimes. Brayn has a small general store if I just need a few essentials."

I nodded but didn't mention that I'd just visited Brayn. I hadn't seen a general store.

"The police chief asked me the same question," he added. "I don't make an effort to get to know anyone, but I have talked to the man who runs the mercantile."

"Did Gril ask you about your property belonging to the State of Alaska?"

"He did, and I told him it didn't. He's researching."

I looked at Lane, wondering if having company was work for him. Had he lived his life so completely alone? "Where were you born?"

"In Brayn." He looked into his mug for a moment. "I lived there until I was grown."

"Then you moved out here? Did you build this house?"

"No, it was given to me. My way of life was taught to me." He took a deep breath. "Where are you from?"

"I moved to Benedict a few months ago, from Colorado. I fell off a horse and wanted to get away. I took over the Benedict *Petition*. Are you familiar with the newspaper?"

"No," he said. He looked so pointedly at me that my eyes opened a little wider. He said, "I read a lot of books, though."

As far as I could tell, there was not one book in the entire place. I nodded and took a drink. Surely I was imagining what I thought I'd seen in his eyes: recognition. I needed to have a firm sit-down with my imagination, rein it back in to where it was just a few days ago, before I knew my abductor's name. There was no reason for me to have veered off the rails like this. Enough was enough.

"I really feel terrible that I hit you. I'm very sorry," I said.

"Please don't worry about it. I'm sure you were scared."

"I was."

We looked at each other for another long, uncomfortable moment.

"I should have torn that shed down last year, but I got so sick last summer that I couldn't leave my house for a month or so," Lane said.

"What kind of sick?"

"Some sort of virus, a flulike thing."

"How did you manage out here? Did anyone help you?"

"I was prepared enough. If I'd been stuck inside much longer, I would have struggled, but I got better. I didn't have enough strength to take down the shed, but I didn't expect it to be such a problem." He frowned. "I don't know the body."

"I don't think Gril would have released you if he thought differently," I said.

"That's correct."

The writer in me wanted to ask him more questions about his

motivation for wanting to be so alone. But I didn't know him, and truth be told, I didn't like being inside his cozy home in the woods, all by ourselves.

What had I gotten myself into? Even if I'd thought through the possible consequences of exploring the shed, I wouldn't have predicted this outcome.

I nodded and couldn't stop myself. "Who's buried out by the shed, Lane? I saw the gravestones."

"Family," he said without a moment's hesitation.

"Who were the baby clothes for? The ones inside the shed?"

Sadness spilled over his face. I bit back the apology that made its way up my throat. I really wanted an answer, but it was clear that I'd asked a painful question.

Lane only shook his head. "You hungry?"

"Oh. No. I should get going. Thank you for rescuing me, and for the hot chocolate. I think my clothes are dry." I moved the blanket off my shoulders. I hadn't taken my clothes off, but the dampness seemed to have dissipated. The fire was very warm.

"No, not tonight. You'll probably be able to get out of here in the morning, but not tonight. Too dangerous."

"People will be worried."

"Yes, but then they'll be relieved that you're still alive and didn't try driving through something you shouldn't have. That's how it works out here."

"No way for me to call anyone?"

Lane laughed once. "No, no signals at all. It'll be okay. Seriously, it's the right thing to do. I have extra beds. I have plenty of food."

I tamped down a good wave of anxiety.

"I have books," Lane said.

He set his mug down on the coffee table and made his way to what I would have thought was the kitchen pantry. A long, narrow door covered some shelves at the end of the short countertop. He pulled the door open; the inside was well packed with books.

"This is my disorganized library. I take some books on trade, I visit the Benedict library book sale every year, some people just give them to me. You might find something to read."

He closed the door and looked at me seriously.

"If you had hit your head, I would have gotten you back to town. You're okay, though, so just wait until the morning. Relax, get some rest."

"If I did anything to make the shed collapse, I'm very sorry."

Lane hesitated. "You shouldn't have been there, Ms. Rivers. You were trespassing, and behaving ignorantly considering the landscape, terrain, and weather, but you didn't destroy the shed. Like I said, I should have taken care of it last year. The police might be angrier with you than I am."

I swallowed. "Yes, I am truly sorry."

I held the mug in between my hands as I sent him an uncomfortable blink. I didn't like the idea of staying here with him, but he was correct; it was the safe thing to do.

He stood and walked toward one of the bedroom doors. "There are twin beds in here. Make yourself comfortable."

He walked to his bedroom door, opened it, and went inside without another word.

I sat there a moment, listening to all the quiet. It was quieter even than snow falling. No television, no music, no other voices. The fire popped and I could hear small whooshes from the flames, but there was nothing else. If this was what he was used to, I could understand how even from a quarter mile away, he had heard my truck engine. I was grateful he had.

I stood and walked to the hidden library, pulling the door open. At first it seemed disorganized, but I saw a pattern soon enough. Stacks and rows of thrillers and mysteries. I'd read many of them. I'd written six of them.

Front and center on the top shelf, my books' spines faced me. "Damn," I said quietly. I looked toward his bedroom door, but it was shut tightly. Had he read them all? Was he a fan? Had he recognized me?

There was simply no way I was sleeping overnight in this house out in the middle of nowhere. No way at all. I would rather die in my truck somewhere on the way back to Benedict than be there a moment longer.

Lane was a stranger, but Travis Walker was in that house, too; sure, he was in my head, but he was there. He wouldn't be in my truck. I wouldn't let him in. I would have some control. I didn't care one bit if I was making another unsafe decision. I didn't care in the least if I was being stupid.

I closed the cabinet door. I grabbed my coat and gloves from a hook by the front door, fished my keys from my pocket, silently grateful Lane hadn't kept them, and let myself quietly outside.

It was still snowing, and an inch had accumulated on my truck, but he hadn't reset his trap, so I wouldn't set off that noise. He'd hear the truck again, but I didn't care. I got in, pushed down the old locks on the doors, and turned the key. It started right up. Thank goodness for the tires, I thought for the millionth time as I steered without much slippage. There were no snowplows out here. But again, I simply didn't care. I turned onto the road and inched my way back toward Benedict without one glance in my rearview mirror. But I knew he was watching me go. He and Travis were both watching. I had to rid myself of both, and thankfully, they got farther and farther away as I drove.

Twenty-Five

I t was dark and cold inside the shed—my shed, the *Petition*. I turned
on all the lights, giving the space a helpful glow, and cranked up the
heat. I'd been there at night before, sometimes writing until the early
morning.

I had made it. It had been slow going, but I'd made it. I had the
proper driving gear—the truck and its tires. However, the drive—I
didn't want to think of it as an escape, but I kind of did—had given
me time not only to calm down, but also to think. I'd cycled through
many things on that short but slow-going trip—fear, anger, embar-
rassment, even some real rage. But I hadn't had any visions, and ultimately, I'd been relieved to be away from a place where I'd felt
trapped, even if it had all been only my imagination.

It was almost midnight by the time I made it to the *Petition*, but I
was wide awake, and I needed the internet. Fortunately, Orin left the
library's server on all the time. If someone needed a connection after
hours, they could park next to the building or sit on the front steps.

A mudslide had occurred, and it seemed to have changed everything. Two girls, a woman's dead body, and a man whom everyone

had been unaware of were now exposed. As an aside, the man had all my books on his shelves and had behaved as if he might know who I was. To be fair, he wasn't the only one. I'd seen many shelves with my books, but it had been the combination of all the other ingredients that made me run away.

A knock sounded on the shed's door. All the work I'd done to calm down fell into an invisible well. My heart rate sped up yet again as I grabbed the glass coffee carafe. This couldn't be good.

"Hey, Beth, it's me," Orin said from the other side.

Air whooshed out of my lungs and my hands started to shake with the release of adrenaline. I cleared my throat. "One sec, Orin."

I was now tired and wired, anxious and nauseous, but I had to pull it together. I didn't want Orin to see me in this state.

I put my hand on the doorknob, took a few more deep breaths, and then unlocked and opened.

"Hey," I said as I pulled the door wide. "I'm sorry I didn't get back to you."

Orin stood there with a folder tucked under his arm and his hands in his pockets.

"Are you okay?" he asked, his breath making a foggy cloud.

I nodded.

"I've been waiting for you. I was working when I saw your truck head down that road. You were gone awhile. I was about to call Gril."

"I am fine, but I had an adventure, and though I'm very sorry you waited for me to return, I can't tell you how happy I am that you were watching out for me. Thank you, Orin."

"You're welcome." His eyebrows came together. "Can I come in? Is it too late to share some information? And, do you want to tell me what you were doing?"

"Come in." I stepped back. "It's not too late."

He hesitated, but then joined me inside.

The typical Orin scent filled the shed, but this time it mixed with the cold. It wasn't unpleasant. In fact, I took it in. Familiar and now comforting.

We took the seats we always took as Orin placed the folder on my desk in between us. I slid my typewriter over an inch or two and gave him my full attention.

Again, he hesitated. He probably really wanted to know what I'd been up to, but he didn't immediately ask again. "All right, I've been at the library all day. I tried to call Gril but he's probably busy. You're the first one seeing this."

I nodded encouragingly.

"Okay, let's start with the Hortons. Do you remember us talking about them? The people whose house burned down in the fire?"

"Yes, and only one girl's body was found."

"And as far as we know, no one knows what happened to the other girl."

"Do you think it's one of the girls who were here?"

"I don't know. Maybe."

"Seems plausible."

"It does. Around the time of the fire, about two months before it, actually, Randy and his wife Wanda Phillips came to Benedict. I don't remember Wanda. I came to town around the same time, so maybe our paths just didn't cross. Randy had their house built before they moved here. I think he wanted to surprise his wife. The house that Randy had built is almost identical to Paul and Audrey Horton's house, the one that burned down; they were neighbors. Remember that detail. Wanda Phillips must have disappeared around the same time the Hortons left, after the tragic fire."

"Wait. Was her disappearance news back then?"

"Nope," Orin said. "I never once heard mention of it. You have to understand that once winter hits, people hunker down. By the time the next spring thaw came, she was probably forgotten about. We take care of our own out here; sometimes that means others do get forgotten. Here, I'll show you what I found. Here's record of the purchase of Randy and Wanda Phillips's land—they bought it from the Hortons. There was no real estate agent involved. Not uncommon out here."

"Okay."

"It took me a while to even remember conversations about Wanda, but I might remember hearing at some point that Randy's wife went back home to New York City. The news didn't make an impression on me. There was no goodbye party. Nothing seemed strange. It just was what it was. Again, never a big topic of conversation." Orin paused and looked at me.

"I'm following."

"Good. Okay, here's the really interesting part."

"Let me guess. You looked and couldn't find her in New York?"

Orin smiled. "Good work. That's correct. But not only that, I couldn't find her anywhere, Beth. I have access to databases that track Social Security numbers as well as credit reports. Wanda Phillips's credit stopped being pinged, used, wasn't checked, not long after the fire. No sign of her using her Social Security card for anything. I can't find her anywhere."

I bit my bottom lip. "Is there a chance she could have just stopped needing credit? Maybe they had a home that was paid for and she just moved back into it. It's a stretch, I know."

Orin nodded once. "You're kind of onto something, though. I found their old address in New York City, and they did not sell it; they are still listed as its owners."

"So she moved back there?"

With a satisfied expression, Orin shook his head. "No one has lived there for six years."

"How do you know?"

"I started with utility companies. Then, I confirmed with their building's co-op board. Their apartment is and has been empty. Once a week, someone comes in to check things, look around."

"How did you do that?"

He sent me an incredulous look. "I have my ways."

"Okay, so Randy must know she didn't go back there?"

"I don't know what Randy knows. But she didn't go anywhere, Beth, not as far as I can tell."

"And now her body has been found in Lane's shed?"

"I don't know. Was it her?"

I suddenly realized I knew things Orin didn't. He might not know about the wrist tattoo. Did he even know Randy had been taken to Juneau? Now I told him everything, including what I'd been up to that evening. He was curious and then visibly angry at my bold move in exploring Lane's now collapsed shed.

"Aw, Beth, please don't do stuff like that. It's just plain stupid," he said.

I blinked. "I know. I'm sorry. But if the shed hadn't collapsed, I'd have been in and out and back quickly."

"It was snowing and you didn't tell anyone where you were going."

"True."

"Never again, okay?"

"Okay."

"Good. Now, Gril has the tattoo as the only distinguishing feature so far?"

"Yes, and the Juneau ME, an interesting woman named Christine, is the one who did the research."

"Ah, tattoo research. She's good. I'd like to meet her."

"There's such a thing as tattoo research?"

"If you're good. If I had a picture, I might be able to track down the same things she has, but I bet she was able to find the artist. Maybe someone nearby in Juneau, and then it's a matter of hoping for accurate and archived sales records. Who knows, but there are ways. I'll ask Gril for a picture. Does she *think* the body is Wanda's?"

"I don't know exactly. She took Randy to Juneau for identification purposes, and maybe booking, I guess. I doubt more than one woman around here would fit the description so precisely."

"Can't think that way. If the tattoo artist was a local, more than one woman with brown hair could have that tattoo."

"It's close to a perfect murder, you know? I mean, they move here and a month later Wanda 'goes back home.' No one in either place would spend too much time wondering. Maybe Randy is sending fake emails to friends. It's well thought out," I said.

Orin tapped his lips with his fingers. "Sort of. If the body had disappeared forever, then it would've been perfect. If it's Wanda, she's been on ice somewhere and just became exposed. Why now?"

"What if a body is thrown into the ocean. Is that a guarantee that it will disappear?"

"It would take a boat and some weights, but currents are strong. A body can resurface and show up on a shoreline somewhere."

"Just like what happened here a few months ago."

"Exactly. A body might not stay hidden that way. Also, water can do different things to bodies. I don't think the body found on shore had been in the water for long, and from the description of the body in the shed, it wasn't waterlogged."

"Randy told me his wife hadn't signed the divorce papers yet," I said. "Maybe he had to get her body out in the open so he could finally . . . I don't know, cut his ties to her? Have her declared dead maybe. Life insurance?"

"I guess that's possible."

"But where has she been on ice?"

"A freezer?"

"Well, maybe, but I didn't see one big enough on Randy's property."

"We have ice caves. Climate change is warming our temperatures, and the permafrost is melting, but we still have ice caves, places where it's always below freezing."

"Where?"

"Around. I'm not sure exactly, but I can work on that. Gril will want that, too."

We each sat back in our chairs and fell into thought. My mind was swirling but I no longer needed the internet; Orin had done all the research, and more.

Orin sat forward. "What if he just didn't know? If it's Wanda, Randy might not have killed her. Someone else could have."

I switched gears in my mind. "Who?"

"Another good question."

"We need a positive ID on the body at this point. There's more in that file. What else is there?"

Orin flipped over a piece of paper. "I think I found the Hortons; maybe. They moved back to the Lower Forty-Eight after their tragedy. I have an address."

"They had a rough go."

"That's putting it lightly." He looked at the paper. "Beth, remember the earlier detail of the proximity of their house to Randy's here in Benedict?"

"Sure."

"Their New York City address is right around the corner from Randy and Wanda's apartment."

"What in the world does that mean?" I said.

"Maybe nothing."

"You believe that?"

"No, but I can't prove anything else."

"I guess just tell Gril."

"I'm going to get this information to him first thing in the morning." Orin gathered the papers and tucked them into the folder.

I looked at the clock hanging on the wall. It was close to one a.m., too late to call Gril unless it was an emergency.

Orin followed my gaze. "That's good for tonight. I'm glad you made it back safe and sound."

"Me too. Thanks."

Orin stood and tucked the folder under his arm. He headed to the door but stopped and faced me again. "Are you going to stay here or go home?"

"I don't know."

"Go home, Beth. It's been some long days, and I think you could use some rest. I'll come back over in the morning. We can talk again. I'll tell you everything Gril shares with me. I promise."

I nodded. "All right. I'll go in a few."

"Good."

It was too cold to linger in the open doorway. I watched as Orin hurried around the corner of the shed, sending me a smile and a peace sign as he went.

I closed the door and sniffed. His scent had lingered inside. Maybe that's what had calmed me down. I smiled to myself, grateful for the calm, but it was definitely time to go home and get some rest.

Twenty-Six

A distinct sound of laughter came from the dining room as I stepped out of my room. I made sure my door was locked and went to explore.

I'd slept well and awakened on my own—finally. I had no headache and my vision was spot-on. My arm was bruised, but not badly. I could hide it with long sleeves and mask the pain with some aspirin.

I could use a good haircut, but the reflection in the mirror wasn't too terrifying this morning. It was a good hair day; I was bound and determined to force it to be one, if I had to.

I didn't have any nightmares. I didn't remember any dreams. So far, a good start.

Viola and Ellen again sat at a food-laden table. Ellen had been the one laughing, seemingly about something Viola had been telling her.

"Good morning," Ellen said. "Come in. I made so much food, I should probably invite the whole town."

"Good morning. You look . . . a lot better," I said.

Ellen smiled, but I could see the tightness in her expression, at the corners of her eyes. She *was* doing better, but it was only by the thinnest of threads. "I hope to God that other me is gone, even if I have to eat her away. I'm bound and determined. I might gain a hundred pounds, but it would never weigh as much as my addiction."

"That should be on a poster somewhere," I said as I grabbed a plate and loaded it with biscuits, gravy, and bacon. I didn't mention that I'd just been thinking about my own determination.

My appetite had been hard to tame when I first moved to Benedict. I was still hungry more often than I ever used to be, but at least I got filled up sometimes now. I was starving this morning.

Ellen's color was almost back to normal and the blemishes on her face already seemed to be clearing up. Her hair looked clean, though it wasn't quite shiny yet. I could see how she had once probably been very pretty.

"I feel like I'm coming out on the other side of something. Well, almost coming out of it," Ellen said.

"You are. That's really terrific," I said as I took a bite of the food and my insides melted at the delicious flavors.

"Well, I can't take any credit for it. I'd still be strung out if I hadn't been sent here. Viola has helped a lot. You too."

"I just threatened to shoot you," Viola said.

They laughed as if they'd already shared a joke about Viola's gun. I didn't ask to be let in on it, but I was mightily impressed by the transformation.

"This food is amazing," I said.

"I know my way around a kitchen," Ellen said. "I haven't cooked in a long time. It felt therapeutic this morning."

"What was your job, your career, before life took a turn?" I asked.

"Took a turn—I like that. I worked in an accounting firm. I'm not a CPA, but I have a degree in accounting. I also know my way around a spreadsheet."

"Good skills to have," I said.

"Like organizing offices?" Viola said as she looked at me over her fork.

No one had witnessed me organizing any offices via Skype, which was the job I had told everyone I had. It was the same sort of career the protagonist in my first thriller had, but she did it in person, leading her to a night of terror inside a high-rise.

But they hadn't witnessed me writing books, either. I did my real job inside the *Petition* shed, behind a locked door. When people asked, and they rarely did, I told people I did my fake job there, using the library's internet connection.

When I first arrived in Benedict, Viola told me she knew I wasn't sharing the whole truth as to who I was or why I'd come to town. She'd bargained with me that I should be truthful to her if she figured it out. I'd agreed.

"I wish I had mad spreadsheet skills," I said, ignoring Viola's obvious poke.

"I hope to get them back," Ellen said. "I hope for a lot. How long have you been here? I mean, I know you're just staying here, not in trouble, but Viola said it hasn't been for long."

"A few months," I said. "You know, you've done the hard part."

"It's all the hard part," Ellen said.

"It's a cliché, but I think it's valid—one day at a time, that's all you can do," I said.

Ellen nodded and looked at Viola. "How long can I stay here? I mean, I'd like to stay awhile."

Viola smiled. "You'll be here awhile, depending on the weather, maybe. And you might not feel that way in a week or so. You might start to get anxious, but that's when you really need to work to keep it together. You might be able to help over at the café. Can you bake, too?"

"I can."

Viola shrugged. "I don't know if Randy will be back to run the mercantile, but selling some baked goods there might be an idea. Everyone needs bread."

"Okay," Ellen said as if she was processing the information. She didn't know enough about what was going on to inquire about Randy. She smiled. "Okay. I can do that. Will they let me?"

"I'm sure they will," Viola said.

I didn't interject and mention that "they" meant Viola would just take care of getting it done.

"Randy still under arrest?" I asked Viola.

"As far as I know."

I looked at her, gauging what else I should share. "Viola, I went to visit the girls yesterday."

"You did?" she said.

I nodded.

"Goodness, you *were* concerned about them. What did you think about their father?"

"He was an imposing figure." I was a little disappointed in my lack of creativity in picking an adjective.

"He tracked the girls through the woods, did you know that?" Viola said.

"That's what he said."

"He was distraught when he made it to town."

"And the girls were happy to see him."

"It was a happy reunion."

"And no one knows who their mother is?"

"According to Tex, there is no mother. Gril called his contacts in Brayn, but no one is telling him anything different," Viola said.

I stopped my fork halfway to my mouth as a memory came to me. "Viola, there was something at the Southerns' house that might be of interest to Gril. There were some old appliances stacked next to it. It didn't look like they'd been used for a while, but there was at least one full-size freezer, I think."

Viola ran her tongue over her teeth. Her eyes unfocused and she put down her fork. She finally looked at me and nodded.

"Excuse me," she said as she stood and walked out of the room. I thought she might be going to her office to make a call on the land-line, but a few seconds later, I heard the front door open and shut.

Ellen looked at me. "What in the world is going on?"

"It's a long story, Ellen. Can I help you clean up? I'll give you the highlights in the meantime."

"Help me carry the dishes into the kitchen. I'll wash them."

Ellen was so very normal. She listened to me just like she hadn't been a messed-up junkie only a few days earlier. I was impressed, but I didn't give her much information, just the gist. I hadn't forgotten her previous state or the fact that I didn't know her at all.

As I was leaving her to the dishes, she stopped me.

"Beth," she said.

I turned.

"I think I know who you are," she said.

I just looked at her.

She smiled. "Back before . . . well, you know, I was also a big reader. *37 Flights* was one of my favorite books. Haley. I read it over and over again. I'm fully aware of the main character's job. When Viola mentioned organizing offices earlier, I put two and two together. Your incident was in the news. I see the scar. I'm glad you seem okay"—she lowered her voice—"Ms. Fairchild."

There was no one else in the building as far as I knew, but I looked around anyway. Was anyone listening? I squelched the idea.

"The man who took me still hasn't been caught. I ran away. I'm hiding," I said.

Ellen nodded. "I figured it was something like that, and I won't tell anyone. I just . . . I just want you to know how much I enjoy your books and I'm really glad you're okay." She laughed once. "You don't look like you, really. I just happened to be a fan, so I figured it out. I doubt many people will, even if they are fans. I like to look at writers' websites, their biographies. I used to be more than just a normal reader, maybe. I'm a true fan. I won't tell. I hope to get back to reading again."

"Thanks, Ellen," I said.

"Thank you."

I left the room with wobbly limbs.

I felt an imaginary creature nipping at my heels as I made my way inside my room before I managed to let go of the appearance of control I'd kept up in front of Ellen.

There was no trusting a junkie, particularly one so recently clean. But I really didn't think she would tell anyone who I was—she didn't know Travis Walker.

I stepped to the window and looked out at the woods as I thought about what I needed to do with this information. Was it time for me to get out of Benedict? Where would I go? How would I get anywhere? The ferry was still running, but I had no plan, hadn't even thought about trying somewhere else.

Something in the woods grabbed my attention. It was just past the morning twilight, but dark clouds kept the light muted. I'd all but forgotten about the figure I'd noticed in the woods outside Randy's house, the one I thought might look like the same one Gril and I had seen in the woods outside Lane's. I had fallen and hit my head at Randy's, and that had been more important.

But here it was again.

I put my face even closer to the glass and squinted. The brown figure was far away—maybe about thirty yards or so—amid the trees. It looked to be covered in fur, but, as Gril had noted, not moving quite right. It seemed distinctly human, with its hunched-over gait, as it walked deeper into the woods.

I wanted to run outside and try to chase it, but I had no doubt I would miss it; it would run away or hide so I couldn't see it. I wanted to grab Viola and see if she knew what it was. Did Benedict have its own version of Big Foot? But Viola was gone.

The figure stopped moving and turned slowly. It was covered in fur—maybe a coat and hat. Though I could see two eyes, or at least understand where they were, I couldn't tell what color they were.

I could, however, tell they were aimed directly at me.

I gasped.

This was my third sighting. Did that mean that I was the one meant to see the thing, that I was the one it was watching, following?

I stepped back from the window, put my hand over my mouth, and sat on the edge of the bed. I could still see out the window. The creature turned back around and continued moving away, at a pace much too fast for me to catch up to it.

What the hell?

I didn't know what to do, except that I now wanted to talk to Mill. I was with Gril the first time I saw the figure in the woods—he saw it too, but with what had been going on inside my head, I couldn't help but wonder if I truly was seeing it again or if maybe I was hallucinating. I didn't want to feel this paranoia, but I couldn't help it. And the first person who came to mind when I wanted to talk about paranoia was my mother. I grabbed the burner phone and moved back to the window, where I might get a signal if I held the phone up.

I texted: *Call me in half an hour? This is my new number.*

I hit send, crossed my fingers that the text would go through, gathered my things, and headed outside, taking a brief detour around the other side of the building to look out into the woods. I didn't see the figure anywhere, so I hurried to my truck.

More snow had accumulated overnight but some already-forged tire tracks told me where the roads were. The previous night's activities felt like a million years ago. I wasn't fine, though. In the last twenty-four hours, in my new home, it seemed maybe two people knew who I was—and something seemed to be stalking me. The universe was trying to tell me something, and I needed to find a way to understand it.

Just as I made it inside the *Petition* shed and cranked up the heat again, my phone buzzed. I opened it. Mill had answered.

You bet.

Twenty-Seven

Thirty minutes after I'd sent the text, on the dot, the burner rang.

"Mom," I said.

"Baby girl o' mine. How are you?"

"I am okay." I forced myself to relax some. I didn't want to freak her out too much.

"Don't bullshit the bullshitter. What's up?" She struck a match.

I could smell her. I'd never smoked, not even tried to, but there was something about the smoky scent of her well-driven old cars that would always be comforting. When I hadn't been with my grandfather, living like a normal person in a small house in a small town, I'd been with my mother in that car, searching, breaking into homes, "investigating." Even then, I could see how strange her behavior was. But I would always think back fondly on those moments, all those greasy fries and milk shakes, that cigarette-smoke-infused smell.

I told her everything, but I only used first names. When I finished, her first comment was concern about my head, and her second was a question.

"Are you sure your fingers didn't touch anything in Randy's house?" she asked.

"I'm sure. I learned from the best."

"Damn straight, you did. Good. It will be fine. And if anyone asks you, deny, deny, deny. Don't ever admit to anyone but your old mother. Got it?"

"I got it. Thanks, Mom."

"No problemo. Now, this creepazoid, Lane. Just stay the fuck away from him. He's probably harmless, but Jesus and Mary on a cracker, Beth, look at the way he lives. It ain't right. It just ain't."

"I understand, and I agree, except . . ."

"What?"

"He's sad about something. He's secretive and mysterious, but he's sad, too. I think the police chief needs to explore that—maybe his sadness has something to do with the body."

"It's possible. I bet he's the one you keep seeing out in the woods. I mean, think about it. It's like Bruce Wayne and Batman—you've never seen them together, right?"

"I'm not sure that theory works in this sparsely populated area, and we saw the figure by his house and then came upon him arriving from the other direction."

"A feasible thing for him to do, circle around that quick?"

"He would have to be in amazing shape." I thought about the figure and how it could have been wearing a bearskin coat exactly like the one Lane had been wearing when I first saw him.

"The man walks through the woods every day. If anything could get someone in great shape . . ." Mill said.

"Maybe . . . but the sadness."

"Tell the police as much. And don't let them give you any crap. You're smarter than twenty cops. Make them listen. You don't need to know why Lane is sad. You don't need to care, but I don't disagree that your police force should. It's not Walker wearing that coat and watching you, baby girl. He hasn't found you, I'm sure, and I can't even get a line on if you're being followed on purpose or it's just all chance. You yourself just mentioned the small population. Wrong times, wrong places, maybe."

She sounded confident and that helped infuse me with some confidence, too. "Okay." I sighed.

"As far as people recognizing you. It's gonna happen. In fact, you should probably own that. Don't let anyone see that it bothers you. People are assholes. Don't let them have something up on you."

"But I'm trying to hide."

"Not completely. Think about it. Yes, you ran far away, and you're hiding a little, but you're not living by yourself out in the middle of the woods, because, different than that trapper, you're a normal human being who doesn't want to be alone all the time. It's actually a good thing. Own it, though. Don't run from running away. You keep the power over your own decisions. Own your own life, Beth."

In her messed-up way, she made sense. "Yes, I understand."

"Here's hoping the police check out that freezer tout suite."

"I think they will."

"Then good. I bet some answers will be found soon. You're fine. I promise you're fine."

I took a deep breath. "You've helped, Mom. I feel better."

"That's what us moms do." She sucked on the cigarette. "Now, I have some other news. You ready to hear it?"

"Yes. Please."

"I don't think Levi Brooks needs any further attention at this time. But it seems that Travis and your dad did know each other. They were friends, darlin'; well, more like coworkers, in a way."

I felt a new wave of sick, but I didn't want to hang up. I didn't want to pass out or have another vision, either. I just wanted to listen and see if her words gave us some answers.

"Okay," I managed to say, pretty levelly. "Tell me more."

Mill took me back in time, back to when I was about four, and my grandfather had stopped by the house and asked me to go outside while he had a talk with my mom and dad. I had no memory of that moment, but Mill did—though it had only recently come back to her.

During that conversation, my grandfather told them he'd become aware of a friendship growing between my father and Travis Walker, a man who'd been born in Milton but had left when he was a child. My father had admitted to knowing Travis, having met him because they both sold the same brand of cleaning supplies and their territories bordered each other's.

My grandfather had become aware that Travis might be selling more than supplies, that he'd ventured into selling drugs as well. My father had claimed not to be aware of such activity. Gramps was pleased to hear that news, but wanted to emphasize to my father that he shouldn't ever be seen socializing with Travis—lunch and drinks at bars, those sorts of things.

My mother told me that my father resented my grandfather's interference, but he also knew who the boss was. My grandfather ruled our small part of the universe. It wouldn't do anyone—including my dad—any good to cross Gramps.

"Dad ended his friendship with Travis Walker?" I asked.

"I don't really know," Mom said, her lips around a cigarette. "But not right away, for sure. That man came over to our house, girlie."

I wished I remembered, but I still didn't. "Okay."

"Now I remember him stopping by. You were in the front yard. He picked you up and carried you to the front door. He knocked on the screen, said he'd found a little pretty one on the front lawn and did she belong to Eddy Rivers."

"Mutherfucker," I said, my teeth clenched.

"At the very least," Mill said. "I grabbed you from him and took you out to the backyard while he and your dad had a convo. Dad later told me that he told Travis that he couldn't be buddies with him anymore, but he wasn't overly convincing. He told Travis that the police were onto him and he might want to watch out."

"How did that go over with Travis?"

"Don't know. Dad shut up after that, told me we could never talk about it again. Until I let that picture Majors showed me soak in, I didn't remember any of it. The moments were brief—the conversations. It all seemed resolved. It's been over twenty years, but I remember some of it now."

"Dad refused to talk about him anymore, or did you put a stop to it?"

"Dad demanded we didn't talk about him, and he never demanded much of anything. We moved on. You know, meals to make, bills to pay. I never thought it was as serious as I maybe should have thought it was."

"You mean that he would eventually take me?"

"Yes, that, and he might have had something to do with Dad disappearing, too."

"Jesus, Mom, did he take me to remind us of Dad?"

"I don't know. I just don't know. We're only speculating here, but I think it's all possible."

"It's old news now. No one cares; no one's paying attention."

"There's some of that. I'm trying to get a local news slut to help me get the story going again."

"You might not want to call her a slut."

"Well, not to her face."

I sighed. "This is pretty big news, nevertheless. Don't you think you should tell Detective Majors?"

"No, ma'am. Not yet. You gonna tell her?"

I thought a long time before answering.

"No, not yet," I finally said.

"All right. Just let me know if you change your mind. I'll have to change how I'm doing what I'm doing if the police know."

I did and didn't want to know what that meant, but all I said was "Will do."

"Now, other than what all this hairy news has done to you, how are you feeling?"

I took stock of myself. "No promises, but at this moment I feel fine. Sore, but not bad. Somewhat liberated, in fact. This has helped. Thank you."

"Yep, truth, knowledge, it's all powerful stuff. That doesn't mean we don't still have work to do, but we're getting closer."

She was correct, and I hadn't lied completely. I did feel a little more power, but also a little more anger; if that was actually part of the power, it might be a toxic mix of it.

I thanked her and told her I loved her. Today, she loved me more than the first fireflies on a Missouri summer night, which was more poetic than her normal declarations.

We disconnected the call. I sat for a long moment. *Should* I call Detective Majors? I'd told Mill I wouldn't. So I wouldn't. Not quite yet.

Maybe this afternoon.

Twenty-Eight

jumped into work. I didn't want to think about Travis Walker and my
father's friendship, or whatever it might have been. However, maybe
it was the idea of it that sparked a creative explosion. I wrote some
good stuff, I thought. My words were creepy, my mood dark. I used
it, I threw it all on the page, and I loved every minute of it. We'd see
in a few weeks if the words held up.

Mill had told me I needed to use what had been done to me inside
my books. I couldn't remember most of the details of what had happened inside that van, but, of course, that wasn't what she meant.
Writing what you know isn't about specifics: it's about writing scenes
that duplicate feelings, with the goal of making your readers feel them,
too.

I went deep today. I lost myself in the frightening world I was creating on the page. If I'd talked to a therapist, she'd probably ask if I
was trying to escape something or face something. I wouldn't have
an answer yet, but I was working on it.

When I came up for air, three hours had passed, and I felt better than I had when I'd started. I stretched and opened the door. It had been snowing again. I looked down toward Randy's house. I couldn't see anything but the white road and woods, but I wondered about him. I crossed my arms and shivered. I turned back and went to the window. I could see Orin was at the library. It was almost lunch and he might be planning to visit me then, but I didn't want to wait.

I packed up my pages for the day, locked up the shed, and drove the short way over to the library.

As usual, the place was packed.

Though it wasn't a large building, it offered a wide selection of all types of books. Orin ran the place, but other locals helped—everyone helped out everywhere.

Except me. I hadn't offered my services more than at the *Petition* and light stuff at the Benedict House. I hadn't thought of my time in Benedict as anything but temporary. But I hadn't left before August 15, which was the recommended departure date if you wanted to be sure to get out before winter set in.

I could still leave. The weather wasn't terrible yet. But I decided—partly because my conversation with Mill had eased my earlier panic—that I wasn't leaving until Travis Walker was found. Maybe it would be soon now, but if it wasn't, how long should temporary be?

Should I offer to help out at the library? The crowd today was a good combination of people reading books and people looking at their laptops. I smiled at some of the familiar faces that looked up as I came inside. I snaked around the rows and shelves of books and knocked on Orin's door.

"*Entrez.*"

Orin had been smoking in his office. It was all I could do not to wave my hand in front of my face.

"Beth, I was going to come see you at lunch. Come in and close the door. Hang on, no, that's impolite," he said, as if he realized the smoke might be too strong. "We've got a break room."

"No, I'll be okay," I said as I closed the door, glad I'd already gotten my writing done for the day.

"Okay," he said as we both sat again. "It's medicinal, in case you were wondering. I probably shouldn't smoke in here, but it doesn't spread out there too much, and I have work to do."

He was correct. It didn't spread out there too much. I nodded. It was the first time he'd ever really even talked about it.

He continued. "It's for pain. I was shot, hit by a couple of bullets in my back. It's a miracle my spine wasn't severed, but it still hurts."

"I'm sorry."

He shrugged. "I manage it well. I'm able to still function, and isn't that what it's all about, functioning?"

I smiled. "Yes. And I really am sorry you have pain."

Orin waved away my comment. "I do all right. Anyway, stuff is going on in Benedict. I can't believe the ancient history that's being dredged up, but first of all, did you hear? The body was not Wanda Phillips."

My eyes opened wide. "What? Not Randy's wife?"

"Nope. I talked to Gril this morning. The body remains unidentified. Randy's coming back over from Juneau, probably as we speak."

"The tattoo?"

Orin shrugged. "Not Wanda's."

"One of Wanda's friends?"

"No one knows yet."

I was thrown. I'd been so sure. If I listened closely, I'd probably hear my grandfather's admonishing laugh.

Orin said, "While I was talking to Gril on the phone this morning, Viola showed up at his office. She sounded like she really needed to tell him something. He told me he had to go. Sounded urgent. Do you know why?"

"Yes, I saw a freezer," I said. "I mentioned it and she took off.

I suspected she was hurrying to tell Gril. He might have wanted to check it out."

"Oh, a freezer where the body could have been kept? We have lots of those, I suppose."

We did, indeed, have many freezers throughout town. The airport, the back of the bar and café, as well as a place where caught seafood was prepared and kept frozen until tourists left for home.

"But this freezer was next to Tex Southern's home."

"Right, and his girls . . . I don't know."

"Me either, but Viola left the Benedict House in a rush when I told her."

"Maybe she knows more about Tex than she told you."

"I wouldn't be surprised. Orin, is there a way to figure out who the girls' mother is? I don't buy that they're fraternal twins."

Orin's fingers moved to his keyboard.

"I've tried to get in touch with the Hortons," Orin said as he typed. "I couldn't find them on social media, but I left a message with their apartment manager in New York. I couldn't find a phone number, which is something I can usually locate easily. Gril knows all of this, too."

"Do you think their New York address has anything to do with Randy's and his wife's?"

"How could it not? Whether it's something as simple as the Hortons learning about the apartment because of Randy or his wife—who's back to just missing, according to other things I'm *not* finding, by the way—or if there's a deeper connection, I want to know. So does Gril. He told me he was going to ask Randy more questions about the Hortons, but I'm not sure when that will be."

"Randy has no idea where his wife is?" I asked.

"According to Gril, with the help of the Juneau police now, too, Randy is searching the world over for her, trying to reach her family. He thought she just didn't want to talk to him. He hasn't really tried hard to get ahold of her for years, and he's not been in touch with any in-laws."

"Does that seem odd?" I said.

"Who knows? It appears, and is consistent with his personality, that he's just lived his life, thinking she was doing the same. Gril is also trying to work with the airlines to see if they can check if she was a passenger back then, but it was a long time ago."

"Bizarre. No one else has lived with Randy since then?" I said.

"Not that I know of, but I've never been to his house. He really keeps to himself."

"That, in itself, could be something weird."

"We're all pretty weird that way, Beth. You know that. We all keep to ourselves."

"Okay, what about Tex?"

Orin typed a minute. "Tex Southern. No social media, but that's not surprising. I can't find a record anywhere that he's been married. I'm familiar with Brayn. It's struggled over the years, trying to keep the Tlingit traditions and ways of life going. It's tricky—this world isn't made for that, unfortunately." Orin paused and sat back and then forward again. "They're currently trying to raise funds for a museum; there's an idea." He typed some more. "Here's a list of donors. Yep, here's his name. Along with his daughters' names." Orin shook his head. "There's one other Southern here. Grettl Southern, but I don't know the relation. I would say chances are slim this is the girls' mother, but it's a possibility. There are no in memoriam listings."

"What about old marriage records?"

"That's where I was headed next."

I waited. A few minutes later, Orin shook his head slowly. "Nothing. No record of anyone named Tex Southern getting married in Alaska. I doubt he got married in another state, but I could be wrong."

I thought about the toothbrushes in Randy's house. I thought about the three messy beds. I thought about what Gril's reaction to my trespassing would be. He'd be angry, but he probably wouldn't arrest me, not right away, at least. Was there a connection between Tex and Randy? As I thought about it, it felt tenuous, but anything was possible when nothing was definite, right?

"Maybe I'll go check in with Gril," I said.

Orin's eyebrows came together as he peered around the screen. "I don't know if you should bother him right now."

"I'll tread carefully."

"Okay. How do you feel after your adventures last night?"

"Fine, thank you, and I'm not telling anyone else what I did."

"I can keep a secret." Orin smiled.

I was standing up to leave when his landline rang. It was old-school, just like Viola's and Gril's; each ring took me back to my grandfather's small table and the stool in his front hallway where the one phone sat, with its forever-tangled cord.

"Hello?" Orin answered. "Yes, thank you for calling me back." He grabbed a pen and poised it on a notepad. "Are you sure? Yes, I see. Okay, well, thank you. If you find any way to get in touch with them, would you mind calling me back? No, I'm not the police, I'm the local librarian and we're doing some research on their old property. It burned down, but we're trying to find plans or blueprints." He sent me a lifted eyebrow and shrugged. "Thank you very much." He hung up.

"What?" I said as he stood, too.

"That was the Hortons' apartment manager. He said they've never lived there, but their names are still on the lease. He's never seen them. Ever."

"Two New York City apartments without residents, close to each other. Now, that simply can't be a coincidence," I said.

"I suppose it could be, but I'd better tell Gril." Orin looked at the time on his phone. "I'll close a little early for lunch and come with you."

As happened frequently when Orin couldn't find someone to cover for him if he had to leave for lunch, he announced that the library would be closed and locked up for an hour. He said everyone could leave their things where they were, and he'd be back.

Without grumbles, everyone left, some heading over to use the airport internet, some leaving their stuff where it was until Orin returned.

That was just how it worked.

Twenty-Nine

We drove separately, in case Orin ran out of time and had to hurry back to the library, but we parked next to each other on the small parking strip on the other side of Donner's and Gril's trucks.

Donner was seated at his desk in the front part of the building when we went inside; Gril was back in his office.

"Can I help you two?" Donner said distractedly.

"Any chance we can talk to both you and Gril?" I said.

Donner looked back toward Gril's open door. Gril stood up behind his desk, his phone's handset to his ear, and signaled us in. We made our way, crowding the small office.

"What's up?" he said, covering the mouthpiece with his hand. "I'm on hold."

"We have some things we think you should know," Orin said.

"I'm listening."

"The Hortons," Orin said.

"The folks who lived in the house that burned down? Yes. You said you were looking for them in an apartment building in New York," Gril said.

Orin nodded. "Still didn't find them, but the building's landlord did just call me back. Their apartment has been empty all these years."

"Both theirs and Randy's apartments have been empty?"

"Yes."

He held up a finger. "Gril Samuels from Benedict. I need to talk to Christine. All right. I'm returning her call. I need to talk to her ASAP. Have her call when she can. Thanks."

Gril hung up the phone. "So, Randy and his missing wife are listed as the owners of an apartment in New York City. The Hortons are also listed as owners of an apartment in New York City. Neither family has lived in their apartment for a long time?"

Orin and I nodded.

"The apartments are located close to each other. The families might have known each other?" Gril asked Orin.

"Hard not to wonder. I need to talk to Randy about that. He should be back soon."

I raised my hand. The three men looked at me.

"I think it's time for me to confess something," I said.

Gril's expressions quickly spanned a spectrum, ending in irritated doubt. "What?"

"I saw something. I shouldn't have, but, nevertheless, I did." I cleared my throat. "I saw some toothbrushes."

"What?" Donner said.

"And three beds," I said.

"Spill it, Beth," Donner said, sounding even less patient than Gril looked.

I sighed. "I'm sorry, but I trespassed on Randy's property yesterday, early. I saw some things."

Donner and Gril made noises that I purposefully ignored.

Orin looked at me and smiled. "Atta girl," he said. "Att-a girl."

"I'll tell you the details, but there's more. I went to Tex Southern's house to check on the girls. I saw something that might have been a big old freezer. I told Viola. Did she come talk to you?"

"Yes," Gril said. He looked at Donner.

"I was going to head out there this morning," Donner said.

"Viola said she was going to check on it, too," Gril said.

They looked at me, waiting.

"Right. Okay. I know you probably saw the three beds in the loft," I said.

"Sure. Randy said he sometimes sleeps up there. Many cabins have lofts, makes it easier when you're having visitors. Randy said the space heaters keep it warmer up there."

"Were the clothes all his?" I asked.

"There was nothing to indicate they weren't," Gril said.

"I opened the medicine cabinet. There were three toothbrushes inside it. Is . . . is that normal for some people? Three toothbrushes? One adult size; two were smaller and pink."

"I didn't notice the toothbrushes, but I didn't look in the medicine cabinet. We'll ask Randy. Donner, head out to Brayn now. I doubt the freezer is anything, but I think it's time we insist upon knowing who the girls' mother is, or who their mothers are."

"Wait!" I said.

Gril and Donner weren't happy. Orin just smiled at me again.

"I suspect we've all had this thought, but do you think the Horton girl whose body they couldn't find survived that fire? What if she, Annie, is actually a Horton?"

"The thought seems to be solidifying some. Son of a bitch." Gril stood and grabbed his jacket off the back of his chair. "Let's both go, Donner."

A few seconds later, after a whirlwind of gathering guns and coats, Gril and Donner were gone, the sound of Gril's truck engine firing up and rumbling away. Orin and I stood in the office, alone.

"I'll be," Orin said. "You are full of surprises."

"Why would Randy have three toothbrushes?"

"I admit, that's weird, but maybe not, Beth. It could just be the way it is. I keep my old toothbrushes to use to clean other things."

"Me too, but I don't keep them with the toothbrush I use on my teeth."

Orin nodded. "I just don't know."

"You need to get back to the library," I said.

"I do. What are you going to do?"

"I don't know. It seems as if I've managed to send a group of people out to Brayn. I feel like I should go, too."

"I hate to sound like your parent, but I wouldn't if I were you. The snow is only going to get worse today. Wait for Gril to come back. I bet he tells you what's going on. All you'll have to do is ask him."

I'd promised Ellen I'd take her to the knitting class anyway.

We walked outside together and said goodbye. I watched as Orin drove away and stuck his arm out to wave. I looked up at the cloudy sky. It wasn't dark like night, but dark enough not to feel like day. I shivered, though I wasn't terribly cold.

I wouldn't drive out to Brayn, not today, but I had another idea. Maybe the coming storm wouldn't be too much of a detriment.

Thirty

didn't regret leaving Lane's house the night before. I wasn't going to apologize to him. If I ran into him again today, on or near his own property, I was more than prepared to behave with zero shame. I'd been bothered and I wanted to leave—I didn't need to explain myself.

I was still curious, though. This time, I left a message for Viola, letting her, letting someone, know what I was doing: that I was driving out toward where the mudslide had occurred.

I had snowshoes in my truck. I had enough winter gear that I wouldn't freeze to death. At least not right away. This time I wasn't going to go inside the shed, because there would be no shed to go into; it was in shambles. I wouldn't go inside any structure I came upon.

As I drove my truck past the places I had passed by more times over the last few days than in all my days before in Benedict, the snow began to fall again. Big, sticky flakes that accumulated quickly. I looked toward the *Petition*, and then Randy's house. He wasn't home; he might not have made it back from Juneau yet. I was glad the body wasn't his wife's, but who in the world was she, this woman who'd been strangled and then hidden away in a frozen grave before being deposited in an old trapper's shed?

And where was Wanda? Just because the body found in the shed wasn't hers didn't mean she wasn't out there somewhere, buried or frozen. Lots of bodies got lost in Alaska.

It was an odd setup inside Randy's house, but that could mean nothing at all. It could just be the way Randy lived, like Gril said. Maybe he slept in the loft sometimes because it was warmer up there. Maybe *he* alternated between all the beds and three different tooth-brushes, two of them pink. We all had our habits and rituals.

Even if he didn't learn about my trespassing, I wondered if I'd be able to look Randy in the eyes again. Would he sense that I'd invaded his space? Would Gril or Donner tell him? Gril might not be done talking to me about it. I felt guilty.

Mill wouldn't feel guilty. She wouldn't be bothered at all. She would say something like, *"I just looked. I didn't touch or destroy any-thing. I just fucking looked. No harm done."*

I continued through the snow, and my tires cut a fresh path down the old logging road. I stopped the truck near the collapsed shed and left the engine running again. If Lane wanted to come talk to me, he could. I wasn't going to hide from him.

I stepped out of the truck, slipped on the snowshoes, and made my way, awkwardly, toward the gravestones. I realized quickly that the snowshoes might have been overkill, but I needed practice walking with them anyway.

I'd gotten in better shape, but I wasn't in snowshoe shape. You'd think that something used to make walking through snow easier wouldn't require an extra dose of energy. But by the time I made it to the graves, I was breathing heavily, and warmth had spread un-derneath my heavy clothing. I slipped out of the snowshoes and dropped to my knees next to the stones. All Lane had said was that family was buried here; it looked as if there were three graves. There were three different stones, the tallest jutting up from the ground a couple of feet. I dug away about seven inches of snow to expose the front.

All three stones were as is; the edges hadn't been carved or rounded or shaped, and only the front of one was remedially engraved with sparse information.

The middle stone read "Beloved Wife." The left stone didn't have any visible carving, but the right one did. It read "Together forever."

"Who's together forever?" I said aloud. If this was Lane's wife, did the epitaph mean that he would be buried here, too, when he died?

I studied the stones a long time, making sure I wasn't missing anything important, but found nothing else.

I looked up and around. There was nothing peaceful about this small cemetery. Nothing violent, either. Only sadness and loneliness, desolation. The ground would freeze solid in the deep winter. I'd heard someone mention that sometimes bodies had to wait until the spring thaw to be buried. Had the body in the shed not shown signs of strangulation, I wondered if that conclusion would have been reached—that she'd been someone who passed in the winter, and for whatever reason, she hadn't been able to get a proper burial.

I looked toward Lane's house but couldn't see it.

When I heard a snap that sounded like a twig breaking, my head jerked around and I looked into the dark woods. Hemlock and spruce trees packed in tightly. I squinted and scanned.

At first I didn't spot anything unusual. I slipped my feet back into the snowshoes. I wasn't sure if I could move more quickly with them or without them, but I didn't want to try to carry them.

Just as I stood straight up, I saw something—the same color and shape I'd seen three other times.

The last time I'd seen it—just this morning, seemingly looking at me though my bedroom window at the Benedict House—I'd panicked. I'd had to call my mother. This time, I swallowed some of that same panic. Whoever was out there, it wasn't Travis Walker. It simply didn't make sense. Mill had pointed that out, and she'd been right.

She'd said something else that rang through my mind. She'd been talking about my reactions to people who might recognize me, but it applied to everything now.

Own it. Own your own life, Beth.

I wasn't going to fall apart. Not again. At least not now.

I had spied quite a few bears in the wild over the past few months, but I didn't know when they went into hibernation. Why hadn't I asked someone? I sniffed, but didn't smell the stink that came with a nearby wild animal.

The dark mass was about fifty yards away, its back to me. It was moving, but not like a bear. I took one step closer to the woods.

"Hey!" I yelled.

The creature stopped and began to turn around, but then moved away, as hurriedly as the snow probably allowed, moving with much more stability and grace than I could have managed.

I opened my mouth to call out again but thought better of it. I turned and hurried back to the truck. I looked out to the woods one more time, but I couldn't tell if the creature was still there.

I started the truck and sat a long moment. Finally, I switched into gear and continued to Lane's house. Without the snowshoes this time, I trudged along the path leading to the house. Walking was somehow both easier and more difficult without them; I slipped more, but now used less energy.

There were no prints around the front yard. I knew where the hole in the ground was, and a quick glance made me realize Lane still hadn't reset the trap, but I was still careful and stayed back from the front porch far enough that my visit couldn't somehow be misconstrued as threatening.

"Lane?" I said loudly.

A few seconds later, the front door opened.

"Help you?" Lane said as he filled the space. He crossed his arms in front of himself and frowned deeply. "I see you're okay."

"I'm fine. I needed to get home."

Lane shrugged. "I wasn't keeping you prisoner."

"I know," I said.

Lane's cheeks were ruddy, but he wasn't wearing a bearskin coat. "What can I do for you, Beth?"

It was a genuine question. He didn't ask it with impatience.

"Were you out in the woods a few minutes ago?" I said. "Out there over by your shed?"

I watched him closely, and I saw a split second of honesty in the set of his shoulders right before he lied.

"That was me," he said as his shoulders loosened some and he ran his hand through his hair quickly. "I was on my way home. I tried to say something to you, but you were too far away."

I nodded again. It was an obvious lie, but why? In fact, if I really thought about it, I would realize that it wasn't truly feasible he could have made it back—was it? Was he able to move that quickly in the snow? Had my journey down the road and then the walking path taken longer than I thought?

"Okay." I paused. Was I going to accuse him of lying? No, but I was so thrown that for an instant I couldn't formulate what I wanted to say next. "Who is buried out there?"

"Family. I told you."

"Your wife? Who else?"

"I'm going inside. Do you need anything else? Are you okay?"

"I'm fine." I stared at him, wanting to say something to keep him talking, but not coming up with the right words.

He turned and made good on his threat—he went inside.

Riled up but not willing to knock on his door, I accepted defeat for this round. I went back to the truck and once again took the road back to town. It wasn't difficult during the daytime, but it still wasn't easy. My mind whirled as I drove.

Who was buried there? Was there a child next to Lane's wife—and had that child been theirs or someone else's?

I couldn't let go of this new idea—one of the Hortons' girls had disappeared. Her remains hadn't been found. Where was she? Was she still alive and with Tex, or dead, perhaps buried on Lane's property? I couldn't piece together how either might have occurred.

Perhaps her body *had* burned away to ashes that had either been overlooked or not found, but I was convinced that the other two options needed more exploration before I could give real credence to the last one.

While Gril was in Brayn, checking on the freezer and hopefully coming to understand the girls' background, their mother, I hadn't been able to stop thinking about the baby clothes and the gravesite. Losing a child is the worst thing imaginable; maybe Lane couldn't bring himself to discuss such a tragedy.

Nevertheless, a child had gone missing six years earlier. Maybe I didn't want to believe that she had burned to unrecognizable or ignored ashes. I believed that, though maybe no one had meant to be negligent, someone had done a hurried and sloppy investigation. There was a child out there somewhere—dead or alive—and it was time the truth was uncovered.

The mudslide was trying to tell us something. I was trying very hard to listen.

Thirty-One

"Ellen? You okay?" I said as I waved away some white fog.

The frantic woman looked up from the dough she'd been kneading. She was covered in flour, her ponytail a nest of flyaways.

"Oh, thank God." She stood up straight. "I . . . oh, thank God."

She wiped her hands on her jeans and came around the table. She pulled me into a tight hug.

"Hey." I patted her back uncertainly. "What's wrong?"

"I was afraid of what I would do. I was afraid to be alone." She was on the verge of sobbing.

I was not equipped for this moment. I held the hug for a few more seconds and then pulled back, taking hold of her arms.

"You're okay," I said with a confident smile. "Look, you did it. You were alone and you didn't do anything harmful."

She laughed, a strangled sound. "That's only because I had the bread to bake. I think my arms will be sore for weeks."

I smiled again, thinking Viola must have known what she was doing by suggesting Ellen cook and bake. "That's how you do it. One day, one sore muscle at a time. There's always something better to do than drugs. If you have to make thousands of loaves, then so be it."

She blinked, her eyes still searching for an answer, something that would be easier than the obvious one of not using anymore.

"All right." I patted her arms. "Where are you with the bread? Knitting starts in an hour. What do we need—I mean knead, ha-ha—to do before we go?"

She blinked uncertainly again, and I was sure I saw flour puff from her eyelashes. And then she smiled. It was brief but genuine.

"Yes, yes, we can do that. I just have to get this loaf in the oven, and I won't start any others," she said.

She had baked five loaves, and I managed to eat almost a whole one by myself as we cleaned. Butter, cinnamon, peanut butter, jam. Apparently, I had to prove to myself that all the toppings tasted good in combination with the homemade bread. They did, and the bread was also delicious by itself.

"You're going to be rich," I said after I chewed my last bite—my last bite for now, at least.

"Only if you don't eat the product first," she said.

I laughed, but didn't think she was joking.

I think both Ellen and I saw how this temporary acquaintanceship could be beneficial. Ellen needed someone she could mostly trust to talk to who wasn't Viola, the woman in charge of her ultimate freedom, and I always needed someone to bake me homemade bread—and keep my secret, of course.

Viola still wasn't back by the time we left. Another inch or so of snow had accumulated while we'd been cleaning and eating. We were getting close to a foot of new accumulation.

I tried to reach Viola's cell phone for about the twentieth time, but there was no answer. I left another message telling her I was back from my explorations and Ellen and I were going to the knitting class.

On a whim, I also tried to call Gril and Donner. They didn't answer, either. I didn't think I'd told any of them my new burner phone number, though; they wouldn't know it was me just by the number.

I wasn't sure whether to be worried or not, but I was. Would they really spend that much time in Brayn? Had Viola run into trouble traveling there on her own?

Or was it simply that no one's phones were in a pocket of service, which was the way things often were? Lane had told me it was better to be safe and let people worry than risk danger. Had everyone gotten stuck in Brayn?

I grabbed one more piece of bread on the way out the door.

The community center had once again transformed. The mats we used for the self-defense class were stored away and chairs had been set out in a comfortable circle. As the class went on, sometimes some people would separate themselves from the others, but there weren't enough attendees tonight to think that smaller groups would break off. Serena was pleased to see a new participant, and Ellen was an eager learner.

In addition to the three of us, Benny from the bar was there. So were Larrie and her daughter, Janell. None of the guys joined us this evening.

The wind blew noisily outside as Serena worked with each of us, one at a time. I had moved from casting on to knitting a scarf or two over the past months, but it wasn't because I enjoyed knitting. I enjoyed the group; the knitting was just the price I had to pay to be around the people.

I was distracted tonight. Since Benny and Viola were sisters, I silently battled with myself—should I let Benny know what was going on and ask her if I should be worried about Viola?

A giant gust of wind rattled the windows.

"Gracious, maybe we should end class early." Serena looked around, then continued, "Well, no one lives too far away. Even if it gets worse, we should all be fine."

"We can crash at the Benedict House if we need to," Benny offered. "Viola won't mind."

We were about a mile from the Benedict House, but it was a paved mile. We all had good tires, mostly reliable vehicles, and Benny was correct, Viola wouldn't mind—that is, if everyone cleaned up after themselves.

I looked at Benny again, but still didn't ask if she'd heard from Viola.

"What is it, Beth?" Serena said.

I blinked. "What?"

"You made a noise," Serena said. "Are you worried about the weather?"

"Sorry. A little, I suppose."

"This is nothing," Benny said. "I'll make sure you and Ellen get back okay. I'm staying in the bar tonight."

Benny had a room in the back of the bar with a bed and a dresser. It was also the room Dr. Powder sometimes used to examine patients, and, before yesterday, the only place I'd ever seen him.

"It's not terrible out there?" I asked.

"No, not really," Benny said over her flying knitting needles. "You really are worried?"

I smiled it away. "It's okay."

Furtively, during trips to the bathroom, I dialed Viola's number a few more times. I also tried Gril and Donner. No one answered; most of the time, the calls wouldn't even connect. I'd found a pocket or two of service inside the community center before, but nothing was working tonight.

The class lasted another hour, and everyone decided they'd be fine to go their own way. But, true to her word, Benny followed behind Serena and me. We made it home surprisingly quickly. Just as Ellen and I stood in the doorway of the Benedict House, waving to Benny, who stood in the doorway to the bar, I heard the landline inside ringing.

I hurried to the phone inside Viola's office, opening the unlocked door without a second thought now, and grabbed the handset. "Hello, Viola?"

There was no immediate response.

"Viola?" I said. Ellen joined me in the small room. She watched me, wide-eyed with her own concern.

"Help!" came Viola's voice over the phone. "Stuck!"

Those were the only two words I got before the line went dead, ringing loudly with the dial tone, a noise I hadn't heard for a long time before moving to Alaska.

I hung up the phone and then tried to dial Viola's number again. No answer.

"Shit, shit, shit," I said.

"What's going on?"

"That was Viola. She sounds like she's in trouble."

"Call nine-one-one."

"There's no nine-one-one here," I said.

"Do you have a number for the police?"

"I do. Yes."

I had three numbers for the police: Gril's cell, Donner's cell, and the police office landline number. I tried all three. No one answered anywhere.

"Goddammit," I said.

"What should we do?"

"I'm going to see if I can find her or find the police." I stepped back out of the office.

"I'll go with you," Ellen said.

"No, you don't have enough winter clothes," I said as I made my way to my room and all my winter gear.

"I'll be fine," she said as she set off at a run to her room. "Don't leave without me. I'll be right back."

I wouldn't have waited for her, but I needed a few minutes to prepare, making sure I had all the proper clothes as well as a couple of blankets and some water. I grabbed another flashlight from one of the key boxes.

I was so into my preparations that I didn't notice Ellen had rejoined me.

"We need to call someone, let them know where we're going," Ellen said.

"Yes, you're right." I was going to call Benny, but for a reason I could only attribute to not wanting to worry her, I decided to call Orin. He didn't answer, either, but I left a message with the best details I could give: we were heading toward Brayn, looking for Viola, who'd called us sounding like she was in trouble.

I wanted to call someone else. I wanted an emergency service I could ask to help us. It all seemed so uncivilized, so backward. Who else could I call?

I couldn't think of anyone.

"Let's go," I said to Ellen.

As she climbed into my truck, I noticed her almost-adequate boots and her thin outer layers. She was not prepared, but she wasn't as unprepared as I'd been a few months ago.

"Are you from Alaska?" I asked as I turned the truck from its parking spot and out to the road again. The snow was falling lightly—for now.

"Born and raised in Anchorage. Never did much outdoor stuff, but I paid some attention."

"Okay."

It was dark in Benedict. Nighttime could be pitch black. When there were clouds above, sometimes the nights glowed with a dusty light. When there weren't clouds, there was the blanket of stars. I hadn't seen the aurora borealis yet.

Tonight, I was simply grateful for my tires and my truck's bright lights. I drove slowly but made my way confidently.

"Keep an eye out. I know Viola keeps emergency flares in her truck. Look for something like that or just a vehicle off the road. I noticed some abandoned ones already when I drove this way, but hers won't be buried in as much snow." I leaned forward and peered out the front. "Maybe."

I hoped to see another vehicle. I hoped to run into Gril or Donner. I didn't understand why no one had called me back. Were they all off the side of the road somewhere? I took a deep breath and let it out slowly.

"It'll be okay," Ellen said. "We'll find her. I'm sure she was prepared for every eventuality."

I looked at Ellen.

"I think I watch too much crime television," she said.

Even in the dark, I could see that her face looked healthier than it had a few days earlier. It was still blemished, but her color had continued to improve, and her cheeks had filled out a little. I hoped she'd been a good mother; I hoped she'd get the chance to be one again.

The thirty-minute drive took about a thousand years longer than it should have, and we didn't see Viola's vehicle. No Viola anywhere. No Gril or Donner, either.

The one streetlight in Brayn hung from a leaning pole above the Southerns' house. Its weak glow was yellow and sickly and lit up the swirling snow. A light illuminated the inside of the house, and the freezer was in the same spot it had been when I'd visited the first time, but it was now open. I didn't see anyone anywhere.

Hot anger bubbled inside me; I wondered if I might combust. It wasn't another vision from my time in the van, but I suddenly remembered the feel of the ropes around me and the seat Travis had tied me to. I'd been under his control. I couldn't move, I couldn't do anything. I hated helpless.

I closed my eyes and tried to calm down, but all that did was bring the edges of Travis's face into view. I opened my eyes.

"You should have done what I told you to do," he said to me. I didn't remember what he was talking about, but his voice sounded in my head, tinged with his deep southern drawl. *"None of you Rivers people ever listen."*

What the hell was that? Had he been talking about my father?

"Beth," Ellen said as she put her hand on my arm.

I jumped. "Sorry. I was trying to calm down, figure out what to do. Do me a favor, remember these words if you can: none of you Rivers people ever listen."

"None of you river people ever listen. Got it."

It was close enough. "Thanks."

"Why are we at this house?"

"It's a long story," I said. "But I'm going to knock on the door and ask the man inside some questions. If I don't come out in about ten minutes, go get some help somewhere."

"What? Where?"

"I don't know. Just find someone."

I got out of the truck before she could ask for more details or protest. I hoped she wouldn't roll down the window. It might never roll up again.

I marched to the front door and put my anger into pounding hard on it.

"It's me, Beth Rivers," I said. "Open up."

I heard someone slowly making their way. Tex pulled the door open wide.

"What the hell?" he asked.

Tex was so large that I felt the need to step back, but I held still. He wore a sweatshirt and some jeans, his long hair pulled back in a ponytail, his long beard falling to his chest.

"I'm . . . I'm looking for my friend, Viola."

"She was here. Hours ago."

I didn't see or hear the girls and I wondered about them. I looked over his shoulder.

He stepped sideways and looked back there, too. "She's not here, and the girls are asleep, if that's what you're wondering."

My entire body quaked with a shiver.

Tex turned to face me again and then crossed his arms over himself. "Are you telling me your friend didn't make it home?"

"Yes, that's what I'm telling you." I matched his pose, but only so my body wouldn't shiver again.

"Come in. I have a landline. You can use my phone to make calls if you want to. You can invite your passenger in, too, if you'd like." He paused as realization squinted his eyes. "Or keep her out there where she can save herself, or you, if she needs to, but I'm not going to hurt either of you."

"Thanks. I'll use your phone. That would be great." I made my way around him and into the warmth of his front room.

It had seemed sparse and stark the last time I'd been there. Now it just seemed small and comfortable.

Tex closed the door. "Sure."

The phone sat on a side table next to the wall. It was old and blue, pocked with years of chips and scratches.

I hurried to it and started dialing the same three numbers I'd been dialing for hours. No answer. I looked at Tex. "She called me when I was back in Benedict. I only heard two words—'stuck' and 'help.'"

Tex's eyes clouded. "That's not good. Did you check her home?"

"We both live in the Benedict House."

"Of course." He rubbed a small part of his exposed cheek with the backs of his knuckles. "She was here hours ago," he repeated. He walked toward me, and I took a large side step.

He looked at me with tight eyebrows. "I'm just using the phone."

I nodded and watched. He placed a call to someone, asking them to come by the house for a while, that he had to perform a welfare search. When he hung up, he made his way to a room down a tiny hallway.

"What's going on?" I said.

"I'm grabbing some clothes. We'll find her." He emerged from the room dressed in the same sort of things I was dressed in, not a bear-skin coat like I expected.

"What did she do when she was here?"

"We talked. She asked about the girls, what she thought might have happened, why they walked so far away from home. She looked around the property outside, too, claiming to just be curious, but I was sure she was looking for something specific."

"What about the police chief, Gril, or the park ranger, Donner. Were they here?"

"Yes, they stopped by a few hours after Viola did. They asked about the girls, but they were curious about the freezer, too. They looked at it and then left." Tex frowned. "Any more questions? Or should we go search for your friend?"

He didn't say a word about any of them asking who the girls' mother was, but at that moment, I didn't much care to ask myself.

"Maybe we need to search for all of them. I can't reach Gril or Donner, either. Let's search. Of course," I said.

A knock sounded on the door. Tex pulled it open again and the woman who'd been at the post office walked inside.

"This is my mother, Grettl Southern," Tex said.

She looked at me. "Ah, you're here again."

I didn't know what to say, so I didn't say anything. I just nodded and made my way to the door.

"Thanks, Mom," Tex said. "I'll be home when I can."

"Sure. I can be here all night, so do what you need to do."

Tex looked at me. "We'll take your truck, but I'll drive."

Ellen and I would either be fine with this man I didn't know, or we wouldn't. I was focused on finding Viola more than my or Ellen's safety with this oversize stranger. "Sounds good."

Tex grabbed a big duffel bag that had been sitting against the wall by the front door. I hadn't paid attention until then, but the word "Rescue" was embroidered in yellow thread over the dark blue material.

Ellen was relieved to see me back in the truck. I did a quick and informal introduction and we piled inside, Ellen on the passenger side, Tex driving, and me stuck in the middle, crowded up against both of them and working hard to arrange myself so that the exposed seat springs didn't cause any permanent damage.

"You come down the main west road?" he asked.

"We did."

"I'm going to take a different route than you took. I told Viola the way I thought the girls had taken to get to Benedict. Some old logging roads were exposed because of the recent weather."

"I traveled one of them from the other direction," I said. "I mean from Benedict. A man lives back there—the police had never heard of him."

"A few people live that way," Tex said. "It happens."

"Do you think the police took this route, too?" I asked as Tex steered the truck over some mounds of snow-covered dirt that I would never have attempted to conquer.

"I doubt it. We didn't discuss the same things I discussed with Viola."

"Did you tell them Viola had been there?"

"I didn't." He shook his head. "Honestly, I didn't connect the two. I should have. I wish I had."

I didn't think Tex had done something to them—I really hoped he hadn't—but it was impossible not to speculate. I didn't have a weapon anywhere. I used to keep a knife under my car seat back in Missouri, but I hadn't even done that much here.

We were being driven into the dark wild night, and I didn't even have nail clippers with me.

"Hang on," I said. "Stop, please."

Tex brought the truck to a slow stop. "What?"

He looked at me with sincere impatience. I couldn't really see his eyes, but I could see the set of them, and his worried forehead. I had nothing but my pure instinct working.

Here I was. I'd handed over my and Ellen's safety to a near stranger. I'd given him the keys to my truck. He was in charge. I didn't like it, but as I looked at Tex's shadowed eyes in that dark and stormy night, I didn't see evil. Not one ounce of it. I hoped I was right.

"Sorry. Go on," I said.

Furtively, Ellen moved her hand next to my thigh. She gave it a quick squeeze. I looked at her and she sent me an encouraging nod.

The old logging road wasn't really a road from this direction. The other direction seemed a more passable route. We rocked and rolled, slipped and slid a little, but as the snow continued to fall, Tex managed the truck so well that I wanted to ask him for pointers. I didn't.

"This road was once used a lot, I remember—back when I was a kid, this was the way we would travel into Benedict," Tex said.

"A mudslide back about six years ago closed it off?"

"Yes."

"Makes sense," I said.

"There!" Ellen pointed. "Look there!"

The front lights from my truck glimmered off the orange plastic of the lights of another truck, one whose back end was tipped up, as if it had gone off the side of the road and now its front part was aimed down into a ditch.

"Viola," I said as I reached over Ellen for the passenger-door handle.

Tex gently grabbed my arm. "Hang on. I know what to do and we need to do it the right way so no one gets hurt. Do as I say, all right?"

Tears burned the back of my eyes but I blinked them away and nodded. "Yes. Okay. Let's get there."

Tex let go of my arm and then pushed on the accelerator again, slowly and purposefully so that my truck got very close to Viola's. We'd put the duffel bag on the floor. Tex reached over both of us, grabbed, and took it with him as he got out. I followed him.

We stood on the edge of the shallow berm as the icy wind and snow swirled around us. It wasn't steep, but it would be a slippery trip down.

"Viola!" we both called.

The cab of the truck was right there, but it was shrouded by the dark night and the couple inches of snow on top of it. We were going to have to walk down the precarious slope.

Tex crouched, reached into the bag for a rope, and then looped it around my waist. "We might not need this, but just in case. I'll hold on. You walk down and open the door. See if she's inside," Tex said over wind.

I nodded and did as he instructed. I was glad he kept hold of the rope—the snow was much deeper and icier than I thought it would be. It wasn't a far walk, but I about fell a few times. Tex held tight, and his feet seemed to be rooted in place.

I wiped away the snow over the door window and looked in but still couldn't see much of anything. I tried to open the door but it was locked. I knocked. I pounded. "Viola!"

The longest second of my life later, the door opened. Inside, Viola's bleary eyes blinked above the silver of her outdoor emergency blanket. "Ah, you found me." She smiled. She was wearing the Indiana Jones hat she'd worn almost every day since I'd met her. "Good work!"

"Let's get out of here," Tex said. "Come on."

Viola was no worse for wear. She'd gone off the road and couldn't get her truck unstuck. She'd made the decision to hunker down and walk back toward Brayn the next day, when there was a break in the weather. It was still early enough in the season that there would surely be a break in the weather. She'd had emergency supplies packed in her truck like any good Alaskan, and she would have been fine through the night, and maybe through another day.

Her truck didn't seem damaged. Just stuck.

"I was going too damn fast," Viola said. "What an idiot."

"You're okay," I said. "That's what matters."

We weren't going to get her truck unstuck tonight, though. As we all packed into mine, even tighter with me now sitting on top of Viola and Ellen, Viola told us more.

"I was going that way because Tex mentioned that's the way the girls went, but I also remembered something from years ago. An ice cave," she said.

Tex had started the truck and was turning it back toward Brayn. We decided not to search further for Gril and Donner, hoping they were as prepared for every eventuality as Viola had been. Tex offered to look for them the next day.

"Hang on again. Stop," I said to Tex. "What do you mean?" I said to Viola.

She looked out toward her tilted truck. "Out there. There's an ice cave. Benny and I used to explore it when we were kids. At least it used to be there."

"I remember it, too," Tex said. "I haven't been inside it for years."

"Would it keep a body frozen?" I asked.

Tex and Ellen both looked at me like they weren't sure what they'd just heard. Viola just nodded. "That's why I was trying to spot it. I shouldn't have tried, should have just told Gril."

"Shit," I said as I looked out at the dark and the falling snow.

"A body?" Tex asked.

I looked at Viola. "Do you think I can tell them?"

"Don't think Gril would be pleased, but considering the way you've already scared 'em, I think it would be okay to share a few details," Viola said.

And so I did.

Thirty-Two

As happens, everything was better in the morning. Well, not everything, but some of the mysteries were solved.

After rescuing Viola, we dropped Tex back at his house, and I drove the rest of us back to Benedict. Mercifully, the snow stopped falling, and we must have done something right at some point in our lives because temperatures stayed warm enough that ice didn't accumulate under the tires. When we got back into town, we immediately drove to Gril's house, another cabin in the woods that reminded me of Randy's place—including its loft.

Gril was there and fine, having made it to Brayn and back easily. He had made sure Donner got home before he went home, too. Sometimes cell phones just didn't work in the wilds of Alaska. It was why everyone talked so much about being prepared, being smart. Gril informed me that before I took off to Brayn, I should have checked his house. It hadn't even occurred to me, but in the muted, cloudy light of the day, it made complete sense. I didn't think I'd ever make the same mistake again.

Gril and Donner had looked at Tex's freezer and quickly determined that it couldn't have been storing a body for any length of time, mostly because its guts, the electrical parts, were missing—had been for a long time, from all indications. Also, it didn't smell like a thawed or thawing body had been inside it ever; there were no suspicious signs.

I should have checked for the electrical guts myself when I first saw it, but again, that hadn't occurred to me. Everyone agreed that it was still something they'd needed to check out; there was no sense that it had been a wild-goose chase.

That Gril and Donner were fine and that Tex hadn't been storing a corpse was all good news, but we still had an unidentified dead body. And now Tex had become even more involved. I'd called him the night before to tell him we'd found Gril and Donner, but he'd hung up quickly, only saying that he'd see me the next day. I didn't call back to clarify when or where, but I wasn't surprised that he was waiting for us at Viola's truck when we got there. He suspected we'd be there soon enough; he'd been waiting in his truck—after he'd taken it upon himself to pull Viola's out of the ditch.

"Mighty kind of you," Viola said to him as she stepped toward him. "I thank you."

"You're welcome," he said. But he didn't make any move to leave.

We were all there. Viola and Ellen rode with me. Gril and Donner followed us in Gril's truck. I squinted at Tex behind the dark sunglasses I'd put on.

Tex looked at Gril. "I heard some about the woman's body and it being frozen."

"Any chance you have information that could help us with that?"

I knew Gril had wanted real answers as to who the girls' mother or mothers were, but I didn't know if he'd gotten the answers from Tex the day before. I hadn't inquired, and it didn't feel like the right moment to bring it up now, but I was certainly curious.

Tex looked out and into the snow-covered forest. It was a cold, clear, and shadowy morning, but it wasn't currently snowing. "No.

I know about an ice cave out this direction. I didn't walk out to it. I thought you should be out here before I explored. You'll see there are no prints in the snow, but I'd sure like to look with you."

"Why?" Gril asked him.

"We've had people go missing over the years. I've participated in many rescue missions that turn into recovery with no answers to tragic questions. It would be nice to be in on helping solve something. I don't have to go inside it, but I can show you where it is."

"I see," Gril said. He pulled something out of his pocket: a few stapled-together pieces of paper. "This is technically Tlingit land, but I got the okay to search the cave. Viola reminded me about it last night. However, I'm going to ask you all to wait while Donner and I check it out first."

Tex didn't act surprised as he nodded, not interested in looking closely at the papers Gril held. "I understand, but you might want to have me along, Chief. I know this land like the back of my hand. I grew up here. True, I haven't been inside the cave for years, but I remember there's a drop-off inside it. I can at least guide you to the entrance. I won't do anything you don't want me to do, but I can help."

Gril studied the crowd around him.

"Shit. All right, let's all go," Gril said. "Tex, lead the way and we'll follow your tracks. I don't I want anyone out of my sight." He looked at Tex. "Other than the drop-off, is it unsafe out there?"

"Not at all. Not if you do as I say. There might be some traps, but I can spot them and move everyone around them."

"Lead the way." Gril looked at us again. "Don't be stupid, people. I understand everyone's curiosity today, but don't be stupid. This is a long, long shot, but it's one I need to explore. You're all here only because I don't think you're killers. You can still piss me off, and I don't want to be pissed off today."

We all nodded our allegiance.

I did learn that Gril and Christine the ME had finally spoken. There was more information that might have made the ice cave a real consideration—I guessed that's really why Gril was here. The body had been quickly frozen after she'd died, but there was no way to know how long she'd been "on ice," other than probably at least a few years. There was no indication that the body had been exposed to wildlife. Christine was stumped, and she didn't like being stumped. Neither did Gril.

"Let's go," Gril said.

Tex led the way. Donner followed him, then Gril, Viola, Ellen, and me. We didn't have snowshoes, but our boots worked fine.

Gril had been most bothered by Ellen's riding along. His opinion of Viola's charges was always set to suspicious. He had a file on Ellen, and his questioning squint toward the woman, who wasn't behaving like a strung-out drug addict, made Viola send him a reassuring nod. That seemed to be enough; he didn't ask Ellen to stay behind. He didn't say much of anything to her, which she seemed fine with, too.

Hiking in a straight line wouldn't have been possible because of the trees, but the trek was mostly as the crow flies, other than one detour to veer around a trap. True to his word, Tex had recognized it before the rest of us. It was well camouflaged by snow, and chances were good I would never have seen it. Another thing I had to get better at.

"Are ice caves common in Alaska?" I asked after we passed the trap, which was about five minutes into the hike.

"They're like extended glaciers," Viola said. "You have to see the land from above to see the glacier on the other side of that mountain." She nodded to our right. "This cave is a long extension of it. It's the only one I've ever been inside of."

"There are others around, but since this path was cut off until the recent mudslide, this one hasn't gotten as much attention as it used to." Tex spoke back over his shoulder.

"Are they dangerous?" I said.

"If you aren't careful or don't know what you're doing, then yes," Viola said. "They can be. They're also pretty. You'll see."

We were far enough that we could no longer see the road or the vehicles behind us when Tex stopped.

"It's here, I'm pretty sure," Tex said as he looked at a couple of dirt mounds on the slope of a hill that eventually turned into the mountain. They weren't as covered with snow as everything else.

Gril handed him one of the small shovels he'd brought. Donner had another one. They got to work. It didn't take long before an obvious cave opening was uncovered: dark but with what seemed like some light coming from somewhere inside. Crouching would be required to enter, but not crawling.

"Should have been more snow and not so easy to uncover if no one has been here awhile," Gril said.

"I agree," Tex said. "Someone re-covered the opening recently; at least that's my guess."

"Okay, Donner and I are going in first. Nobody do anything stupid out here. Viola is armed," Gril said as he pulled a flashlight from his pocket and flipped it on.

She lifted the flap of her coat to prove that she was, indeed, armed.

I wasn't scared of anyone there, including Tex, but I understood why Gril was being careful.

We secured ropes around them, though Viola and Tex said that probably wasn't necessary. Nevertheless, we held on to the ropes as Gril and Donner went inside the cave.

"That seems terrifying," Ellen said with a loud gulp.

"It's not that bad," Viola said. "At least it wasn't back when Benny and I explored it."

"No, it shouldn't be terrible," Tex said.

A second later, Gril reappeared and undid the rope. "It's an easy one. High ceiling, good walking space. Plenty of light only a few steps in. We're going to walk a little farther, but it's okay if you all want to take a look. It's stunning."

"Sounds good," Viola said.

"Sure," I said.

"Do I have to?" Ellen asked. "I'm not into closed spaces."

"I'll stay out here with you," Tex said.

I was too curious to stay outside, but no one seemed to mind Tex and Ellen remaining behind.

I followed Viola inside. It was mostly dark, but only for a few steps. Once we turned a rounded corner, the world was lit brightly, the space open enough for us to easily stand. It was like stepping into a place made of frozen blue water.

"Wow," I said as I looked down the tunnel, walled and topped off in blue ice. I knew how it worked, that the ice absorbed all the colors of the light spectrum except for blue. That's why the glaciers also looked blue from some angles. I hadn't seen any glaciers yet, but it was hard to believe they could be more spectacular than this cave; it was more like a sculpture than a simple hole in the land. It could have been mistaken for Atlantis, a place where it wouldn't surprise me if sea creatures swam by. But there was no swimming; everything was frozen in place, and in time.

"It's something, isn't it? Come on, if I remember correctly, it slopes gently until the drop-off," Viola said.

Sort of crowded, but side by side, Viola and I made our way down the chute. The ground was stone, not slippery, but slightly rocky here and there. It was cold, but I didn't think freezing. The light reflecting off the ice was so bright that there was no need for flashlights.

"Could a body stay frozen in here?" I asked Viola.

"I don't know," she said doubtfully.

Shortly after we moved around another curve in the tunnel, we met up with Gril and Donner. They were standing to one side, their backs to us as they seemed to be looking at a cubbyhole along the bottom side of wall.

"Uh-oh, that's the drop-off," Viola said. "Something's not right."

We'd probably traveled about thirty yards from the opening, but now with each step toward Donner and Gril, the temperature lowered, seemingly by many degrees. It fell below freezing, I was sure. I no longer wondered if a body could remain frozen here. There was no doubt in my mind that it could. The downward slope steepened, too, but if this *was* the drop-off, it wasn't the drastic fall I'd imagined.

"What's up?" Viola asked Gril.

"Hang back, Vi," Gril said.

"What did you find?"

Gril turned around and looked at us. "A purse, and some other things."

"What?" I asked.

"A purse, handbag," Gril said. "Donner's going to gather it, but now the cave is considered a crime scene. You two need to head back the way you came. We'll be out when we can."

"Was her body kept here?" I said.

"It's possible. We have an ID," Gril said.

"Who?" Viola asked.

"Not ready to share," Gril said.

"It was carried out, as well," I said.

Two things occurred to me. It *had* been easy to clear the opening, and Tex had known exactly where it was.

"Be careful, but head on out," Gril said again. I heard the regret in his voice this time. He wished he hadn't let us join them.

I felt the need to hurry out to Ellen.

"Let's go," I said as I turned around to hike back up. But as I turned, I caught sight of the purse in front of Gril. I didn't look at it long, but I tried to memorize it. Brown leather with a red stripe.

"Gril, I've also got a man's wallet," Donner said.

Gril moved closer to Donner. Viola and I halted, too curious again.

"Whose is it?" Viola asked. "Is there an ID inside?"

"There is," Gril said a moment later. "With a picture and everything."

"Who?" Viola asked.

"A wallet and a purse, both with IDs," Gril said, mostly to Donner.

"Whose?" Viola asked again.

Gril hesitated but then finally said, "Paul and Audrey Horton. Remember them?"

"The fire," Viola said.

"Aw, damn and double-damn," Gril said as he looked at the ID in the wallet. He showed it to Donner. "He changed some. Remember this guy?"

It took Donner a long minute, but he finally answered. "Damn. That's him."

"Who?" Viola said.

"Remember the body on the beach a few months ago?" Gril said.

"Yes, he wore a white dress shirt," I said.

Everyone looked at me.

"It's what I remember the most. Was that Paul Horton?"

"It appears to be. He didn't look familiar to me when we found his body. His hair had grayed, he had aged. He's in the same cooler in Juneau his wife—at least that's who I think she is now—probably is, waiting for someone to solve something. He might be in the drawer right next to her."

"The body on the beach had been killed shortly before it was found, stabbed. If the woman was Audrey Horton, she was frozen for some time, right?" I asked.

"That's what I'm beginning to think," Gril said. "Neither of them were recognizable."

"What in the world is going on?" Viola said.

"What, indeed," Gril said. "Go on, ladies. Get out of here."

Silently and carefully, trying not to touch anything, Viola and I made our way out of the cave.

Thirty-Three

"verything go okay?" Tex asked as Viola and I emerged.

Ellen didn't say anything but seemed pleased to see us. Not relieved, though; she hadn't been concerned.

Viola had already told me to let her handle talking to Tex and Ellen.

"Remember the fire we had six or so years back?" Viola said.

"No," Tex said. "Wildfire?"

"House fire," Viola said. "Two girls were presumably killed, but only one body found. Jenny Horton."

"Jesus. No, I don't remember that at all."

"Were you in Brayn back then?"

"I've lived in Brayn all my life."

Viola looked at me and then back at Tex. I looked at Tex, too. So did Ellen. He noticed the audience, but he only looked at Viola.

"Only one girl's body was found. The other remains seemed to have been burned up completely," Viola said.

Tex brought his eyebrows together tightly. "That's . . . horrible."

I wondered if I was the only one who saw the moment when Tex's eyes gave him away. What had that news made him feel? Surprise, shock, fear? I didn't know, but I knew that in that briefest of instants, something had changed. I wondered if Viola should have waited for Gril and Donner. What had Gril and Tex discussed the day before? I was torn between being anxious for Gril and Donner to join us and hopeful that Tex would explain more about his girls.

"That's just terrible," Ellen said.

Viola and I shared another glance. I suspected she'd seen what I had.

"Viola, when was this exactly?" I asked. "Do you remember?"

"Six years ago. July." We both watched Tex again. "The girls would have been about two at the time. They'd be eight now."

I couldn't see his neck, but there was something about the way the hair on his face moved that made me think Tex had swallowed hard.

"Terrible," Tex said.

"You don't know anything about that, do you?" Viola asked.

"No."

Viola put her hands on her hips and stepped toward Tex. She was a big woman, but still not at big as he was.

"Tex, I gotta ask you, are both of those girls yours?" Viola asked.

"Yes, Viola, they are mine," he said.

"Where's their momma?"

"She didn't stick around."

"White woman?"

Credit to Tex, he didn't behave as if he was offended by the questions. He'd heard them before probably, but he didn't answer, either.

Gril and Donner emerged from the cave, both of them carrying bags of evidence.

"Tex," Gril said. "I need you to come with me. All right?"

Tex looked at Gril with steely eyes. "Why?"

"I have some questions for you."

Tex hesitated. "I need to call a tribal representative if I'm going to be talking to the Benedict police."

"Whatever floats your boat," Gril said.

"What's this about?" Tex asked.

"We found some things in the cave we'd like to talk to you about."

"What?"

"Why don't you call your tribal rep and have them meet us in Benedict, at my office. Want the address? You come with me, if you don't mind."

Tex hesitated, but then said, "I'm sure they can find it."

"Your truck running, Viola?" Gril asked.

"I think so."

"You all get back to Benedict in Beth's truck. Donner will take your truck, and Tex will come with me. We'll let Tex's representative know his truck is out here."

"Am I under arrest?" Tex asked.

"Not yet."

There was no cell signal out in the woods. Or at least not one reliable enough for Tex to call his representative. Gril loaded Tex into his truck, offering to drive back to Brayn first. Donner took Viola's truck and headed back to Benedict. Tex's truck was pulled to the side of the road, inasmuch as there was one.

Finally, Viola, Ellen, and I piled back into my truck.

We were silent for a long time.

"Did Tex say anything when we were inside the cave?" I asked Ellen. "Did he seem nervous?"

"No. He didn't say much, and I didn't feel the need to talk, either. Mostly, we were quiet. I thought I saw something in the woods and for a second I was worried it was a bear or something, but he looked and said it was probably just someone checking traps."

"Why did you think it might be a bear?"

"Looked like one, sort of." Ellen shrugged. She sat in the middle space and I could tell she was continually readjusting to save herself from the springs.

"How far away were they?"

"What? How far out into the woods?"

"Yes."

"I don't know. Half a football field or so."

"From which direction?" I asked.

"Back there." She pointed.

The other way, the way that would eventually lead to Lane's house.

"I'm going a different direction," I said as I maneuvered the truck.

"Why?" Viola asked.

"I want to see if someone has been spying on us."

"What?" Viola asked.

"It's just a hunch."

"It was probably just a trapper, Beth. They're out here," Viola said.

"What trapping season is it?" I asked.

"I don't know. But people trap out of season, too. There's not much regulation."

The way might have been "cleared" by the mudslide, but it was still rough going. I didn't want to give up, though.

We bounced our way over rough terrain. It was a semi-miserable journey. I finally came to a stop and we all looked around the woods.

"You see anything out there?" Viola asked aloud.

"Nothing like someone in a bearskin coat," Ellen said.

"When do bears hibernate?" I asked.

"Depends," Viola said. "They don't all hibernate. If food is available, bears don't need to hibernate. The pregnant females will anyway, but not all the males. If you head to the northern parts, you'll find more hibernation. Here, it's not as necessary. However, an early winter might be an indication that the bears are headed in. Bottom line, it's hard to know for sure."

We saw no animals, no people covered in animal skins. Nothing but the snow-covered woods. Another time on an easier ride, it would be a pretty sight.

"Hang on. We're going to cross the river," I said as I put my foot back on the accelerator.

"What?" Ellen said. "That doesn't sound wise."

"I hear there's a low point. Right, Viola?"

"It's been a while, but give it a shot. I'll tell you if you need to turn around."

"Oh boy," Ellen said.

A long and bumpy few minutes later, we came to the river and the low spot. The water *was* low, and the rocky riverbed was high; a hump, of sorts, where the water slowed to almost a trickle. I thought I could drive across it—it would probably be easy to walk across.

"Will we get stuck?" I asked Viola.

"Don't think so, but there's only one way to find out. Hang on and go."

"Wait! Want me to get out and check it?" Ellen said.

"Nope. Just hold on tight," I said.

We made it halfway when my tires started to slip. As Ellen and Viola waited silently, I put my foot back down, nice and easy.

In what seemed like an inch-by-inch infinite journey, we finally made it to the other side.

"Nice," Viola said.

"Phew, that was something," Ellen said with a laugh.

"Where to now?" Viola asked.

"I want to see if . . ."

We came around a sharp curve, and there it was, the place I was looking for. Lane's house.

I stopped the truck again. "That didn't take long."

"What?" Viola said.

"It only took about ten minutes to get here, even getting over the river. How is that possible?" I looked around, trying to understand the distances.

"It's just a shortcut," Viola said.

"Why weren't these roads paved instead, then?"

"I'm not a civil engineer, Beth, but I'm guessing because this area was dangerous with the possibility of mudslides. The river might flood. I don't know."

"Lane has been hidden out here for years. Now he's not."

"Happens," Viola said.

"Come with me to the door? Make sure he sees your gun."

"Sure. Why not."

"Oh boy," Ellen said again. "I'll stay in the truck."

"And I'll leave you the keys," I said.

I pulled the truck around to the front of the house, and Viola and I got out.

"What's going on, Beth?" Viola asked as we walked to the door.

I veered her around the hole in the ground, and we stepped over the now obvious string that had been restrung to arm the cookware alarm. She didn't seem surprised to see the homemade setup.

"Something that, for some reason, no one wants to tell anyone about," I said. We stopped walking and looked up at the smoke curling up from the chimney. Even so, the house didn't seem particularly welcoming.

I knocked on the door and heard noises inside.

Lane opened the door and looked at me, at Viola, and then at her exposed firearm. He didn't seem to be bothered by it. "I don't understand why you keep showing up."

"Were you out in the woods over there toward Brayn a little bit ago?"

Lane crossed his arms in front of himself. "Look, what I do is none of your business. Where I do it is even less your business. Time for you to leave me alone. Got it?"

Viola didn't introduce herself, didn't need me to prompt her with a full story, either, apparently, but said, "We were out there, by the ice cave, and thought we saw someone. We wondered if it was you."

Lane blinked at her but seemed to relax. "I wasn't out there. Now, that's the last time I'm answering your questions. Please don't come back to my house ever again."

A noise sounded from the back of the house, as if a door had been slammed shut.

"You live alone?" I asked.

Lane sent me a look that would kill, if looks could do such things. And then he closed the door, surprising me by not slamming it, too.

I stepped backward toward the truck and contemplated walking into the woods to search behind the house, but the slamming of the door might have meant someone had gone *inside*, too.

Just because I wanted answers did not mean they were any of my business. What was I sensing—what connection? What was the missing piece that would pull it all together?

"What does it matter if he was out there?" Viola asked.

"I don't know yet, but I'm working on it."

"Come on. We've got Ellen. I don't know this guy."

"He does come into town, shops at the mercantile."

"Well, there aren't many options. That doesn't tell me much of anything."

"I know." I looked into the woods another moment. "All right, let's get back."

Ellen was still sitting in the middle spot on the truck's bench seat. She might not have heard what we'd said, but she'd watched out the windshield.

"You okay?" I said.

She laughed once, nervously. "Well, I'm keeping very distracted."

"That's good," I said.

"That's very good," Viola said. "Let's see what's going on back in Benedict."

Thirty-Four

I looked at Randy's house as we passed by it. He still wasn't there; maybe he wasn't even back from Juneau yet.

"Viola, does Randy have any hobbies? Does he hunt or trap?" I asked.

"I don't think so. He owns the mercantile. It's his life."

"Have you remembered his wife, Wanda, any better?"

Viola thought a long moment, then shook her head. "She was unhappy, unfriendly, but that's the only impression I remember."

"Where in the world would she have gone? Anywhere around here you can think of?"

"I have no idea. I didn't have one real conversation with her."

"Do you remember the day she left?"

"No, Beth. I just don't. She wasn't here long as far as I know. Why?"

"I just wondered if it was ugly, if there was a public argument."

"Not that I'm aware of."

We were coming up to the *Petition* and the library. "I need to check in with Orin. Do you mind if I stop there a minute?" I asked.

"A library?" Ellen said as the hand-carved sign came into view.

"Yes, a great one," I said.

She looked at Viola. "I know you have no real reason to trust me, but could I stay here awhile? I'd love to find some books. I'm not sure I can get a card, but I can read here."

"Sure," Viola said. "Just remember, there's nowhere to run."

Ellen laughed again. "I know that even more than I did before. We just got back from nowhere. Thank you."

"You're doing great, Ellen," Viola said.

She took a shaky breath. "At the moment, I'm not so sure, but there's no fix in the near vicinity, so I'll battle through. All addicts should be lucky enough to have so many strange adventures."

I thought about Orin's medicinal painkiller and hoped it wouldn't cause a problem.

"I'll just wait here," Viola said. "Hurry up, Beth. I want to get to Gril's office. I need my truck."

I guided Ellen inside and saw her eyes light up as she looked at the shelves, and then dim when she saw the crowd.

"Lots of people," she said quietly.

"Internet access is like gold around here," I said. "Everyone will head over to the airport at lunch if Orin shuts down for an hour. You going to be okay getting back to the Benedict House if you need to? Just down the road we were traveling."

"I'm going to be fine," Ellen said. "Maybe I'll never have to leave this library. That might be the best. Oh, but I have to cook dinner and I wouldn't even think of shirking that duty."

We were standing right inside the doorway, not speaking too loudly, but probably too noisily for the library setting. I put my hand on her arm and lowered my voice even more.

"Are you okay?" I asked.

"No. I mean, yes, I'm fine, but now I'm overloaded with regret and sorrow. I'm trying to ignore it. I mean, people have been killed and I can't seem to stop thinking about me and all the time I have wasted."

"Well, I don't have the right answers, but you can only do better from here on. It's up to you."

Ellen looked at me. "Thanks. I'll try." She took another deep breath. "I hope to find some good books." She leaned close and spoke even more quietly. "I think I'll pass on *your* books for today, though. Too scary."

"Sheesh, that's the truth." I smiled. I gave her the phone number of the burner phone I'd been using. "Not sure it will do you any good, but if we both happen to be in pockets of coverage, or you use a landline, I'll try to answer it."

"Thanks."

I left her with the readers, the books, and the open laptops, and made my way to Orin's office.

"Come in," he said when I knocked.

"Hey," I said. I closed the door behind me.

"Beth! I got your message. I tried to check on you but no answer. I'm glad to see you. What's going on?"

I filled him in on the latest.

"Gril thinks the body from three months ago is Paul Horton? What in the hell does that mean? How bizarre," he said.

"Orin, someone was watching us in the woods. I thought it was Lane, but now I'm not so sure. We just stopped by his house and he said he wasn't out there by the ice cave, and then I heard a door slam in the back of his house."

"And we don't know who that might have been, coming or going?"

"No clue."

Orin shook his head once. "And two women are missing—Wanda Phillips, and Ashley Horton. Ashley's purse was found in the cave?"

"He assumes she's the female body. And Gril took Tex Southern in for questioning. What if one of Tex's daughters is the Horton girl who disappeared? What if *neither* of those girls are his?"

"That could get very ugly, indeed." Orin sat back in his chair and rested his chin on his steepled fingers.

"What?"

"I'm going to research some more, but I'll call Gril the second I find something helpful."

We said we'd talk later. As I left the library, I saw that Ellen had scored one of the comfortable chairs and was nose-deep in a romance.

I rejoined Viola, but then did something that surprised even her. I told her I didn't want to go with her into Gril's office, that I had some things I wanted to get done.

I dropped her off at the police cabin, noticing that Gril's and Viola's trucks, along with some vehicles I didn't recognize, were parked out front. Presumably, Tex was in there, too.

I told Viola I'd see her later and took off back to Brayn. I didn't tell anyone where I was going.

Thirty-Five

Though I didn't completely understand why, I didn't want Tex Southern to be guilty of anything. Nevertheless, I hoped he would remain with Gril and Donner for at least a little while.

The dark clouds promised more snow or maybe rain, but none was falling yet. It would, probably when I least wanted it to. For now, I traveled the thirty minutes to Brayn confidently, the road mostly clear, or clear enough.

I drove directly to Tex Southern's house and knocked on the door.

As I'd hoped, his mother answered. "Hello again," she said, but not with a friendly tone. People were tired of me knocking on their doors today.

I paused a moment and then stuck my hand out. "My name is Beth Rivers."

"My son told me your name."

I took back my hand. "Right. May I come in, Grettl? I'd like to say hello to the girls if they're here, but that's not the real reason I've stopped by. I'd like to ask you a couple of questions."

"No, I won't invite you in," she said. "The girls are upstairs, and I

don't know you. Tex doesn't really know you. What right do you have
to ask questions?"

"The girls know me and they trust me."

"They're children."

I put my hands in my pockets and tried to see behind Grettl, but
it was too dark.

"Exactly." I paused. "Maybe I've just made them my business."

We stared at each other, neither of us willing to blink.

I pulled my hands from my pockets and crossed my arms in front
of myself. "Who's their mother?"

She squinted and then sighed, giving up the battle much more
quickly than I anticipated. "All right. Come in for a minute, Beth. But
I'm only inviting you because I can see you might cause trouble for
my son. There's no need. He hasn't done anything wrong."

I followed her inside and heard faint noises from upstairs. Music
played—something kids would enjoy, and I heard toys being scooted
across the floor as well as being dropped on it. I didn't hear any
little-girl chatter, of course. I didn't hear laughter or any of that
strange screaming sound.

Grettl sat on the couch and nodded toward the chair. "Sit."

I did as she instructed.

"I'm not exactly sure why the police want to talk to him, but he
has done nothing wrong. I'm sure he will be home soon," Grettl said.

"Okay."

I waited. She knew why I was there, and she'd invited me in.

"It's a simple story," she said finally.

"Then why doesn't Tex talk about it?"

Grettl frowned. "They are his girls. He loves them deeply. But he's
lived his life afraid that someone would take them from him." She
sighed again. "The girls were both adopted."

"I see. A single man was able to adopt them? Is that why he's concerned?" I asked.

"The girls were left here in town, at the post office, when they were
about two years old. They were relinquished to the tribe by the birth

mother, and she didn't give us a specific birth date, but claimed the girls were fraternal twins."

"Who was she? Where did she go?"

"No one knows," Grettl said. "I was at the post office the day she brought them in. She said she was looking for a hospital but there wasn't one close by. She said she couldn't care for them, thought that maybe we could. She was hurt—an injury on her face—but she kept trying to hide it. She ran off before I could chase her—my priority quickly became making sure the girls were okay. The woman was long gone by the time I managed to get outside to see which way she'd gone.

"My son offered to pay for their care if a woman or a couple wanted to adopt them, but no one did. It's a tough life out here, and many of us are poor. Tex offered to give them a home, agreed to allow our tribal leaders to visit and inspect. Time went on, and the girls just stayed. They are well taken care of. They are well loved."

"May I ask what the state authorities did? Did they try to take them away, put them in an orphanage or foster home situation?"

"The Alaskan state authorities were never informed. We didn't feel the need."

My heart fell and soared at the same time. Surely, the girls' situation hadn't been handled appropriately. But Tex Southern had stepped up and taken care of them. They seemed healthy and happy.

"They've never spoken?" I asked.

"Mary spoke a little when they first arrived, but Annie didn't. When Annie continued not to speak, Mary stopped talking, too."

"That's . . . that might have been helped," I said.

"We've had them work with a speech therapist and it hasn't helped."

"Psychologists?"

"No."

This wasn't right, but maybe other solutions were worse.

"Why don't you all just tell everyone the truth?" I asked.

Grettl frowned. "I see what you're thinking. I see your judgment. Any time we've shared the truth, particularly to those outside the tribe, we've received the same judgment, as well as threats regarding contacting authorities. It's best just to let everyone wonder."

She wasn't wrong. I didn't mean to judge, but I was, even if it was silently and to myself. How had something like this happened? How had these girls fallen through the cracks so deeply? Where was their mother?

But I knew this sort of thing happened all the time. Maybe the details were different, the circumstances, the situations, but children fell through the cracks every day. And they weren't always ultimately taken care of as well as Annie and Mary had been.

"Do you know anything else about their first two years?" I said.

"I don't," she said.

The fast pitter-patter of footfalls came from the stairs. I righted my expression so Annie and Mary wouldn't think I was bothered.

Mary was the only one who emerged from the stairway. She held a doll and was looking at it with concern. She smiled when she looked up and saw me. She ran to me and hugged me genuinely.

"Hello," I said as I pulled her close.

She pulled back and smiled and then took the doll to her grandmother. She pointed at the head, which was almost torn away from its neck.

"I can sew that," Grettl said. "Why don't you run up and get Annie to come down and say hello to our guest."

Mary frowned and looked at Grettl. She shrugged and shook her head.

"What do you mean?" Grettl said.

Mary repeated the shrug and head shake. She tucked the doll under her shoulder and signed something.

"What?" Grettl stood and made her way around the child. Mary followed her, and then I followed behind them both.

We all jetted up the stairs and into the large children's room.

"Annie?" Grettl said. There weren't many places in the room to search, but she looked under the bed and behind the closet curtain. "Annie?"

Mary seemed suddenly concerned, too. She started to cry.

"Where is she?" Grettl said as she put her hands on the girl's arms. "Where is she?"

Mary was too frightened to respond. I grabbed a piece of paper and a pencil and took them to Mary.

"Can you draw it?" I said.

Mary blinked at me and then took the paper and pencil. She sketched quickly, but her simple drawing was easy enough to translate.

She'd drawn a bear—but there was no doubt in my mind that the bear's face was human.

Thirty-Six

have never experienced anything like the relief I felt when Donner answered the phone at the police station.

"One of the girls is missing," I said before could finish his greeting.

A brief pause was followed by "Beth?"

"Yes, yes, it's me. Listen, Donner. I'm in Brayn. Annie, one of Tex's girls, is missing. The best I can understand is that she and Mary were outside playing when their grandmother came over. She told them to come inside and then went back into the front room to answer the phone. Tex was calling to tell her that he'd made it to Benedict. She heard the back door open and then footsteps up to the girls' room, so she thought both of them had come inside. But Annie hadn't. Mary has now communicated with her grandmother, and the best we can understand is that someone with a bearskin coat or something like that took Annie. The girl might have gone willingly. Mary wasn't too upset until we were upset, so I sense it wasn't anything violent. It's not possible for me to understand her sign language, but I know Annie is gone. We looked everywhere around here for her. We've called the tribal representatives, too, but no one is here yet. You and Gril and Tex need to get here. Tex's house."

"We are on our way," Donner said without further hesitation or question.

Mary was falling apart now. Grettl and I hadn't considered how she might respond to our panic, but it couldn't be helped; we were distraught and having a hard time hiding it. Mary and her grandmother communicated with sign language, and they were both so upset that I couldn't separate anger from fear from confusion.

I tried to get Grettl to tell me what Mary was saying, why the child thought it was okay for Annie to go with "the bear." But Grettl only said that Mary thought the bear seemed nice.

These were not toddlers. They were young girls, but eight-year-olds would know not to go with strangers, if that's what they'd been taught. I couldn't know for sure, but that seemed like something Tex would teach them. Maybe it wasn't an important lesson so deep in the Alaskan wilderness.

After the long wait for Gril, Donner, Tex, and the tribal representatives, I became convinced that the girls must have known the person wearing the bear coat. Maybe Mary could explain it all better to Tex.

With the force of a hurricane, he came through the front door. Overflowing with fear and anger, he kept it well contained—better than Grettl and I had—his fiery eyes the only things giving him away. Behind him, Gril, Donner, Viola, and a man I assumed had been acting as Tex's tribal representative followed.

"Mom, what happened?" he said as he gathered Mary into his arms and held her tight.

Grettl relayed the story to Tex, but now she was so upset I wondered if we should call Dr. Powder, too.

"Mom, relax," Tex said, though he wasn't relaxed at all. "We will find her. You need to calm down." He put his daughter down and crouched to her level. He put his hands on her arms and looked her in the eye. "Sweetheart, tell me everything. It's going to be okay, but I need to know what happened."

They spoke in sign language, but Tex also translated the words aloud.

"The bear" came for Annie. The girls had been talking to the bear for a week or so now. It was the bear who guided them over to Benedict after the recent mudslide. They knew the bear. They liked the bear. The bear gave them treats, played with them.

"Mary," Tex said, righting his features after cringing over Annie and Mary's seeming ease of going with the stranger. "It's not a real bear, is it? It's okay. It's a person in a bearskin coat, right?"

For whatever reason, perhaps because a magical bear would be more believable than a person, Mary hesitated. But then she nodded.

"Good, that's good," Tex said. "Do you know the person under the coat?"

Without hesitation, Mary shook her head. No.

"A man or a woman?" he said.

Now Mary hesitated, but I could tell she was going to answer. We waited in breathless anticipation. I realized I hadn't been fully breathing the whole time they'd been talking.

Mary signed. Tex spoke, "A woman. A momma." Tex looked back over his shoulder at the rest of us. "Let's go find them."

Grettl, Viola, and the tribal representative stayed with Mary. Tex told his mother she would need to make sure Mary remained calm. Giving Grettl that task, or maybe trusting her with it, helped her focus. Viola was there to take care of all of them. They'd be fine. For all their sakes, though, I hoped we'd find Annie, alive and well, but if we didn't . . . No, it wouldn't do anyone any good to dwell on ifs.

Gril, Donner, Tex, and I headed out the way Tex had gone to track his daughters a few days earlier. Tex's still-wild eyes scanned the world around us. I knew he saw things I didn't, things I'd never see, even though I saw things differently than most people, too. When I first heard he'd tracked his girls to Benedict, it had sounded as mysterious as magic to me. As I watched him today, it still seemed unreal. In the remains of the fallen snow, he didn't hesitate, seemed confident in the way he chose to go.

I had to work hard to keep up with him, Gril, and Donner, but I managed okay, as I remained silent. I had many questions, but Gril and Donner were quiet, letting Tex do what he needed to do with full concentration, so I followed suit.

I glanced at the time after we crossed the river and as we came upon Lane's house. It had only taken us twenty minutes to walk to the place that would have taken ten minutes to drive to this way and at least thirty minutes to drive around the other way. The shortcut was real.

"Hey," I said breathlessly as the back of Lane's house loomed ahead. They all stopped and looked at me. "Gril and I have seen the man who lives here in a bearskin coat. I also thought I heard someone leaving out the back door earlier when I was here. Do you know if a woman lives here? Is Lane, by chance, married?"

"When we brought him in for questioning, he said he wasn't," Gril said. "He told us his wife died about six and a half years ago, in the woods. Her leg got caught in a trap and he didn't find her until too late. She had been mauled by a bear. Her remains are buried up by the shed. He didn't tell anyone at the time."

I nodded, not taking the time again to ponder the gore or how, once again, the proper authorities weren't always notified out here. "I saw the grave—but there seemed to be more than one. Did he talk about a child?"

"No," Gril said. "I asked. I saw the gravesites, too, Beth. Lane claimed there are no children buried there, but . . . Jesus." Gril raked his hand back through his hair. "Lane said their dreams of having a child were buried there. If the body we found in the shed had been hers, we would have arrested him, I would have pushed him more, but I was convinced he didn't know the dead woman."

"If someone is living here with him, who would it be?" I asked.

"It might just be someone else who wants to remain off the grid," Tex said.

"Let me talk to him. Come on," Gril said.

As we approached the back of the house and the room that still hadn't haunted my dreams but was bound to at some point, Gril called out.

"Lane! It's Police Chief Samuels and three others."

Even with smoke curling up from the chimney, I thought the house might be empty, but Lane did open the door a minute or so later. Dressed in a short-sleeved shirt and jeans, he would be cold quickly if he stayed outside for long.

"Chief? What's going on?" he said. His eyes moved suspiciously over Donner, Tex, and me.

"I need to ask you a couple questions," Gril said. "Can we come in?"

Lane didn't want to invite us in, but his better judgment won out. "All right. Come in."

We followed him through the back door and into the work room. Thankfully, there were no animals in there. Once in the front room, Lane stood next to one of the chairs and stuffed his hands into his pockets.

The warmth inside was too much, and I took off my hat and gloves. I caught Tex's eyes as they moved over my scar.

"Lane, have you seen a young girl walking through your property, maybe with an adult?" Gril asked.

"No," Lane said. "Is someone lost?"

"Yes," Gril said. He moved himself so he was in between Lane and Tex. No one could stop Tex from doing anything he wanted to do, but Gril could slow him down. I could see restraint in Tex's eyes and the set of his shoulders. Whoever had taken his child wasn't going to fare well. Gril knew that, too.

"A lost little girl. I'm sorry. How can I help?" Lane sounded sincere.

"I need to know something and it's very important, Lane. We are looking for a woman who might be wearing bearskin. Do you have any knowledge of such a woman?"

At first he was going to lie, as if he'd practiced doing it. He looked at Gril. This wasn't me, a nosy neighbor asking questions—this was the Benedict police. That still might not have been enough to get Lane to answer honestly, but there *was* a missing child. "Shit." He swiped his hand through his hair. "I've made a promise to keep it a secret and I'm sure she has nothing to do with a missing child . . . I don't live with anyone, but . . . yes, I believe I know who you are talking about. Chief, I would never suspect her of taking a child. Never."

"What's her name? Who is she?" Gril asked.

Lane shrugged. "I only know her as . . . Woman. She never gave me a name. She's a white woman. I don't know much about her, and I'm not sure who she is or was. She's kind, gentle, not someone who would take a child," he repeated.

"Give me more here, Lane. How do you know her?" Gril said.

"When she first came to my house about five or six years ago, she was in bad shape, upset, and her face was burned on one side—not a recent burn; it had mostly healed. She wouldn't tell me what had happened, but asked for shelter. She stayed a few nights, then left. She came back—comes back—I don't know how many times. There's never been a set schedule. I don't know where she stays when she's not here, but she does not live here."

"You didn't let the police know?" Gril said.

"No," he said as if the idea hadn't even crossed his mind.

Gril sighed. "Woman? That's it?"

"That's it."

"We think she took the girl," Gril said. "I know you don't think so, but you gotta help us. I need to know where she might have taken her. Give me your best guess, at least."

"I don't know," Lane said. "I don't have any idea where she goes when she's not here. She doesn't want me to know."

None of us had a vehicle. We'd walked from Brayn. Lane walked everywhere. I couldn't imagine his life, even as it was right there in front of my eyes.

"What did she tell you back when you first met her?" Gril asked.

"Nothing about her past. She wouldn't tell me where she was from. Nothing. She wanted to learn how to trap, so I taught her. And then we . . . we became friends, I guess." He looked pointedly at Gril. "There's never been anything more than a friendship, like a partnership. I help her with her traps, she helps me with mine. We eat meals together sometimes. We've never talked much."

"You aren't a couple?" Gril asked.

"No, but she was at my house earlier today, and yesterday, too. I've seen a lot of her over this last week." He looked at me. "You have, too. I was just trying to protect her privacy."

"You mean her secrecy?" I said.

Lane sighed and his mouth made a straight line. "I guess so."

"Do you think she had anything to do with the body in your shed?" Gril asked.

"I don't," Lane said quickly. "At first, I wondered, but when I told her a woman's body had been found, she said she knew nothing about it. I have no doubt she was telling me the truth."

Gril rubbed his hands over his beard. "Can you think back to three months ago? How was she then? How did she behave?"

Lane was quiet a long moment.

"Lane?" Gril said.

"Three months ago, I found her in my work room. I came home and she was cleaning blood off her hands, but there were no animals in the room. She said she got hurt releasing a wolf back into the wild, but she wouldn't show me her injuries."

"That could happen," Gril said.

"Dangerous, though," Tex added.

"You're coming with us," Gril said to Lane. "We're walking back toward Benedict. I want you to help us find her, bring her out. I'm sure she'll be watching. Somehow."

"Of course." Lane quickly grabbed and donned his gear. He led us out of the house. Once we were back outside, both he and Tex looked around with identical intensity; they were both trackers and trappers.

"Did you ever ask her more questions?" Gril asked as we approached the land with the collapsed shed and gravestones.

"No, Chief, that's not how we communicate. We leave each other alone for the most part."

"Did you have a daughter?" I interjected.

Lane's eyes shot to me. The pain there was hot and not diluted. "I had a daughter and a wife. They died in the wild."

"You told me about your wife. When did your daughter die?" Gril asked.

"The same time as my wife. My daughter was two years old."

"Shit," Gril muttered. "Lane, you weren't straight with me when I asked you about a child. That's not smart."

"I know," Lane said, no apology to his voice.

"Let me see if I've got this straight, Donner. Lane's family died six and a half years ago. We had a house fire about the same time and a strange woman with a burn on her face showed up at Lane's a few months later. Sound about right?"

"Yes, Chief," Donner said. He'd been quiet, but apparently, he and Gril had been working through the timeline, working the case or cases.

They were good cops. I was impressed.

"You buried both of them?" Gril looked at Lane.

"I buried my wife. My daughter's body was . . . gone."

"You never saw her body?" Gril said.

"No, but she had gone out with my wife and I found her doll with my wife's body. The bear took her away."

"Shit," Gril said. "Well, I'm sorry for your loss, Lane, but goddammit, you should have told someone."

"I don't tell the police anything," Lane said. "I took care of it. I tried to find my daughter's body, but it was gone. I buried my wife and, with her, my daughter's spirit. I know the woods, Chief. There was no sign of her. There was so much . . . blood."

"Jesus fucking Christ," Gril said.

Of course, he was thinking the same things I was, the same thing Tex probably was. Somehow, Lane's child had lived and Tex had raised her. But there were two children.

"Was your wife Tlingit?" I asked.

"She was. I am, too, but I haven't been a part of a tribe for years. I . . . there were issues."

"I need to know the issues right this minute," Gril said. "No time to waste."

Lane nodded. "My father was abusive. I ran away when I was twelve. My father is dead, Chief. I'm sure that has nothing to do with what's going on now."

"Your missing daughter might," Gril said, with more anger than compassion.

"I don't know what to think about that. I'm afraid to hope. But I will do whatever you want me to do. I was . . . so upset, and then the woman came. We were both hurting, but she never told me the reasons for her pain. I'm . . . sorry."

"Tex, when did you adopt your girls? Six years ago, right?"

"They came to Brayn in July, six or so years ago. I adopted them shortly thereafter, but there are no official state records of the adoption."

"Gril, why did you take Tex back to Benedict to be questioned?" I asked, hoping he would tell.

"We found one of his traps in the cave."

"With the purse and wallet?" I said.

"Yes."

"How did you know it was his?"

"His name had been etched into it."

"I have no idea how it got there, but it was a trap I haven't seen for years, and I didn't put it in the cave. I'm happy to keep answering those questions, but right now, I need to find my daughter."

"Look." Lane pointed.

We all looked up the road at the same time. Ahead, black smoke filled the sky.

"Son of a . . ." Gril was the first to take off in a run, but the rest of us followed behind quickly.

Thirty-Seven

The shed and its contents were gone by the time we got there.

We came upon ashes and leftover black smoke. Tex moved close to inspect the building's remains, but the rest of us grabbed his arms and held him back.

"Hang on," Gril said. "It's not going to do you any good to get hurt, Tex."

The smoke cleared a million long moments later. There was no sign of Annie, no sign of her body. I felt my legs wobble with relief.

"Who would burn this down, Lane? The woman?" Gril asked.

We'd let go of Tex and all of us moved closer to the shed's remains.

"I don't know why she would," Lane said. "Except maybe this is the place I once showed her, a place where we kept some of our child's things. I truly don't know."

I looked at Lane. For an instant, I thought his image might have wavered, its edges transforming into someone else—Travis Walker.

I wasn't going to let that happen. I gritted my teeth and took a loud breath in through my nose. This wasn't going to happen. I blinked rapidly and my stomach turned, but Travis Walker didn't appear in place of Lane.

"Beth?" Gril asked.

I hadn't fallen into a memory or a spell this time, but coming back to the moment wasn't instantaneous. I made it through. I had kept my captor at bay. He wasn't here. I might have pushed away an important memory, a message, but if I *could* push it, him, away, maybe I could retrieve the important parts later.

Control. This was what it felt like, and it felt good. Was it because I knew, without a doubt, that a child's welfare was more important than my own, so my own issues had to be forced away? I doubted it was anything that noble, but I'd take it, no matter what had given me the strength.

"I'm fine," I said. I was, for now.

Gril looked at me. He knew what I'd been through and he knew I'd just remembered something.

"I'm okay, Gril," I said. "Really."

"All right." He turned to Lane. "Come on, you gotta tell us where that woman is, what she might have done with Annie."

Lane's eyes wavered with real fear and concern. "I truly don't know. I'm sorry."

"I have an idea," I said.

They all looked at me. I could never have seen this moment coming in my life. But what do we ever really see coming? There's a beginning and an ending. The in-betweens can be anything. If I knew anything at all, I knew that with certainty.

"Let's check Randy's house," I said.

"You think Randy took them?" Gril said.

"No, I don't," I said. "But I wouldn't be surprised if we find the woman and Annie there. It's just a hunch, but we don't have anything else at this point. Is Randy back from Juneau?"

"He was at the mercantile earlier," Donner said.

We had no phone. We had no vehicle. We could only gather Randy if we walked back to Benedict first and found him at the mercantile.

"I'll go get him," Donner said without needing instruction. "I'll bring him to the house."

He started running down the road. He had boots, but it wasn't going to be an easy trip. No one protested and Gril didn't stop him.

"Let's go," Gril said to Tex, Lane, and me.

The four of us were silent again as we hiked quickly toward Randy's. I could feel Tex's anxiety, Gril's concern, Lane's confusion.

"Why do you think they're at Randy's house?" Tex asked. "Who is Randy?"

"He runs the mercantile; he's a great guy, but he's not home much. My hunch could be wrong, but I think the woman is Wanda, Randy's wife, and I think she's been spending time in that house when Randy's not there."

"Wanda?" Lane said.

"Ever heard her use that name?" Gril asked.

"Never."

"You think she's lived out in the wild all these years?" Gril asked me.

"I think so. But . . . Gril, have the identities of the bodies been confirmed? Are they Paul and Ashley Horton?"

"Probably, but I only told Christine who I thought they were today. She'll let me know."

"You didn't recognize Ashley's body?" I said.

"I didn't, for a few reasons." Gril paused, but only a moment. "The Hortons weren't here long, and if I had any interactions with them, I don't remember. They had their house built before they arrived. But my wife died right before their house fire. I was in Chicago, taking care of her funeral when it happened. Donner wasn't working for me yet. The folks who investigated the fire came over from Juneau. I see now that they didn't do a good job with the investigation, but I'm afraid I didn't follow up when I got back to town. I was . . . I probably should have taken some time off, but there was no one else. I got Donner aboard, but the fire was behind us by the time I got back at the end of August, and then winter was on its way. We had other things."

If Gril had been here, if his wife hadn't died, maybe none of the subsequent tragedies and mysteries would have occurred. I would never point that out to him, but he knew, and it would wear on him. It was a perfect storm of bad things.

"I think Randy's wife left Randy, but I don't think she ever left Benedict. I think she's a murderer, although"—I looked at the three pairs of curious eyes—"I have no idea why she would have killed either of the Hortons. Lane said her face is burned—she was somehow involved in the house fire. The good news is, I don't think she would hurt a child." I looked at Tex. "I really don't."

"How did you come up with all of this?" Lane said.

"I trespassed, Lane. If I hadn't gone into Randy's house because I was curious, I wouldn't have seen three beds in the loft and three toothbrushes in the bathroom. That's all I have, so I could be wrong, but . . . I don't think I am, at least not completely."

"Are you in law enforcement?" Tex asked.

"I used to be." I looked at Gril, who nodded.

"Let's go," Gril said as he pushed his way to the head of the line.

Randy's house looked empty and quiet. There was no sign of Donner, but I calculated that he might have only just made it back to Benedict. If he rounded up Randy and a vehicle, he would be back in about ten to fifteen minutes.

We weren't going to wait.

We stood behind a few trees on the perimeter, but we were too large a group to be hidden.

"You all stay here a minute. I'll check it out," Gril said. He pulled his weapon from its holster.

"Chief Samuels, I'm not the type of man to tell law enforcement what to do, but please don't shoot anyone in there," Tex said.

Gril looked at Tex and then did something my grandfather would have done. He holstered his weapon, though he kept the snap undone. "All right, I hear you, but none of you can get in my way. Understand?"

We all nodded.

A bead of sweat rolled down my back. I was warm, but would be cold quickly if I didn't get moving again soon.

Gril stepped around the trees and made his way toward the house.

"Hello? Anybody in there? It's the police chief. Come on out," he said.

Nothing. The house was dark and quiet. I looked up at the loft window. The green paper was still there. I'd all but forgotten about it.

I tapped Tex's arm. "Does that look familiar?" I pointed.

"It might. Hard to tell. My girls make stuff like that all the time."

No one had answered Gril's calls, so he kept moving forward. He was careful, but I didn't think he put much stock in my theory.

"I'm going around back," I said to the men beside me. I raised my voice. "I'm going around back, Gril."

"Hang on a second," Gril said.

"I'll go with her," Lane said.

"All right," Gril said a long moment later. "Heads up, though. Got it?"

Lane and I assured him that we understood.

"Want to come?" I asked Tex.

"No, I'll stay on this side. Be careful."

Walking along the perimeter and keeping ourselves amid the trees, Lane and I moved around the house.

"I saw a back door," I said quietly. "There are windows. We need to stay to the side so we're not seen."

I could still hear Gril calling from the front, still announcing his arrival. And then I heard the rumble of a truck. It was Gril's, I knew the engine. Donner was here, with Randy, probably.

"Let's go back," I said. "We'll go in with Randy."

The back door of the house slammed open.

A woman emerged. She wasn't anything like a wild animal. Her hair was pulled back into a messy ponytail and her face was clean; one cheek was scarred. She wore jeans and a faded blue shirt underneath a well-worn brown sweater. There were no bearskins in sight. She saw Lane and me and she stopped, her eyes flashing with surprise.

"What's going on?" Lane asked her as he stepped around me.

She looked at me again, and then at Lane.

"Where's the girl?" I asked.

She still didn't say anything, just shook her head as her mouth pulled into a tight line. Tears filled her eyes. She took off, running into the woods.

"Hey!" I yelled. "She's back here!"

I took a step in the direction she'd gone, and then I went down. My foot had caught on something. I looked back, wondering what it had snagged on. At the angle Lane was standing, it looked like there were two possibilities: either he had put his foot in my way, or the toe of my boot had caught on a rock.

Had he stopped me from going after her?

Lane reached out a hand to me. "Should I chase her?"

I let him help me up. "It's probably too late now." I looked out into the woods. She was fast and agile, darting behind trees, making it difficult to keep track of her, and she had a good head start now.

Gril, Randy, and Donner came around the house another second later.

I pointed out to the woods. "She ran!"

"I'll go," Donner said, and again, he took off.

I looked at Gril. "The girl?"

He stepped up the small stoop and went in through the back door. The rest of us followed. Tex had gone in through the front door. We didn't have to go far to see him—with his daughter.

She seemed fine as Tex held her tight in his arms.

The shared relief was palpable, emotional if we let it be. But there wasn't time.

Gril turned to me. "What the hell happened?"

"She came out the back door and saw us. Lane asked her what was going on, but she didn't answer. She took off running."

"It was the woman?" Gril asked Lane.

"Yes. I didn't know if I should chase her."

I inspected Lane's face, but couldn't discern if he was lying or pretending. I didn't voice my recent suspicion.

Gril looked out to Donner. "Dammit."

Randy ran a hand through his hair. He walked over to the desk and opened a drawer. He pulled out a picture and brought it back to the rest of us.

"Is this . . . her?" Randy pointed at the woman in the picture. She wore a wedding dress and a happy smile as a tuxedo'ed Randy stood next to her.

"Yes," Lane said.

"Yes," I added.

It was the same woman, and in fact, to me she looked younger now than in the picture, even with the scarred face. For a moment I tried to make sense of that—the woman I'd just seen for the first time didn't wear makeup, and she was older than in the wedding picture. She wasn't tanned, but she wasn't winter pale, either. She reminded me of the outdoors, but that might have only been because of what I knew about her.

Randy's eyes were wide with confusion. I put a hand on his arm. "You okay?"

"I don't understand what's going on," he said.

"We'll get to the bottom of it," Gril said. He walked to Tex and Annie. "Come and sit down. We need to see what we can learn from your daughter, as soon as possible."

Somehow, Randy got past this new shock and went to the kitchen to gather waters for everyone. Donner hadn't been able to find Wanda, lost her tracks quickly, and he joined us, too.

"I wish I could tell you where she goes," Lane said. "I would. I swear I would."

I studied him. He seemed sincere.

Gril turned to Tex. "What can Annie tell us about the woman?"

Tex nodded. He and Annie had been conversing in sign language. When Tex spoke to us, he didn't sign.

"The girls met her the day after the recent mudslide. They saw her across the river—she waved them over. Annie said she was kind to them, asking them if they wanted to play or if they wanted something to eat." Tex paused. "I know this isn't the most important part of all of this, but I *have* taught my daughters to beware of strangers, not to talk to them. The only thing I can come up with is that they truly hadn't run into any strangers until they met this woman. Our community is small. No matter what I taught them, until now, they must not have understood."

He felt responsible. I couldn't share how I'd opened my front door to a stranger and had learned the ultimate lesson that, thankfully, Annie and Mary hadn't had to learn as violently.

"It's okay, Tex. Kids are kids. The girls are fine, that's all that matters," Gril said. "Can Annie tell us anything else about her?"

Tex nodded. "Annie said that Wanda—she said the woman told her her name today, Wanda—was very nice to her and Mary. Wanda took the girls to Lane's house, at least that's where I think she means, when Lane wasn't there. And then brought the girls here when Randy wasn't here. They brushed their teeth, and played up in the loft." He looked at me. "You were right about the toothbrushes. Wanda bought them for the girls."

"You didn't notice them?" Gril asked Randy.

"I guess not," Randy said. "I brush my teeth in the kitchen, shave there, too. The light is better. It's what I've always done; Wanda would know that. I haven't slept in the loft since last winter. I admit, there have been times over the years when I wondered if someone had been in the house. I spend so much time at the mercantile, though. And, honestly, nothing seemed damaged. I have wondered if someone just needed temporary shelter. If things had been damaged or stolen, I might have had a different attitude, but nothing ever was."

"What about the construction paper on the loft window?" I interjected.

Randy shook his head as his shoulders slumped. "I just thought it was something on the window. I'm not here much during daylight hours, haven't been for at least a week until today. I saw something up there but didn't bother to explore. If I'd thought it was construction paper, I would have . . . told you, Gril. I'm sure I would have found that strange, but I just didn't notice."

"All right," Gril said. "Go on, Tex."

"This hasn't been going on for long." Tex looked at Annie, who signed something. "Just since the mudslide for the girls, but Wanda did tell them *she'd* been coming here for a long time."

"Did Wanda ever hurt either of you?" Gril asked Annie. "You have done nothing wrong, Annie. I just need to understand if she ever hurt you."

Annie shook her head vehemently and then signed something.

"She was nice," Tex said.

"Okay," Gril said. He still looked at Annie. "Do you know where we can find her?"

Annie shook her head again and held her arms akimbo. She seemed sincere. Then, she signed something to Tex. We looked at him for interpretation.

"She sets traps. She took the girls with her to check them the night they didn't come home. They lost her when she told them to stay back as she checked a trap. She didn't want them to be scared, but when Wanda didn't come right back, the girls took off. That's how they got lost, how they ended up in here and then in Benedict. They were afraid to tell me the truth, afraid they'd be in trouble, and Wanda told them she was their special secret."

"Of course," Gril said. He smiled at Annie. "I can understand you being scared, but, see, your dad isn't mad. We aren't mad. Can I ask"—he looked back and forth between Annie and Tex—"do the girls make a high-pitched screaming noise sometimes?"

"Yes," Tex answered quickly. "I taught them to do it, in case they need to get someone's attention. They can't yell."

I was surprised that the question hadn't been asked before now, and I didn't understand why they could make that noise and not speak. Nevertheless, it was good to know with certainty that that's what Randy and I had heard. It also made me, and probably Randy, realize that the noise wasn't meant to be disturbing, even in the middle of the night. It was just communication.

Gril nodded. "Okay, Annie, I really need to know if there's anything else you can tell us about Wanda."

Annie fell into thought a moment. We held our collective breath.

Finally, she looked up and frowned, and then tears filled her eyes. She signed to Tex.

"Oh, sweetheart, that wasn't your fault. She did that, not you. Not your fault," Tex said to her. He looked at us. "Annie says that Wanda set fire to the shed right before they came here."

"Got it," Gril said. "Annie, we know you had nothing to do with that."

"Exactly. Okay, what else did you and Wanda talk about?" Tex asked Annie.

She signed and Tex smiled. Her tears slowed. He looked at us. "Fishing and hunting, some of the same things we talk about at home."

"And you have no idea where she lives when she's not at one of the houses?" Gril asked.

Annie shook her head again.

Gril looked at Randy. "I'll find her."

"You think she ki—" Randy began, but stopped and looked at Annie before continuing, "was responsible for what you found in the shed?"

"I don't know what to think," Gril said. He sent Lane a critical frown. Lane didn't seem to notice.

He was staring at Annie. There was a chance he was looking at his biological daughter. I wanted to ask if she looked familiar to him, perhaps like his deceased wife, but now wasn't the time. However, I saw the scrutiny, I saw the pain and confusion. If Gril or Donner noticed Lane's struggle, they didn't make it a priority.

Gril looked at Donner. "We need to find her. We'll call in some Juneau folks and we'll track her down. You all can come into town, stay at my office if you're worried, but if you don't want to, make sure you protect yourselves. I don't want any harm to come to her, but . . ." He looked at Annie. "Wanda should currently be thought of as dangerous."

"I'm going home," Lane said.

"I'll be here or at the mercantile," Randy said.

"Annie and I will be going home," Tex said.

Gril took a deep breath. "Look, folks, I'm trying to be delicate here, but I don't want any misunderstanding. I want her alive. I need answers. Got it?"

Everyone nodded that they did.

Thirty-Eight

"Unbelievable," Orin said.

"I know," I agreed.

It was late, but I thought Orin deserved an update. After using only Gril's truck to get us all where we needed to go, I hopped in my own and went to the *Petition*. I left Orin a message to meet me there after he closed the library. He joined me and reached for the whiskey. He downed two shots as I relayed what had happened.

"But if Wanda killed either or both of the Hortons, why? And how did so much time pass between the two murders? There's something bigger here," I said.

"I agree." Orin smiled. It was distinctly Cheshire.

"What? You know something else."

"I do. I found some interesting information."

"Should we call Gril?"

"I already sent him an email, though he might not have read it yet." Orin thought a moment. "His goal is to find Wanda, though, and my information won't help with that."

"What do you have?"

"Randy and Wanda and the Hortons were related. Randy and Paul were second cousins. I tracked them all back to a small town in Texas, and then I tracked Randy's career to New York City. He was extremely successful, made lots of money. From what I could discern, his cousin Paul tried to follow along behind, but he wasn't nearly as successful. And when he and his wife had children, they decided on a different sort of life. They moved here."

"Wow. That's a big move. They must really have wanted to raise their children away from everything."

Orin shrugged. "I get it."

"I kind of do, too."

"But then, Randy visited them out here and decided he wanted to live that way, too—I bet Gril didn't ask Randy a thing about the Hortons until now."

"No, probably not. Gril's wife died right before the fire. Big things fell through big cracks."

"Sounds like it." Orin reached into his back pocket and pulled out a piece of paper. "I wasn't the librarian at the time, but I searched just on a hunch. It's a copy of Wanda's library card. It wasn't even a computer search. I just looked in my old files and there it was, with the date and everything. It's dated about three months before the fire; they weren't here long at all."

"What do you think this means?"

"Well, according to the records, Wanda checked out only kids' books. She must have read them to the Horton girls. My small interpretation from this is that she cared for those girls, even when she didn't want to be here. I don't know, it's just another thing, I suppose."

"We've got to find her."

"Gril's got to find her."

"Of course." I fell into thought.

It was late enough that I let Orin pour me a shot, but just as I downed it, my open laptop pinged with an email.

It was either junk or something from one of the few people who had the address. I resisted looking at the screen.

"Go ahead, take a look," Orin said.

Before I could, though, another email pinged. I was too curious to ignore two emails.

Aiming the screen so only I could see it, I clicked it to life. The two emails were from my mom and Detective Majors.

Mom's subject line was "Shot the fucker." Detective Majors's subject line was "Your mom is on the run. Help."

"Oh. Oh no."

Orin swung his feet off the desk and sat upright. "Everything okay?"

"Fine," I said.

He downed the last drops of whiskey in the shot glass and set it on the corner of the desk. "I'll leave you to it, then. You probably have some work you need to get done. Organizing offices knows no hours."

"Yeah," I said distractedly as I set the laptop to the side of the desk.

I followed Orin to the door. He hesitated a moment. "You really okay? You know you can talk to me."

I smiled. "I'm fine, maybe better than I've been for a long time. And I know I can. I'm not . . . there yet."

"Got it. Okay, then. Later, gator." He sent me a peace sign as he took off into the darkness, back toward the library and his truck.

I locked the door and hurried back to my laptop.

I clicked open Mill's email.

Girlie—I have to be quick. I shot him. I shot our man. He was coming out of the Piggly Wiggly and I got him. Unfortunately, I hit his leg and a goddammed security officer starting firing at me. I wasn't hit, but I had to get away. I'll be in contact later, but I HURT THE MUTHAFUCKER! Love you more than chocolate sundaes.

"Oh, Mom," I cried. I was at once elated that my kidnapper had been shot and devastated that my mom had been the one to do the deed. Maybe I had wished a little for her to have the chance, but the reality was that he wasn't worth her freedom. I could try to reach her—phone, text, email—but she wouldn't respond, not until things cooled down. She had hidden from the law before, but as far as I knew, never because she'd shot someone. No, her violations had been more along the lines of trespassing or fisticuffs assaults. I'd wanted to tell her how I'd managed to push him away; only once, but that it was a beginning. Now I didn't know when I might hear from her again. She would go dark.

My grandfather had once said that Mill couldn't stay away forever, even if it would be best for her to do so.

She'd get back to me.

I opened the email from Detective Majors, but wasn't surprised by the contents.

> Hello—I need to inform you that your mother shot a man we assume was your kidnapper. We believe he was shot in the leg. Both your mother and the man got away from a security guard who was in pursuit of both of them. I'll keep you up to date, but please tell me if your mother gets in touch. I'll do what I can to keep her out of trouble. Thank you. Hope you are okay.

Detective Majors always kept it brief and ambiguous. No names, no identifying specifics. I appreciated that, but even with her sparse words, I could sense her anger. She'd been worried about my mother from day one, and Mill had just confirmed all her concerns. How had Mill found him? Was it truly the right man? I doubted I would know for a while.

Anxiety sent a shiver through my system, and my arms quaked. I didn't like what I was feeling—the sense of control ebbing out of me. I took a deep breath and tried to center myself.

And then I heard a strangled cry. I thought about the noise the girls had made before they knocked on the door that night, but this wasn't the same. This time it was a scream.

"What the hell?" I said quietly. I perked my ears, listened hard.

It sounded again. Was it coming from one of the girls? Surely, they were home with Tex. I hurried to the door and unlocked it, and then I stood there, my still-shaking hand on the knob. I was afraid to see what was in the dark. I was afraid to open the door.

I was afraid.

But if the noise was coming from one of the girls, I needed to see if she needed help. I could do this. Travis Walker was somewhere in the Lower 48, a bullet wound in his leg presumably slowing him down. An involuntary smile twitched at the side of my mouth. "Good job, Mom."

I pulled the door open. There was nothing to see. I peered into the darkness, wanting to see something, wanting to see nothing. I was going to have to go out there.

One foot in front of the other, and I made it. I was outside the building, though I made sure to leave the door open wide in case I had to run back in.

I looked all around as I walked away from the building, but all I could really see was more darkness. Until I looked toward the library.

"Orin?" I squinted.

It was dark over there, too, though it was neither snowing nor raining. It was cold, but I barely noticed. The library lights had been turned off, but there was one small one on the outside of the building, illuminating the improvised parking strip. Orin's truck was still there. I looked at the building again. There was no doubt; there were no lights on inside the building. Orin would turn on the lights if he was in there.

"Orin?" I called as I started to walk that direction. "Orin?"

Shapes moved in the darkness a few feet from his truck. I couldn't make out any specifics, but I thought I was seeing a body—a human body.

I didn't think about what I was doing as I set out in a run over the snowpack. As I got closer, I heard the noises of a fight, a physical fight. Grunts, slaps, groans. Two voices, a man and a woman. I was pretty sure the man's voice belonged to Orin, was almost as sure the woman was Wanda.

"Hey!" I said as I ran. I still couldn't make out the details of what was going on, but the fighting noises stopped briefly.

"Get help," Orin gurgled.

I was going to have to be the help for now.

They came into view. It was, indeed, Orin and Wanda who were fighting. Orin's face was covered in dark smudges that were probably blood. Wanda's ponytail had come loose and her wild hair made her now seem untamed.

Orin was on the ground, holding tight to Wanda's pant leg. She was trying to wrest it away.

"Get help, Beth," Orin said.

I ran at them. I didn't know what else to do. I tackled Wanda, both of us falling to the ground with an *oomph*, our lungs releasing air.

"Get off me," she said as she squirmed beneath me.

"What's going on, Orin?" I yelled as I somehow managed to pin Wanda's arms to the cold, snowy ground.

He was rolling over and trying to make his way to us. "I caught her coming out of the library. I thought someone had been breaking in at night."

"If you'd just stayed away a little longer," Wanda said between clenched teeth.

She was squirming enough that I wasn't sure I'd be able to keep ahold of her. She was lots stronger than me. I thought about what Cecile Throckmorton had taught me, and I moved my knees so I was straddling her better. If I could keep hold of her arms long enough to get Orin's help, we'd be okay.

"Did she hurt you?" I said to Orin.

"She stabbed me. She didn't hit any organs, but I'm losing blood."

Anger burned up through my gut and into my throat. Strength came with the anger; the burn helped me ignore the cold ground.

"You bitch," I said, sounding more like Travis Walker than I could have ever predicted I would. I punched her then, so hard I might have broken a bone in my hand.

I hit her only once, but it knocked her out. Orin pulled me off her before I could hit her again. He held back my arms.

"Good shot, Beth. She's out. I need help, though. You need to get inside the library and use the phone to call for help."

I blinked away the blinding, searing anger and looked at Orin. "I will."

"Good." He let go of my arms.

I scrambled up and then hurried to the library doors. I turned and looked back at him.

"Don't you fucking die."

Orin laughed once. "I won't. Make the calls."

I made the calls.

Thirty-Nine

If murder isn't addictive, it's at least an acquired taste.

Once Wanda had killed one person, Audrey Horton, she found it easy to kill Paul, too, particularly since she believed they deserved to die.

I got to be in on the interrogation. Actually, I think Gril just wanted to make sure I was okay; he didn't want me out of his sight. It was just him and me with Wanda inside the police station.

He had answered his office phone on the first ring. He was working, trying to figure out where Wanda might have gone. Once I told him what had happened, he then got ahold of Dr. Powder. They, along with Donner, Viola, and Ellen, were at the library in record time. Gril made a quick beeline for Wanda—I'd tied her wrists and ankles. The doctor hurried to Orin, who was still conscious; he and I had kept enough pressure on the puncture wound at the top of his shoulder to mostly stanch the bleeding.

Even if it had been snowing, I suspected the Harvingtons would have flown Orin to Juneau, but it wasn't snowing and they, along with Dr. Powder, had him on a plane in record time. An ambulance would be over there waiting for them, and Orin would be delivered to a real hospital.

He was going to be fine. Dr. Powder had called before the interrogation began to tell us Orin was stable and would get back to normal soon enough. I blinked away tears of relief; even Gril worked to keep his emotions in check.

When Wanda regained consciousness, she was none too happy. And now she wasn't pleased to be handcuffed to a pole, a handle, something like a reinforced towel rack, on the side of Gril's desk. There were no holding cells in Benedict. Gril sat in his chair and I sat in one like the one Wanda was occupying, though I was on the other side of Gril's desk, out of her potential reach, and I wasn't being held against my will.

"You're under arrest for lots of things," Gril said when she was completely coherent. "Want an attorney?"

She glared at him. "No, I'll tell you everything."

"Well, that's refreshing," Gril said. "Go ahead. Start at the beginning. I'll jump in if I have questions."

Wanda nodded as she sent me a look that could kill. I sent her one back just as full of murderous intentions. I could have killed her; I knew it. She knew it. We could have killed each other. I was done with people like her, and I was probably more like my mother than I wanted to admit.

"When I first came here, came to this empty world, I just knew I couldn't stay. It was all such a shock. I just wanted to go home. I wanted to go back to civilization."

Gril nodded once. "You were here for how long before you came to these conclusions?"

"Two weeks."

"That's not very long."

"It was long enough." She sighed. "I told Randy I was leaving, that I wanted a divorce. He didn't even fight it. He loved it here from the beginning, loved being far away from all those people. We still had a home in New York. I was just going to go back. We didn't have any kids, so no harm, no foul, really. He's quite a bit older . . . anyway, it just didn't need to be the way it was and there was a fix for it that really wouldn't hurt anyone, at least not too badly. You don't even remember me, do you?"

Gril looked at her a moment. "I don't, but there's a reason for that."

"Exactly. You weren't here for the two to three weeks I was part of the community. Your wife had died and you were out of town. I wanted to talk to someone in an authority position, but back then, you didn't have any help—no park rangers filling in as deputies. Viola, the woman who runs the halfway house, was the closest thing, and I knew pretty quickly I didn't want to talk to her. I didn't like her at all."

"I'm sorry I wasn't here. What did you want to talk to me about?"

Not long ago, Gril had told me his wife died several years ago, but it sounded like it was less recently than that. I could still sense his pain, but now wasn't the time to express my sympathy.

"I . . . something felt off about Paul and Audrey," Wanda said. "I wanted you to keep an eye on them, on their girls. I was leaving and I knew Randy would be working all the time."

"Did you tell Randy that you thought something was off?" Gril asked.

"No." She shook her head. "Until the morning after I told him I was leaving, I didn't have any proof, and then . . . it was all too late."

"Go on."

"That morning, Randy went to the mercantile, and I went over to tell Paul, Audrey, and the girls, Jenny and Josie, goodbye. I was going to take the ferry back to Juneau and then figure out how to get home from there. My plans were pretty fluid. I just knew I had to leave. I never booked a flight or anything."

"We couldn't find your name on any passenger manifests."

"Exactly. Anyway, I knocked on Paul and Audrey's door, but they didn't answer. I heard noises from inside, and they sounded . . . wrong, like people were rushing around, maybe talking quickly. I simply opened the door and went in. That wasn't unheard of; it didn't take but a day or two to realize we wouldn't need locks on our doors out there. We were the only two houses in sight. In those two weeks, we'd just walked into each other's houses a number of times. This time, though, I didn't announce myself; something told me to be quiet. I walked toward the back of the house, where I thought the noises were coming from." Wanda stopped talking and her head bowed. She looked at her hands on her lap.

"Wanda, what happened?" Gril asked a moment later.

She looked up at him. "Jenny was dead. Audrey had killed her. Audrey and Paul were trying to figure out what to do with her body."

"Hang on. How had Audrey killed her daughter?"

"Threw her from the loft."

"Jesus," I said.

Without looking at me, Gril lifted a hand to tell me to hush. I hushed.

"How did you know that's what happened?" he asked Wanda.

"I . . . I ran to her little body, but it was too late. I freaked and started yelling, 'What did you do? What did you do?' Paul told me what happened as Audrey sat on their couch, in a daze, and just listened. And, then I couldn't stop myself . . ."

"What do you mean?" Gril asked.

"I pounced on her, jumped on her and strangled her to death."

"Why didn't Paul stop you?"

"He helped me," Wanda said as tears filled her eyes. "Right there, in front of Jenny's body and as their other daughter, Josie, watched— she was so upset—Paul helped me kill his wife."

My stomach was sick, but I swallowed hard. I needed to know the rest of the story.

Wanda leaned toward Gril. "Listen, it was all so unreal, and happening so fast. Even now, I look back and it doesn't seem like time moved appropriately—it's like time kept folding over itself and things just kept getting worse, and I don't understand much of any of it . . ."

"All right. I get that," Gril said. "But we still need to know what happened."

Wanda nodded. "He wanted to get rid of Audrey's body, so we drove it out to an ice cave they'd visited the week before and dumped her in there. He was just going to say she wandered off. Someday, someone might find the body, but people would think she went into the ice cave on her own and just died. He thought he could make that work."

"Was she dressed?"

"Yes. I undressed her later, just recently. I . . ."

Gril interjected, "Why not Jenny's body, too?"

"He thought that would be too suspicious—both of them dying in the ice cave didn't seem as possible as just Audrey. And he thought Jenny should get a decent burial. He wanted to give her that. It was July, the ground would have allowed it, but we never got to that point."

"Where was Randy?" Gril asked when she stopped talking and fell into thought again.

"Randy was at the mercantile. We dumped Audrey's body and were back at their house by noon." She shrugged. "No one saw us do any of it. No one."

"But you didn't bury Jenny's body?"

"No, Paul told me that he would not tell the authorities what I'd done to Audrey if I helped him dig a grave for Jenny and then just left, just got out of there. He didn't even know that I was coming over to tell them goodbye. He never even knew."

"But he helped you; you killed Audrey together," Gril said. "He would have been in trouble, too. He couldn't have gone to the authorities without being in trouble, too."

"I know, but you have to understand the way things were happening—time was moving funny, we didn't see anyone else. I was caught up in the horror of it all, but by the time we got back to his house, I just wanted one thing: Josie."

"Okay?"

"I didn't want that little girl to be raised by him. I told *him* to leave, that if he just left, I'd take care of Josie. He didn't want the little girl anyway."

"So he did that, just left?"

"Yes, he did, but it wasn't easy to convince him. He fought me some, but I didn't give him much choice."

"But he did leave?"

"I told him to go back to Texas, back to family that Randy didn't know well. I told him to tell Randy that he and Audrey just couldn't take their loss so they had to leave."

"The loss of the girls? So he set fire to his house to make it look like the girls died in the fire?" Gril said.

"No. Not exactly. I mean, yes, the loss of the girls was their loss." Wanda frowned at Gril. "But I set the fire. He couldn't figure out how to make his own disappearance work, make it feasible, so I set the fire, told him to leave, that I'd take Josie and take care of her. He shoved me into a burning curtain." She put her hand up to her cheek. "I got hurt, but then I got away with Josie. Back then, the last I saw of Paul was him trying to get out of the fire. I took that girl and ran."

"The authorities would have talked to him, would have wanted to talk to Audrey," I interjected.

"You mean after the fire?" Wanda asked me.

"Yes."

"The fire died out on its own. No authority even looked through the house until two days later. Jenny's body wasn't found until then. Paul was gone. I assume he finally talked to the authorities on the phone and told them Audrey was with him—that's what I told him to do. You don't understand; this world is ignored out here."

"No, it isn't," Gril said.

"It was then. You were gone. You had no help back then."

"But Randy?" I said. "He would have wondered about everything— where had his cousin and his family gone? Why was there only one girl's body found?"

"As far as I know, Paul handled everything over the phone with Randy, too. Ask Randy. All I know is what I told Paul to do. I left and never looked back; well, not until recently."

Gril and I were silent for a long moment. Did what she said make sense? Almost anywhere else in the rest of the world, no, it didn't. But here, when Gril was gone and he had no help, maybe it could have happened the way she was saying. It wasn't an impossibility.

Gril sat back in his chair. "You took Josie to Brayn."

"I did."

"With another little girl?" I said.

"Yes. I was walking through the woods with Josie, trying to figure out what I was truly going to do." She laughed one phlegmy laugh and then wiped her arm under her nose. "I'd come to the conclusion that I was just going to go back to Randy and have him help, but then . . . I came upon another child. She was there, amid the gore of what must have been her mother's brutal death. She was crying but with no sound. It was so strange. I didn't even give it a second thought, but I picked her up too and just kept walking. I didn't even know where I was going. I was being somehow guided, and I just went with it. I came to Brayn and stopped in the post office. I turned over the children and hoped they'd be okay." She blinked at Gril. "And they were! They were well taken care of!"

"You've been hiding in the woods since then?" Gril said.

She laughed again. "Yes. I think it must have been the trauma of everything that happened, but I stayed. I survived one night, and then another. I could sneak into Randy's house, my house, during the day. I eventually befriended a man named Lane who taught me how to trap."

"Where did you sleep during the brutal winters?" I asked.

"I made a camp. I'll show it to you. There are other caves out there, not all of them made of ice. I was going to watch the girls from across the river, but shortly after I dropped them off a mudslide cut off easy access to them."

"You didn't have anything to do with the mudslide?" I asked.

"No, I wouldn't even know how to create a mudslide. It just happened."

"But you still stayed?" Gril said.

"One night turned into another, one year into another. I thought I would die every night, but I didn't. I woke up and just kept living, kept finding a way to eat, ways to keep warm. I just kept surviving," she repeated as if she herself was surprised.

"How did you get Paul to come back up here so you could kill him, too?" Gril asked.

"Eventually, I figured out how to break into the library at night. I used one of the computers and emailed him. He still had the same email."

"Okay, why did you want him to come back? What did you say to get him to return?"

"I told him I would turn him in to the police for murdering Audrey and abandoning his daughter if he didn't help me move Audrey's body."

"To the shed? Lane was sure it hadn't been there even a week ago."

Wanda shook her head slowly. "No, I didn't really want Paul's help. I just wanted to get him here. I told him to meet me by the tourist boat dock, at night. Again, no one was around. Trees even cut off the view from the lodge. I got him there and I killed him."

"Why?"

"Because he shouldn't have been allowed to live. If my time here has taught me anything, it's that the bad guys shouldn't get the breaks. I'd somehow given him a break. I wasn't willing to let it continue."

"That is wicked," I said.

Wanda looked at me. "I see the way you look at me. You could kill me. When I hurt that man Orin, you wanted to."

I didn't say anything, but I'd already acknowledged that fact to myself.

"So you moved Audrey's body by yourself?" Gril asked.

"I did. After the latest mudslide, I could get through to Lane's more easily. I made a sled and brought her over. I took her clothes, burned them, just in case there was any evidence. I kept hoping her body would be found, but it wasn't."

"Why did you want her found so badly?" I asked. "She might have stayed in that cave forever."

Wanda shrugged. "No. The mudslide exposed the way to the cave. People would have found her. Maybe even the girls. I didn't want it to happen that way."

"So you put her body in Lane's shed?" Gril asked.

Wanda shrugged again. "After I got to know Lane, I realized that it was his daughter that I took. You have to understand that when I realized what I'd done to him I was devastated. I wanted to put things right, but there simply was no way to do it. I didn't intend to leave her body there—I just knew he wouldn't be visiting the shed for a while. I was going to move her over to Randy's house at some point, but then I lost track of the girls when they were out checking traps with me . . . and things spiraled from there. I never got her moved."

"You burned the shed?" I asked.

"I did. I had the girl with me. It felt like the right thing to do, burn away the past."

I wanted to point out how that wasn't normal but I didn't. I looked at Gril. "Didn't Randy identify the body?"

"He said he didn't recognize her," Gril said. He looked at Wanda. "But wouldn't he have recognized her? You two had matching tattoos, right?"

Wanda twisted her wrist inside the handcuff, exposing her tattoo. "We did, but Randy didn't know. One of my first days here, we escaped over to Juneau, had too much to drink, and got these done. Randy never even saw mine—that should tell you even more about our marriage."

"But he would have recognized Audrey?" Gril said.

"You'll have to ask him," she said. "Chief, I just wanted to put things right. I don't know how else to explain it, but I thought Randy should know about Audrey. Once that became clear to everyone, I was sure the authorities would figure out that Paul was the man stabbed on the shore. But then Audrey's body was found in the shed, which really threw a wrench into everything. I decided I needed to do something else to make things right, so I decided I would just get Lane's daughter back to him. That's what I was going to do when you found me. This was all just me making things right."

"Why now?" Gril asked.

I thought she might say she was sick or she wanted to leave Benedict and needed to do these things before she left.

"It was time," she said. "I know you won't believe this, but I was traumatized. I've only recently felt like I was coming out of it, feeling better. It took me the time it took."

I hoped it wouldn't take me as long to get over Travis Walker.

"Six years?" Gril said.

"You keep saying that. I'm not sure how long six years is supposed to feel, but it doesn't feel that long to me. And, when this mudslide happened and I could see the girls, watch them from across the river, I was shocked by how much they'd grown. Six years is nothing, a blink or two, but those girls had grown so much. It's simply how I got better."

"I'm not sure I would call this better."

"I can't explain it any other way."

"The paper on the loft window?" I asked.

"That was Annie's. I thought Randy might actually notice it; maybe it would mess with his head a little. Did he see it?"

Gril and I looked at each other but didn't answer.

"So, not just make things right, but mess with your ex-husband, too?" Gril said.

"We're still married."

"Randy might have helped you find a way to save the girls." I said.

"I can see that now, but back then I just couldn't, and you have to remember that my suspicions weren't confirmed until after Jenny had been killed. It was all too late, too ugly."

"You put an animal trap inside the ice cave. Where did you get it?" Gril asked.

"It was right outside the cave when I retrieved Audrey's body. I know some trappers etch their names on their traps. It was just another way to try to divert the police—I knew it wasn't Lane's, and I didn't want anyone to think he'd done anything wrong."

"It belongs to the girls' father, the man who has raised them," I said.

Wanda's eyebrows rose. "Well, that's ironic."

"You caused him some trouble," Gril said.

"Didn't mean to," Wanda said unapologetically.

"The baby clothes were for a boy," I interjected.

"They were just baby clothes, no thought given to gender. Lane took me to the shed a couple of years ago and showed me. He was still torn up. It was very sad."

Gril officially booked Wanda and then made another call to the Harvingtons. Gril was going to need the plane again. It was finally time for Wanda to leave Benedict. For good.

Two Weeks Later

It was so cold. I probably shouldn't have been running outside in those temperatures, but it wasn't snowing. I didn't want to miss the window of somewhat milder weather. I'd tried the exercise equipment, but that had been torturous, each treadmill minute feeling like twenty real ones.

But I had to get in better shape. I'd promised Cecile. I'd promised myself. I was going to get as strong as I could, be in the best shape possible. I couldn't help but think a face-off was coming. I was going to be ready.

I hadn't heard from Mill again. I hoped she was okay. I suspected she was. The police had lost the man she'd shot; everyone was working from the assumption that he had, indeed, been Travis Walker, my kidnapper.

I hadn't told anyone about the memory of my kidnapper's words: *None of you Rivers people ever listen.* Along with my physical fitness,

I was working on my memories. I wanted to remember—maybe that would be enough. Maybe wanting to face terrible things would allow them to surface, and then go away again when I wanted them to. I was either getting better or worse, but I hadn't been able to bring back that moment.

Dr. Genero was calling me later today, just to check in, she said. I would tell her I was fine.

Wanda was gone. Randy was trying to understand what had happened. He was struggling with what Paul, Audrey, and his wife had done, and also how Wanda had been right there the whole time. He knew he should have recognized his cousin's wife's body. He should have known it was Audrey, but even now, he couldn't see the woman he'd once known as being the frozen body found in the shed. Gril reminded Randy that he hadn't recognized the body, either, and he had met Audrey briefly before leaving town to attend to his wife's funeral. Denial mixed with the passing of time were all they could chalk it up to. Donner didn't recognize or remember her either, and he got the best look at her body. He hadn't been working with Gril six years earlier, but he'd lived in Benedict.

Denial. Boy, I knew plenty about that.

Lane was . . . I wasn't sure. Gril would figure out a way for him to remain living where he was, but it would take some policy changes; the land did, indeed, belong to the State of Alaska.

The road was clear, though, and he was going to see more people coming his direction. He'd been fine making his way into town if he needed something, and then hiking back home. He'd enjoyed the road to his place being cut off, and I guessed he wished for another mudslide to keep traffic away. He had lots of healing to do himself. Wanda had messed up many lives.

I had run all the way to the *Petition*. Well, almost. I stopped just as I caught sight of Orin's truck at the library. He was fine. In fact, he'd been not only shot before, but stabbed, too. He'd shown me the scars, proudly.

I was relieved he was okay, but every time I tried to say those words aloud, tears burned behind my eyes. I couldn't bear the thought of him not being here.

Satisfied that he would stop by later for a shot of whiskey and some conversation, I turned my attention to the *Petition* building—just as someone was walking out of its door. There was no vehicle parked outside my shed.

"Hey!" I said as I hurried toward Tex Southern.

He looked over at me, smiled, and waved. "Beth, hello."

"How did you get in there?"

"I just turned the knob," he said. "It was unlocked. I left you a note, but I'm glad to see you in person."

I was rattled. I'd left the door unlocked? To my knowledge, I'd never left any Benedict doors unlocked. I looked at Tex, at the door, back at Tex. He didn't seem to be making it up.

"I usually lock the door."

"Um. I apologize if I shouldn't have gone inside."

"No, no, it's okay," I said. I should have invited him in again, but I couldn't rouse up any manners. "What's up?"

"Oh. I just wanted to thank you. You saved my daughters."

"Well, I don't know about that, but it was certainly a pleasure to meet you all." I tried to smile. The panic was dissipating a little. I looked down the road. "Mind if I ask what's going to happen with Lane?"

"Sure. We're working things out." Tex looked out toward Lane's, too. "The girls are at his house now. I walked here. By the time I get back, they'll be ready to go home, back to Brayn. Your town doctor has been working with them. They have both said a few words. It's going to take some time, but I think we'll get there."

"That's the best news I've ever heard," I said. "Really wonderful."

"Well, thank you again, Beth," he said as he slipped his hands into his jeans pockets. "I . . . uh, wondered if you'd like to join us in Brayn for dinner. I'm a really good cook and the girls want to see you again."

I blinked at Tex. Our eyes locked for a moment, and just like in those sappy movies, the rest of the world fell away. But just for an instant. My reality always found its way back.

"I would love to. Thank you." I sounded so excited, but I didn't care. Not that I ever had been, but I certainly wasn't into games or playing hard to get now. I was going to live authentic moments. If I was excited, I was going to damn well show it.

"Wow." Tex cleared his throat. "I mean, that's wonderful. Maybe this Saturday?"

"I'll be there. What can I bring?"

"Just you, Beth. That will be perfect. I'll come get you."

"No, I'll drive there. I like the drive."

"Great. See you then." Tex turned and started walking down the road, toward Lane's house and those fateful mudslides.

I watched him a long moment.

"What just happened?" I muttered quietly. I answered myself just as quietly. "Well, this should be interesting."

With a silly skip in my step and Tex out of sight now, I hurried inside the shed. It seemed fine, no different than I'd left it the night before. I thought back to the previous evening. I'd been in a hurry to pick up Ellen for another knitting class. She was already out-knitting me by about twenty scarves. She would probably be here through the winter, and that would be the best thing that ever happened to her. Viola told me that she'd passed her test already. The Benedict House was reopened to low-level female felons. Either I needed to find another place to live, or I was probably going to have more criminal roommates soon. I didn't want to leave.

I didn't remember leaving the *Petition*'s door unlocked, but I didn't remember the specific moments of locking it, either.

I walked to my desk and saw Tex's note. No, there were two notes, both of them folded with my name printed on each outside flap. *Beth.*

I opened the first one. It read, "I stopped by to say thanks. Hope you are well. Talk to you soon. Tex."

I smiled too goofily for my own good, glad we'd been able to talk in person.

But then I opened the second note. It read "Travis Walker"—and then listed an address in Missouri.

There was no signature. I had no idea who wrote the note, but the only person who possibly *should* have was Gril. He and I hadn't discussed Travis's name, but he might have known, might have talked to Detective Majors. I looked at the door. I looked at the note. Had someone picked the lock and left me the note with the address?

I threw it back onto the desk. Who was giving me Travis Walker's address?

I fell into my chair, sick to my stomach. Then I stood and locked the door. I slipped a chair under the knob.

I grabbed my burner phone and sent a text, hoping Mill would answer soon.

Acknowledgments

As always, thank you to my agent, Jessica Faust. I continue to be amazed by and grateful for you.

A special thank-you to two editor Hannahs, Hannah Braaten and Hannah O'Grady. I can't believe how fortunate I am to know and have worked with both of you.

Isn't this cover amazing? Thank you to Jonathan Bush, the cover designer, who even hand lettered the words. You are so talented.

Thanks to copyeditor Ivy McFadden.

Any mistakes I made and any exaggerations I might have included, particularly about ice caves, are mine alone and things I thought necessary for the story line.

As I finish up the edits of this book, the world is in the middle of unreal events. I'm sure that most writers hope to offer readers an escape, perhaps something else to think about while we're staying home, staying safe. Writing these stories certainly helps me cope. If I could have a wish, it would be that reading them also offers some sort of break from reality. Thank you, readers, for coming along for the ride.

My family has been my rock. Thank you to Charlie, Tyler, and Lauren—and even Lola. I love you all, so very much.